Once a Homecoming Queen screenplay garnered 16 awards and recognition, including:

- ♥ Stage 32 + Catalyst Studios Empowering Women Script Competition, Quarterfinalist
- ♥ The Big Apple Film Festival, Winner
- ♥ LA International Women in Film Screenplay Awards, Finalist
- ♥ NYC Screenplay Awards, Finalist (top 10% of over a thousand entrants)
- ♥ Cannes International Cinema Festival, Official Selection
- ♥ Toronto Independent Women in Film Festival, Official Selection
- ♥ WRPN.tv Women's International Film Festival, Official Selection
- ♥ Storyline - Finalist; Paris
- ♥ Women's Festival, Semi-Finalist
- ♥ Las Vegas International Film and Screenwriting Festival, Official Selection
- ♥ Emerging Screenwriters Drama Screenplay Competition, Semi-Finalist
- ♥ Page Turner Screenplay Competition, Semi-Finalist

". . . a powerful script with a badly needed message. With more stories about elderly addiction it gets easier to help people in need. Before you get the chance to experience the film for yourself, get to know more about the writer behind it and learn what you can expect from the story right here."

—**Film Daily**

Once a Homecoming Queen

a novel

JOAN MORAN

TOUCHPOINT PRESS
RELAX. READ. REPEAT.

ONCE A HOMECOMING QUEEN
By Joan Moran
Published by TouchPoint Press
www.touchpointpress.com

Copyright © 2024 Joan Moran
All rights reserved.

Softcover ISBN: 978-1-956851-66-3

This is a work of fiction. Names, places, characters, and events are fictitious. Any similarities to actual events and persons, living or dead, are purely coincidental. Any trademarks, service marks, product names, or named features are assumed to be the property of their respective owners and are used only for reference. If any of these terms are used, no endorsement is implied. Except for review purposes, the reproduction of this book, in whole or part, electronically or mechanically, constitutes a copyright violation. Address permissions and review inquiries to media@touchpointpress.com.

Editor: Paige Ripperger
Cover Design: Sheri Williams
Cover images: Joan Moran
Author Photo: Joan Moran

Visit the author's website at www.joanfrancesmoran.com

@joanfrancis.moran   @joanfmoran   @joanmoran

First Edition

Library of Congress Control Number: 2024930018

Printed in the United States of America.

Dedicated to

THE TRIUMVIRATE

Part One:
Deep Freeze

Chapter 1

Carlos and Ida

The blurry image of a composite of muted colors and slow movements of teenagers crowding a dimly lit dance floor. Flashes of prom gowns and black and white tuxedos. Soft sounds of teenage laughter can be heard over a 1950s song by Nat King Cole. *Unforgettable, that's what you are. Unforgettable tho' near or far.* A priest indicates with his hands that one of the couples has to separate. They are dancing too close. Dim lights dissolve and refocus onto the stage with clear illumination. A lovely young girl walks elegantly on stage with a bouquet of red roses. Her handsome escort follows behind. Cheers erupt from the teenage dancers in the gym. They shout: *Francine, Francine, Francine.* Francine blushes and smiles with excitement as she looks out over the crowd and waves. The student body president stands in the middle of the stage and holds a crown. Francine proudly walks to center stage. The young man holds the crown above Francine's head. Her face is beaming. The crowd cheers in the background.

Francine Fisher-Reynolds-Richelli-Freeman woke up from her dream and stretched her arms over her head as she wiggled her body under the covers. Her face was covered by a white bed sheet draped over her face. Every time Francine took a breath, the sheet puffed in and out, deftly moving a cloud of cigarette smoke hanging above her body. Her bedroom was like a sealed vault, stuffy, stale, and impenetrable to the outside world.

She broke the silence with a series of hacking coughs. A sharp pain jolted her body. When the pain gradually subsided, she threw the sheet off her face and body and tried to catch her breath. Her two small dogs, Sasha and Boo Boo scurried off the bed and waited for her hacking to stop. Francine pushed herself up on her elbows, and with her thumb and index finger, pulled a Marlboro cigarette out of the crushed package on the nightstand. It was her last cigarette.

"Get up here, my darlings," she said as she hugged the two small, white fluffy dogs. "Did my babies sleep well?"

She lit her cigarette with a 7-Eleven generic skinny, yellow lighter and deeply inhaled with pleasure—leaning into the pillows, staring at the ceiling, and mentally digging into her late morning ritual of staring down her memories. It was a game to see how much real emotion she could muster up for her sins of omission. She inhaled and waited for inspiration to recall one self-inflicted wound to entice her ire. Pausing, she exhaled a long stream of smoke. She waited for some scrap of memory to conjure up old wounds. Nothing came to mind. Nothing brought up an image of her youthful infractions and unholy rebelliousness. At this stage in her life, Francine did not have enough bandwidth to devote her morning musings to wonder why she could not muster any defense as to why decades ago she lacked passion and ambition—only to realize that passion and ambition were not her calling. That mindset turned into a curse and the curse became her fate.

Francine was comfortable with her life in the older, conservative suburb of Zeeland, Michigan, and still pleased that decades ago she was able to convince her last and third husband to purchase her final home only twenty minutes from the city of Grand Rapids. It was a sufficiently upscale home for her taste, and she was partial to the idea that Zeeland was a city founded by Dutch settlers. Although it was surrounded by forest farmlands, it maintained a quaint vestige of the nineteenth century through its architecture and dedication to growing tulips. Because Francine never had any airs about having money, she did not need the best house on the block; she only needed her privacy and the embrace of natural beauty. She lived far enough away from her daughter in Forest Hills that they were not on top of each other, but close enough to have regular contact, especially when her grandchildren were young. She and Rachel were not likely to casually run into each other. And since Douglas and Ari both attended the University of Michigan, she noticed her visits to Rachel were less frequent. Francine ruminated lately that the relationship with her daughter had moved from mutual affection, tinged with accommodation, into unfamiliar emotional territory. Francine knew why. She damn well knew why. The night Francine missed coming to Rachel's house for Christmas dinner was the cause. The day after Christmas, Rachel voiced her strong displeasure, verging on condemnation that her mother failed to attend dinner.

Rachel wanted to know what happened. Why didn't she attend Christmas dinner? It wasn't like her to miss Christmas. Was she sick? Everyone was concerned. Douglas asked about her. He has not seen her since he went off to Ann Arbor. And Ari had a new boyfriend.

Francine told Rachel she was sick, but that she shouldn't worry.

Rachel told her mother that she was setting up some tests for the following week, so maybe they'll be able to find out what's wrong.

Francine was caught in a lie. She would have to make amends for missing dinner. Of course, it was irresponsible of her, like all her other wrong-headed decisions she made sporadically during her life. Francine hung up on her daughter and poured herself another drink.

It was not Francine's nature to beat herself up for long. She had a decent social life at seventy-seven. Lunching with friends once a week took up time, as well as visiting seniors living on the margins of poverty in the poorer sections of Grand Rapids by delivering Meals on Wheels. She inspected their homes to see if they were safe as she looked after their physical needs, often bringing simple meals to them. Mac and cheese was a big hit. And so was

Francine. She flipped through a calendar that lay next to her bed to see if she had anything to do that day. Relieved that she was free of commitments, Francine picked up her latest book and read until her memories receded.

∽

At midday, Francine rose from her bed with all the effort she could muster. She rubbed her hands and arms, massaged her legs and feet, and gauged her ability to stand. It was cold in her room, so it was difficult to move her body with agility, as if that was an option, not having exercised in her life. She loved winter, but her old bones had no love for the cold. The dogs jumped off the bed as she reached for her ratty powder-blue bathrobe crumpled on the bed and wrapped it around her frail body. Tenuously standing, she took a breath and began to cough again. She barely made it to the second-floor landing before she could stand up. Catching her breath, she grabbed the banister and descended the staircase, hoping her right hip wouldn't give out.

Her late morning routine began in earnest as Francine put the tea kettle on, lit a cigarette, and headed for the front door to get the newspaper.

The winter cold engulfed her body as she bent down and picked up *The Grand Rapids Press* from the stoop. On her way to a standing position, she noticed Carlos standing in the middle of the street. He was in his late thirties, of medium height with a full head of dark black hair, dressed insufficiently for the freezing cold, and shivering as snow fell around him. She had seen Carlos before in the neighborhood and believed he lived with that prick, Ray, across the street. She figured Ray threw him out. Piece of work, that Ray. Francine placed a hand on one of her knees and helped herself up to a standing position in front of the doorway. He hugged his duffle bag close to his body to ward off the cold. Carlos was probably waiting for a ride because he only glanced at Francine and did not try to make eye contact. Francine couldn't help thinking he was not in a good place.

After she drank her tea, Francine became distracted and checked to see if Carlos had moved. When she saw that he had not, she put out her cigarette and lugged her large black garbage bag through the front door. She set the bag on the top step. The dogs raced outside and greeted Carlos in the street, barking and jumping with the joy of finding a new friend.

Francine shuffled gingerly up to the dogs and pulled them off the man's legs.

"Sasha, Boo-Boo, get down, my sweet darlings."

The duffle bag slipped through Carlos's frozen fingers.

"Why in hell are you standing out in the street in the freezing snow, Carlos?"

"I'm thinking what to do, ma'am," said the man.

"You can call me Francine. I can tell you what to do. You can get my garbage bag at the front door and take it to the bin, and then come inside. Your nuts must be frozen."

Francine wrapped her bathrobe tightly around her thin body, nudged the dogs inside, and left the garbage detail to Carlos.

As he picked up the Hefty bag, it split open from the weight; liquor bottles rolled out on the walkway, clanking and breaking. He recovered the bottles, picked up pieces of glass; he cut himself a few times and deposited the garbage into the outside bin. He noticed he was bleeding as he retrieved his duffle and walked to the front door, shivering like a leaf in a storm. Francine opened the door before he knocked.

"What are you waiting for?" asked Francine. "Get inside. I'm not going to bite. It's colder than a witch's tit out in the tundra."

"You might say that," said Carlos.

"And thanks for helping me."

"Yes, thank you, ma'am. Very kind of you to let me in."

"Francine. Call me Francine." She turned around to speak directly to him. "I seem to remember you lived across the street with Ray for a few months. Did the prick kick you out?"

"He's not really a bad guy."

"Then why did he kick you out?" asked Francine. "Hey, you're bleeding. Stick your hands under the cold water."

"He got sick of me. I couldn't pay for the room anymore. Lost my job."

"I'll get you some hot tea and a bite to eat."

Carlos continued to hold his cut hand under the water while Francine fed Sasha and Boo-Boo. "Good babies. Eat it all up and make me proud."

She hugged the dogs before she put the kettle on and pulled out a couple of tea bags from the cabinet. After toasting two English muffins and setting out butter and strawberry jam, she put plates and utensils on the table. Her guest broke the monotony of the day. He was a stray, and like all strays, she assumed he would be around for a few days. Besides, she already had a run-in

with Ray and wanted to right the wrong perpetrated by her neighbor.

Carlos wrapped a paper towel around his hand and sat at the table. After he was sure he was not bleeding, he smothered his toast with jam and inhaled the food. Francine watched with satisfaction that she rescued yet another stray. When he finished, she took his dish to the sink.

"I'll get this. You sit."

Francine tightened the sash on her bathrobe to make sure she was covered properly. As she began to walk to the sink, her right hip got stuck and refused to cooperate as she tried to move forward. She hit her hip a few times with her fist to wake it up and continued.

"Thanks, Francine. Ray said you were a bitch, but I think you are the kindest person on Earth." Carlos made the sign of the cross and kissed his thumb.

"Oh, God, you're a Catholic. Listen, for your information, I am a bitch, but not to everyone—only to people who are assholes. Like Ray."

Carlos looked down into his lap, unable to respond.

"What's on your mind? Don't beat around the bush because I think I know what's coming next."

"This is pretty bold of me, but if you have a spare room, would it be possible for me to stay a few days until I can find a job? I'd be full of gratitude." He crossed himself for a second time.

"For God's sake, Carlos, please don't cross yourself again. I get sick to my stomach with that pious pretense. I had thirteen years of Catholic school and a mother who never stopped clutching her rosary beads. I'm no saint, far from it, but I'll help a guy when he's down. It's what I live for."

Francine let out her Phyllis Diller laugh, which frightened Carlos out of his ratty shoes.

"Let's get down to it. Where do you come from?"

"I was born in South Central Los Angeles, raised there. Got in trouble with the gangs before I got out of high school. Wandered around and tried to stay away from the bad guys."

"Quite a resume," said Francine. "Eat some more if you want, and we'll figure something out."

Francine was intrigued by the idea of having a house guest for a few weeks. But not months on end. She liked her privacy and her routine. And she liked to drink alone.

"I've been helping a priest at St. Francis de Sales in Holland. I closed up at night until my car got towed."

Francine opened a cabinet over the sink and lifted out a bottle of Jack Daniels. She opened the freezer, grabbed a handful of ice, threw it into a glass, and swirled it around.

"Damn, I'd better not be out of 7 UP."

"I noticed it on the counter next to the honey," said Carlos.

"Shoot, I forgot to put it back in the fridge last night."

Carlos didn't blink. It was several hours past noon.

"I drink, Carlos, so get used to it. What were you saying about a car? Where is it?"

"It was parked too long outside the church, and it got towed. I was sleeping at the rectory sometimes."

"You get around, Carlos," she said as she poured 7 UP into her glass. "I'll do my bit for charity and get your car out of impound, and you can change my oil in exchange, maybe fix my fence, and help me shop. I won't charge you rent. When you get a job, save your money. I'll hold it for you until you can get your own apartment."

"It's nice here in Zeeland—small and quiet."

"Oh, God, you have no idea. I'm orgasmic living here. More parks and lakes than most suburbs. I fancy myself a lake girl. We have a lake house on Lake Michigan. It's what keeps my motor running."

They bonded and settled into a rhythm the first two weeks. Carlos took care of her basic needs: shopping, cooking, fixing things in the yard, gassing up her car, and puttering around the garden. He never said a word about her drinking. Anyway, it was not his place to comment or to have an opinion. And if he even mentioned it, Francine would kick him out. He was not curious about her past life and never asked personal questions. She never mentioned to him that due to her consumption of alcohol, she'd had a few falls: a fractured pelvis, which was why she had a slight limp and another fall broke her arm. A year ago, she fell backward down the stairs and broke her neck. That was her own damn fault. She should have slept on the couch instead of going upstairs to bed that night. There was no permanent damage, but she lied to Rachel and told her she had a routine appendectomy. After ten days of detoxing, a week of physical therapy for her neck, and a promise to go to AA, she was released. Francine was supposed to wear a collar brace, but it itched, and besides, Rachel would be suspicious if she saw her in a brace. This was her own damage. This was who she was.

One morning, about a week after Carlos arrived, Francine's best friend, Ida, came over to the house. She was a small round woman in her early seventies with a full head of white hair and skin as thick as a rhinoceros. No taller than five feet one inch, and she carried too much weight. But she looked healthy despite the small red blotches on her cheeks. She was dressed as if she lived in Miami Beach.

"You're late," said Francine after opening the door. "And why do you knock after all these years?"

"Some of us are polite, Francine," said Ida with a wink. "I got here as fast as I could."

Ida took Francine's arm and walked her to the Jack Daniels bottle on the counter.

"You haven't had one yet, right?" asked Ida.

"Of course, not. We made a pact. Ida, pay attention. Carlos is outside fixing my fence. He's the man who needs a job. I'll call him in, and you can tell him about your cousin."

Francine opened the outside slider and called for Carlos to come inside as Ida wandered over for another look at the bottle of Jack Daniels.

"Ida, get away from the bourbon. You're working yourself up."

Carlos walked into the kitchen. "Ida, this Carlos. Her cousin works at a construction site and her cousin said they needed to hire."

"Glad to meet you, Ida."

"Want to interview for the job, Carlos?"

"Are you good at holding a job, young man?" asked Ida.

"I try, but, like the last job, the boss was never pleased with what I did."

"Don't buck authority," said Francine. "Stay in your lane because I don't have any more contacts for you. Ida is your guardian angel."

"I'm not good with people," he said. "Leaving school at fifteen was a bad move."

"That's your whole story?" asked Ida.

"No. A year later, I got picked up in a police round-up in Long Beach. I gave up my gang, you know, turned in the leaders, in exchange for reduced jail time."

"That's a better story, Carlos," said Francine, "but there are a few holes."

"How did you get all the way from California to Grand Rapids?" asked Ida. "That's quite a distance you traveled."

"After eighteen months of hiding from gang members who knew me, I hitched a ride to Colorado. Got a construction job in Fort Collins for a year and met some people. One of the guys I worked with was moving to Grand Rapids, and he gave me his contact. It was Ray. Told me if I ever got to town to look him up, but I got profiled before I made it to Ray's."

"Don't tell me," said Francine. "You landed in jail again. They play your story every night on the old reruns of *Columbo*."

"The cops said I was loitering. I spent a few nights in jail and realized I needed a car before I looked up Ray. I'm good with cars, so I got a job in an auto shop. One day a guy brought in a car that was a piece of junk and left it. I claimed ownership and fixed it, but before I could register the car, I was caught driving without registration and a license."

"How fast did you talk to get out of that nightmare?"

"I got fined, and I have to pay that before I can drive legally."

"You're a pain in the ass, Carlos," said Francine. "We have to get you that construction job. What's your last name?"

"Menendez," Carlos told her. "What's your last name?"

"Fisher-Reynolds-Richelli-Freeman."

"That's a lot of names," said Carlos.

"I had a lot of husbands," she responded. "Ida's had only one husband. Lucky her."

"May he rest in peace, poor Sam," said Ida. "He died right before I met you, remember?"

"We've been attached at the hip ever since," said Francine.

"I'll drink to that," Ida responded.

They shared a private laugh. Too many rescues, too many secrets to count.

"Is construction your main interest, Carlos?" asked Ida.

"Those jobs are easier to get, so I guess I work more in construction," he said.

"How do you want me to do this, Francine?" asked Ida.

Francine ripped off the post-it and gave it to Ida with a pen.

"Write down the details," said Francine. "I'll go with you to lobby your cousin."

∽

Francine drove her 1999 Ford SUV into a dusty parking lot and stopped in front of a bungalow in need of serious repair. She pulled out a box from the back seat with cardboard containers and several bags of groceries and trudged to a front door in disrepair.

"Hey, Linda. It's me. Francine. Open up. My arms are killing me."

Linda opened the door immediately. She is in her late seventies, five-foot-ten, with gray, straggly hair, wears an old flowered printed house dress.

"Well, for goodness sake, Francine, I thought you would never come," said Linda.

"Help me with these, will ya? Don't get on my ass because I'm in no mood."

Linda took the groceries and entered the bungalow. Francine followed her, set down her purse, and lit a cigarette, blowing out the smoke with satisfaction.

"Calm down, calm down. No worries. I'm just happy you're here."

Francine walked into Linda's bungalow with a single bed in an alcove and a tiny kitchen.

"I love what you've done to the place. Jeez, Linda, ever heard of a coat of paint? I suggest you ditch the falling down wallpaper."

"I do my best, Francine. Just because you live in the lap of luxury." Linda scurried around trying to clean the room up.

"Next time I come by, I'll bring you a form from Meals On Wheels."

"I should quit smoking, huh? I'm making a mess of my place and killing myself at the same time."

"Don't worry about that stuff. Take care of yourself as best you can." Francine hugged Linda.

"Thanks, Francine. Love ya."

"Love you, too. Hey, babe, can I use your phone. I don't have a portable phone, and I have to make a call."

Linda pulled her phone out of a cabinet and handed it to her. Francine dialed and waited.

"Ida, call me about what your cousin thought about hiring Carlos. Hope you get this message."

The day Francine and Ida went to see Ida's cousin, Mr. Marshall, in his construction office, Carlos was working on his 2015 Camry in the driveway. An SUV Lexus pulled up to the curb. Rachel got out of her car and walked to Carlos.

"Hi, I'm Rachel. Francine's daughter. Is my mom around?"

"I'm Carlos Menendez. She's with her friend, Ida, and they are looking into a possible construction job for me with Ida's cousin."

"Are you staying with her?" asked Rachel.

"Just until I get on my feet. Not long."

"Where do you come from? I mean how did you arrive here?"

"I lived down the street with a neighbor and your mom was a saint to help me out."

"I'm presuming this situation is temporary."

"Yes, ma'am, it isn't meant to be long."

"Good luck on your job search," said Rachel as she walked to her car.

∽

Francine was not much of an eater, and Carlos was concerned about her health. He hovered around her and catered to her needs. Best of all, he didn't want sex. Francine carried on her life as she lived it—smoking and drinking and reading the news and watching "Jeopardy." The grim reaper was coming for her, and she didn't give a damn when he took her.

The odd couple compromised. Francine liked to eat out most nights, and she took Carlos with her for company. There was a direct correlation between ordering food and eating it. When a full plate of food, preferably Chinese, was set down in front of her, Francine could smell it and the odors stimulated her appetite.

A few nights after Rachel met Carlos, they went out to Francine's favorite Chinese restaurant.

"Is there anything you'd like to tell me, Carlos?"

Carlos stopped reading the menu and met Francine's eyes. "Yes, I'm sorry I didn't mention it sooner. Rachel dropped by and we talked. She's nice."

"She's wonderful and understanding so don't piss her off. She's not kindly about your living with me. Mainly because I'm old, and I have to be careful of people who might take advantage of me. If you see her again, remember that courtesy is your best approach."

"I'm not going to hurt you, Francine. I'm grateful for your kindness. Besides, I have a mother, you know."

The waitress sauntered to the table.

"The usual, Francine?"

"When have I ever ordered anything else, Rita?"

"Bourbon and 7, easy on the ice and Chicken Chow Mein, it is." Rita turned to Carlos "And you?"

"Meet Carlos. He's my house guest and he'll have the same. Only bring him a coke."

Rita winked at Francine, smiled, and walked to the kitchen.

～

Carlos was working at the construction company for about two weeks when he was profiled by a local cop on his way to the church to close up. The fact that he was a U.S. citizen did not make a difference to the cop because Carlos had no papers on him. Carlos argued that he had a license, but the cop was unmoved. What Carlos did have was a rap sheet that showed he was previously incarcerated in Long Beach and Fort Collins. Carlos made a phone call to Francine to rescue him from jail. He had not been living with her for long, but he'd been good to her, and he hoped she had some mercy for him.

"Damnit, Carlos, you didn't have your papers with you?" she said when he called her from jail. "I thought you were smarter than that. Get a grip."

She picked up Ida and together they went to the jail to see what they could do. It was too late to get him out on bail or help him find his legal papers. Carlos had a swift hearing and was incarcerated for thirty days.

"Bad luck and lack of skills kept Carlos in bondage," said Francine.

Ida was holding Francine's arm as they walked down the stairs of the Grand Rapids Police Department. It was a bright, sunny afternoon with a bouncy blue and white sky that belonged in a watercolor painting by Joseph Turner.

"What are you saying, Francine? Because you picked this guy up on the street and he's living with you and you get him a job, you give him a get out of jail free card? Are you nuts?"

"He's a good guy, Ida, and I felt sorry for him."

"What is he, your boyfriend? Sex at your age is not an option. And besides, he's using you. And he could kill you when you turn your back or when you're sleeping in bed."

"Don't be so dramatic. Or a racist. Both attitudes are unbecoming a woman of your age. I'm not about being abused anyway. This guy is sweet like marshmallows. Let's go to our usual place. I'm starving. It's on me. I didn't thank you for taking care of my dogs last year when I landed in detox after the accident."

"Accident, my ass," said Ida. "You were drunk when you fell down the stairs. I don't know why you don't sleep on the couch like you're supposed to when you've had three too many."

∽

Francine and Ida had been going to Chez Moi for decades. They knew the menu by heart and the waitress by name. It still retained its old musty smell after forty years in business. The furnishings hadn't been changed in twenty years. The brown leather sofas at the front entrance were falling apart. The leather was peeling off the sides like skin from a dead animal. But the menu was better than Applebee's. More important were the bartender's generous shots of bourbon in their drinks.

"Look, Ida, you're my oldest friend since I moved to Grand Rapids, and you need to be on my side with this Carlos business. Rachel already met him."

"I won't say anything to Rachel if she calls me, but you promise me you'll be careful. You never stayed sober when you got out of the hospital after your fall. So you'd better not drink so much while he's around. Things happen."

"Well, I kind of detoxed, but my physical therapist and I had a thing going on with the orderly. Not sexual, so get your mind out of the gutter. We laughed and played cards, and he brought me little booze bottles, like from the airplane, and a thermos of tequila. God, it was fun."

"You cheated through physical therapy, Francine. They could've expelled you."

"Oh, well yes and no. And you wouldn't have taken a drink or two if you'd had the opportunity?"

"Probably true, but luckily, I've never detoxed, so I can't relate. But we did make a promise after you got out of recovery that we would only drink after five in the afternoon."

"How's that going for us?" asked Francine.

"I'm no saint," said Ida. "But I don't drive at night when I drink. And I hope you don't because I don't know what I'd do without you."

"We don't have to drink today," said Francine. "Not even a glass of wine. God, I hate wine."

Jane, their favorite waitress, stood at the table listening to most of the conversation. A skinny, long-legged dirty-blonde woman in her fifties, she bore the marks of alcohol and cigarettes on her face. Lines pinched her eyes and exaggerated the abundance of fatigue she was obviously feeling.

"Let's have our usual, Jane, except no drinks," Ida said.

"You sure?" asked Jane as she glanced at Francine.

"For now," said Francine, glaring at Ida.

Jane nodded, smiled, and walked away to place the order.

"Jane looks like she had quite a night," said Ida. "Poor thing shackled to this job day in, day out. We're lucky we ended up on the right side of the coin. You more than me, Francine."

"It pretty much cost me my life. Remember my crazy third husband trying to light himself on fire with the oxygen pole? Third time was the charmer. Good old Peter."

"Good old Sam. He saved my life more times than I can remember. I shouldn't drink, Francine. I don't hold my liquor like I used to. Doesn't take much to make me feel dizzy."

"You keep talking like that and I'll order a drink."

"You crack me up, I'll tell you." Ida giggled.

"Did I tell you Rachel announced that she hates her marketing job at Spectrum Healthcare? She wants to become a farmer?"

"What are you talking about? Why would anyone want that?"

"She wants to grow vegetables, have a garden, and sell them at Farmer's markets. And just when Mark is about ready to make partner in his exclusive downtown law firm."

"Could be a perfect life," said Ida. "At least, Rachel doesn't confront your drinking like my Karen did."

"I think Rachel went to Al-Anon."

"How do you know?"

"You know how you know. You just know."

"AA for a year, and my daughter was in Al-Anon for years. And just like Karen, Rachel probably keeps her secrets, and I'll make you a bet she is angry."

"I don't care what Rachel thinks, nor do I feel the need to explain my choices. I drink. So be it. I'm sure Rachel hates my drinking. I got balled out for missing Christmas dinner because I had a gorilla of a hangover. But she's my good girl and wouldn't walk out on me. We planned a trip in the spring to Louisiana on one of those gambling riverboats. I love hanging out with her."

"I'd rather travel to exotic places," said Ida. "I wish I could have done that with my daughter. I really screwed this life up, Francine."

"I don't know, Ida. Maybe we both did. But at least we did it together. Ida and Francine. Francine and Ida. Screw the world."

"We're in control, then. Right?" asked Ida.

"Let's renew our pact not to drink until five, but let's start that promise tomorrow. I mean, after all, we are at our favorite place to eat lunch."

"What about a bottle of Chardonnay?"

"Chardonnay tastes like piss, Ida. Let's go for a bottle of Merlot. If I have to drink wine, make it wine with teeth. Merlot is the only wine I can tolerate."

"Anything else?" Jane asked as she set down the food order.

"A bottle of your best Merlot," said Francine.

"Those are my girls," said Jane as she left the table.

They got drunk that afternoon and kept their promise not to drive while intoxicated. Jane called them a cab.

~

Carlos lost his job while he was in jail. Several weeks before he got out, Francine decided to try to plead with his boss, Mr. Marshall, to reinstate him. She went to the construction office and remembered the name of Mr. Marshall's secretary. She loved when her memory worked to her advantage.

"Nothing's easy, Joanne, when it comes to doing favors for friends," Francine told her. "But I have to thank Mr. Marshall for hiring Carlos."

"Mr. Marshall is in his office if you want to go begging for your friend's job back. And good luck with that."

Francine nodded to Joanne in agreement and entered the office. She looked at pictures on a wall to the right of Mr. Marshall and waited quietly until he got off the phone.

"Hi, Mr. Marshall. Do you remember me? Your cousin, Ida's friend."

"Who could forget you, Mrs. Freeman," said Mr. Marshall.

"I think Carlos got a bum rap," said Francine. "And he was a good worker until the asshole cop decided to make an issue out of him. No papers and all. But he had papers. I know because they're in my house. He rents a room from me, and I need the money to help out with monthly expenses and all, so can you please take him back? It would mean a lot to me."

She didn't know if Mr. Marshall believed her or not. He probably did not because he gave her a smile that indicated she was working him. He thought about it for a minute as he checked a few papers on his desk.

"I'm a sucker for ladies with big hearts like you, Mrs. Freeman. He gets one more chance. Have him come see me when he's out."

That night Francine and Ida celebrated the event by meeting for dinner and ordering their bourbon and sevens complete with a petite filet. They both had one too many and rode home in a taxi.

The next day, Francine got up later than usual. It was four o'clock before she had her first drink. She read and talked on the phone with Ida and Rachel. While Francine sat at the kitchen table and studied the news, a sharp pain surged through her stomach. She had felt the sharpness a few times before and paid no attention. But instead of drinking water, she made herself another bourbon thinking she would lie down on her bed for a while. After a few sips, she decided to take her drink upstairs.

As she was climbing up the stairs, Francine felt another flash of pain in her stomach. Dizzy and unstable, she gripped her glass instead of the banister and fell backward, and landed on her back.

Several hours later, she awoke in a state of confusion with a fierce headache. The glass of bourbon was still in her left hand, empty but not broken. The dogs were nudging her and the stray cat sat on her chest. She was momentarily confused and shaken. After calming her dogs and petting the cat, Francine tried to crawl to the phone cord dangling from the kitchen table. She inched herself closer to the cord and tried to grab it with her left hand. Overcome by pain in her neck and arm, breathing heavily, and lacking bodily strength, Francine stretched her arm to the cord again. With the tips of a few fingers, she jabbed at the cord several times, causing the phone to crash land on the floor.

With difficulty, Francine dialed. "Ida! Ida! Help!" Realizing she was about to mimic a commercial, she parlayed it into a joke: "I've fallen, and I can't get up." She started laughing not because of the joke, but because she was relieved that she could move her body. The fear that she might have broken her neck again and was paralyzed terrified her. Was there a god of retribution lurking around her? She knew religion was a pile of crap.

"Can you take me to the hospital? I can move a bit, but I'm in pain."

"I'm in no shape to help, Francine," said Ida, slurring her words. "I can't drive. Where's Carlos?"

"Still in jail. Please call 9-1-1, Ida, and please take care of my animals until Carlos gets back. And when he's back, tell him he has his job back. Promise me, Ida. Promise me."

"I promise," said Ida. "I promise with all my heart. I'll call you after I call 9-1-1."

While she waited for Ida's call and for the ambulance to arrive, Francine panicked because she should have been paralyzed or dead. After she hung up and knew she would be taken care of, the immediate terror passed. She was able to feel her fingers and arms and recognized that her old body was not completely broken. But she was in pain, a welcoming pain, but maybe the pain was a gift. And then, she remembered falling backward, parachuting down, suspended in space, but she couldn't remember hitting the floor. She wished Carlos was there to clean up her mess and take her to the hospital. If Carlos were with her, she wouldn't be in trouble. She forgot she told Ida to call 9-1-1 and dialed for an ambulance herself.

"9-1-1. I need an ambulance."

"Your address," answered the emergency assistant.

There was a knock at the door.

"How did you get here so fast?" asked Francine.

"Mom, it's me, Rachel." Rachel grabbed the phone. "The address 1147 Linden Lane, Zeeland. And hurry. My mother fell down the stairs."

Rachel cradled her mother's head. "This can't continue Mom. It's not right."

Francine fell unconscious.

"Mom, Mom, please wake up." Rachel rocked her mother in her arms.

Part Two: Detox

Chapter 2

Out of Darkness

Where in the hell am I? I can't open my eyes. I can't part my lips. I can't move my damn hands. Fucking toes won't move. Jesus Christ! I'm dead. Or between living and dying. Or between Purgatory and Hell. I was born to land in hell, so I must be on my way.

Damn! I hear something. That must be a sign I'm alive. I recognize that sweet voice—it's my best girl, Rachel. I've got to get out of here. Help! I'm screaming. Can anyone hear me? Rachel, my darling Rachel, get me out of here. I hear Mark. Mark! You have some sense. You're a smart goddam lawyer.

Oh, my God! I can't lift my head. I'm choking. I'm suffocating. Help me! Please!

Francine thought she saw light through her eyelids, but she was not running on full brainpower. She held her breath for as long as she could to see if she was still alive or had crossed to the other side. A phantom silence engulfed her brain as if she was underwater. She was unable to breathe until she heard her daughter hyperventilating.

Rachael stared out the window. Her husband, Mark, put his arm around her. "Are you alright?" he asked.

"I want to be someplace else," Rachel whispered.

Francine was disappointed that she was not dead. *Maybe next time.*

Curiosity about what was happening in the room was getting the better of her, and with great effort, she struggled to open her eyes.

"Hey, Rach," Mark said, "She's coming out of the anesthesia. Your mom's face is moving, and her eyes are fluttering."

A willful Francine forced her eyes open and stared intently at her daughter.

"Mom? You're back."

"Among the living again, dear daughter," replied Francine in a faint, raspy whisper.

Rachel was always present and available for her mother. Her love was unconditional until this very moment. All she could feel was anger that her mother was again in the hospital as a result of her own fault. More confusing was how she could willfully escape death again.

"Well, don't just stand there. Where am I, and how did I get here? Jesus, I can't move a damn thing on my body."

The white plastic collar fitted tightly around her neck and made it difficult, but not impossible, to speak.

"I'm choking to death, babe, help me get this thing off."

"I can't, Mom. You broke your neck again, and the doctor said it didn't heal properly from the last fall. That's when you told us you had your appendix out, remember?"

Francine's steely eyes surveyed the room: white walls, a small window with Venetian blinds the color of eggshells, and garish fluorescent lighting. It hurt her eyes to look at it, and the sickening glow nauseated her. She looked with disgust at the threadbare, white sheets and the well-worn blanket, so thin that her cat would reject it.

"Get me out of here, Mark," she whispered, "or I'll disinherit Rachel."

"No can do," Mark replied. His handsome face was strained, and he looked uncomfortable listening to Francine try to talk her way out of her situation.

"And why is that?" Francine hissed through clenched teeth. "You're a lawyer, so why can't you?"

"Don't you remember how you got here, Mom?" Rachel asked.

"If I remembered, darling, I wouldn't be asking," Francine fidgeted with the tubes taped atop her right hand. "Dammit! Get this damn tape off me."

"You can't do that, Mom," said Rachel. "This time you did a number on yourself. Same stairs, different day, but it's worse."

"Rub it in, darling," Francine shot back. "You think I don't know that I fell?"

Rachel felt helpless in the face of her mother's indifference to her accident. Mark, a tall, handsome man with slicked-back hair and a serious countenance, put his arm around Rachel in support, but she was not in the mood for loving gestures.

"You're not taking this life-threatening situation seriously, and you damn well should."

"How many times have I fallen, huh? Tell me that? Just how many times?"

"In total?" asked Rachel as she inched her way to the opposite side of the room. "Four."

"Oh, for Christ's sake, that's not true," Francine shot back. "Mark, tell her she's wrong. This is the second time. I remember."

"Second time for the broken neck," muttered Mark. "I have to run. You two work this out. Good luck, Francine."

"What do you mean good luck? I'm leaving this place in a few days. Back again—good as new."

"Not quite, Francine," said Mark.

They both watched Mark leave the hospital room, head down, pulling his collar up around his neck..

"What's he talking about, Rachel? Work what out?"

"You lied to us the first time you fell down the stairs and broke your neck," Rachel said quietly. "You still have your appendix. You had other falls, Mom. The arm and fractured pelvis, two broken necks. Four in all."

"They don't count because everyone over seventy has something broken, some goddamn thing going on with their old decrepit body."

"They count, Mom. Every fall counts."

"Don't lecture me, Rachel. You remind me of my mother. You don't look like her one bit, but you damn well sound like her."

"I'm not amused by your non-stop sarcasm and adolescent antics," Rachel told her mother. "The first time you fell backward on the same staircase, I didn't know for a week that you were in the hospital. Then you made up a fake medical story, said that you would be going home in a few days, and not to worry because Ida was on stand-by to pick you up. When I saw you next time at home, you were wearing a neck brace."

"I told you I had a car accident months back before I got appendicitis," Francine lied. "It flared up when I was in the hospital."

"You lied, Mom. You have no appendix scar."

Francine didn't care if Rachel and Mark bought the lie or not. She remained steadfast that never taking a drink again was not an option.

"You have no right to put me in here," said Francine.

"You put yourself in here," Rachel told her. "A third fall would kill you. And your falls are about your drinking. Mark told me that if we let this go, we'd be criminally negligent. And jail is not an option. It's long past the time that I should have intervened. I am now your legal guardian until you get out of rehab, or until you're not a danger to yourself."

"What are you talking about? Danger to myself is absurd."

"Self-destruction is not your birthright. At this moment, I feel no guilt about finally facing your alcoholism. I feel calm in the face of your tricks and manipulations, and constant resistance to being told what to do or not to do. Even though you are tougher than a brick wall and could fend off a Roman army, you are finally where you are supposed to be, but only barely, because you've had the wits to escape your punishment.

"I'll call my lawyer and he'll get me out," said Francine.

"Mark is your lawyer, Mom. You are officially in intervention mode, and you are not getting out of here for at least three weeks. Two weeks for detoxing and some time for physical therapy. You have to heal, learn to walk again. Then you're off to recovery for one month. And I'm not talking about occasional AA meetings when you are in the mood to be on stage. It should be a three-month sentence, but we're hoping you're a fast learner. A month tops is your purgatory."

"You see this shit-eating grin I have on my face," Francine said. "It says,

'I didn't hear one damn word you said. This is my fucked-up life, and I'm welcomed to it.' I'm sure you need to go to work today."

Francine continued to pick at the bandage covering her IV tube.

A short squatty man wearing blue doctor scrubs and a cheerful smile entered the room as

Rachel turned to leave.

"Doctor," said Rachel, "I'll leave my mother in your good hands."

"I resent this, Babe. You're supposed to stand up for me. You can't be serious about intervening or whatever you call it."

As Rachel walked out of the room, the doctor stepped aside to let her pass. They nodded and Rachel offered a forced smile.

"Good morning. I'm Doctor Franklin."

"We met already at intake."

"Yes, of course. Everything all right, Mrs. Miller?"

"I'm sure your protocol is according to hospital regulations. Take good care of my mother, please." Rachel passed in front of Dr. Franklin and left the room.

Francine made no recognition of the doctor's entrance.

"Welcome to Queen of Angels Hospital. How are you doing?"

"How do you think I'm doing? And it's Mrs. Freeman to you."

Doctor Franklin picked up the chart hanging on a post at the end of her bed and shook his head.

"I don't know how you're alive, Mrs. Freeman." He placed a thumb against her veiny wrist and took her pulse. "Normal."

"What'd you expect?" asked Francine. "That means my alcohol level is consistent with my good health. So, why am I lying in this poor excuse for a hospital when I'm good to go home?"

Francine was nauseated by the smell of talcum powder and Listerine coming from Doctor Franklin.

Ignoring her attempt to rant, the Doctor studied her chart. "No paralysis, no broken bones, but three fractures on the cervical spine. We'll probably want to keep your neck in traction for the next few months."

"I'm a miracle, don't you think, Doc? But you're crazy if you think I'm going to wear this albatross around my neck for anywhere near a month."

Doctor Franklin looked at Francine gravely. "I'm reading in your chart that this is the second time that you fell on a staircase and broke your neck. Was the first fall also alcohol-related?"

"I run on alcohol."

"I'm sure you know alcohol requires detoxing in a hospital. It's a medical procedure and can be dangerous to the heart. Once you are sober and get some physical therapy, you'll be able to enter a rehab center and get counseling for your addiction."

Francine ignored Doctor Franklin and returned to peeling off the tape from the tube on her right hand. With what little energy she had, she pulled the tube off her right hand.

"I will do no such thing. My daughter is not the boss of me."

"I'm afraid she is," said Doctor Franklin. "You are the subject of an intervention signed off by your daughter. You are an alcoholic and a danger to yourself and others."

"Over my dead body. You think you can tell me what to do? You can't. I won't give you my permission."

"It's too late for protests," Doctor Franklin told her. "When you lose control of yourself with alcohol or other drugs, you lose the ability to make decisions."

Francine fell back into her pillow, closed her eyes, opened her mouth to scream, but no sound came out.

"Do you understand the circumstances of your stay in the hospital?" asked Doctor Franklin.

"You mean, my imprisonment," Francine said. "I hereby state that I am incarcerated at Queen of Angels Hospital against my will. I swear I will be non-cooperative, noncompliant, and non-helpful to the staff, to myself, and to my family for the duration of my stay." Francine paused. "How's that?"

"Not what I wanted to hear, but I'll take it as a beginning," said Doctor Franklin. "Small steps."

"By the way, I don't start drinking until five o'clock. I expect my bourbon on the rocks with a splash of 7 UP on the dot."

"Keep up your quirky sense of humor Mrs. Freeman. It's a good coping skill and might keep your spirits intact as you move into recovery."

Francine was exhausted from engaging with her daughter and a doctor who was a generic version of Doctor Kildare. She knew how detox worked—been there before and knew its brutal consequence. Dread was about to consume her. Detox was going to rear its ugly head. Nauseated by the overpowering gross smell of chemicals mixed with some kind of smoke coming from the oxygen bag, more than ever in her life she wanted her freedom, a cigarette, and her dogs. She hoped Ida remembered to take care of Sasha and Boo Boo. She hoped Carlos was going to get out of jail. She needed to put her world back together.

"Can my family come back and visit me?" asked Francine to Doctor Franklin. Her voice was weak, and her mood depleted.

"Get some rest, Mrs. Freeman," said Doctor Franklin. "That's the best medicine a hospital can give you. When you start the DTs, ring that bell next to your head on the left. The nurse will come and give you something."

"Like a bedpan to throw up in," Francine said. "You think I don't know about addiction? I know more about addiction than you do, Doc, because I am an alcoholic. You know the play *A Delicate Balance* by Edward Albee? Probably not. You're a hick from Grand Rapids. There's a character in his play named Claire. Claire is an alcoholic, and she doesn't give two shits who knows. No one is trying to save her. No one is trying to make her a better person. No one is trying to transform the bitch. She is an alcoholic."

"Fascinating story, Mrs. Freeman," said Doctor Franklin.

"Is that said with irony, Doc, because if it is, you show promise as a man I might be able to relate to after my release from Riker's Island."

Francine closed her eyes and began a long, slow drift into memory.

Chapter 3

The Dream That Never Was

Before she fell asleep, she remembered one hot spring day in eighth grade when she and her two best friends were eating their lunch on a bench in St. Norbert's schoolyard in Paoli, Pennsylvania, and Francine announced that she was going to marry a truck driver.

"You're joking," Carol Ann said as she bit into her tuna fish sandwich on whole wheat bread and made a face.

"Oh, God," said Kathy laughing, "you think up some wild stuff. No one marries a truck driver, least of all you."

"I mean, we're going into high school in four months," said Carol Ann, "and we've got the world in front of us. Jeez, don't limit yourself to marriage, especially to a truck driver. Why not a doctor?"

"I'm not joking," Francine said. "I'm making a point about how my life is going to turn out."

"You've got everything going for you," said Kathy. "You're smart, smarter than me, and pretty, and have a great figure."

"You didn't mention how funny I am," said Francine.

"Yeah, you're a riot," Carol Ann told her. "You must have practiced hours in front of a mirror to get that Phyllis Diller laugh just perfect."

Francine shot Carol Ann a dirty look. She knew she had a big personality and wit that most girls her age did not possess, and she was the funniest girl in her class. Francine's words mattered. All the girls wanted to hear what she had to say. And her Phyllis Diller laugh gave her status comparable to the beloved standup comedian whom they all worshiped.

"Why would you even say that you'll marry a truck driver?" asked Kathy.

"Because, you guys, I come from Grand Rapids, and people there can barely speak the King's English. My options are limited. And just because you guys were born near Philadelphia and moved to the fancy suburbs, it doesn't mean you have any better opportunities. So a truck driver sounds good to me."

"That's not even logical," Carol Ann countered with a laugh. "Nothing's preordained."

"Where'd you learn such a big word, Carol Ann?" asked Francine. "You're smarter than I thought." Francine gave her big laugh, prompting both Carol Ann and Kathy to join in.

"What makes her smart is that Carol reads Russian novels," added Kathy. "Who does that?"

"Good God, you're a kiss ass, Carol Ann," Francine teased. "I saw you carrying Sister Mary Bitch Face's briefcase this morning when she got out of the taxi, walking with her into the faculty room. Do you do that every day? Kathy told me you used to hold the rosary beads hanging from Sister Alberta's belt when you were in second grade and followed her around the playground. That's the definition of a kiss ass."

"You'd last about a month in the nunnery, Carol Ann," Kathy said. "Then you'd be horny as hell for a boyfriend. Who would you make out with in the last row of the Devon Theater? Your boyfriend, Ronnie, would be long gone."

The three best friends could get mean and bully each other, but they were always *The Triumvirate*, inseparable, the golden clique, the most popular girls in grammar school, and then in high school. They locked their leadership down with the force of their personalities, their looks, and epic reputations for being at the top of the social ladder, making them untouchable.

Before Francine came along, Carol Ann and Kathy had been best friends since they were three years old and lived on the same block. They shared secrets and dreams while they walked to kindergarten, rode bikes every day to first and second grade, and played together with the conviction that their friendship was sacred and would last forever.

One night during Christmas vacation in their freshman year, they had a slumber party at Carol Ann's house. Elvis and Chuck Berry blared from the phonograph, and they danced the bop, told off-color jokes, used the F word, drank cokes, and ate junk food.

"Sometimes I feel like a third wheel with you guys," said Francine. "I mean you grew up together and shared everything and know each other's deepest, darkest secrets."

"We have history, Francine," said Kathy. "But now, you're part of our history. You'll see. It will all work out."

———

Her memories were receding, and Francine finally dozed off into a deep sleep. She was aware that a nurse came into her room and did something to the tube taped to her hand. It itched and hurt, and Francine wanted to scream at her to stop. She opened one eye and caught Nurse Celya in the act of checking her phone.

"I probably need a drink. Any chance of your getting me one." Francine's voice was low and raspy. "I'm sure it's five o'clock somewhere in the world. I also need a cigarette."

Nurse Celya said nothing.

Francine's eyes swept back and forth from the bandage covering the feeding tube to the almost empty bag hanging from a pole.

A war of wills was starting to heat up, but Nurse Celya held all the cards. The idea of a contest of wills sent an electric shock up Francine's spine and caused her to scream in pain. The nurse's thin, colorless lips held firm.

"What's your name? I can't read it on your badge."

"Nurse Celya."

"You're sure it's not Nurse Ratchet," said Francine.

"I saw the movie. Ratchet had some redeeming qualities. Everyone has some redeeming qualities, Mrs. Freeman."

Francine needed to stake out her territory—the victim was held against her will, but the will was fading fast. Nurse Celya looked at her watch, then back to Francine. Their eyes locked tight, and no one blinked.

"Let's get this straight, Mrs. Freeman," said Nurse Celya. "You are in this hospital to dry out, get on your feet, and heal your broken neck. Then you're going to enter hell."

Francine conceded nothing to Ratchet. She was the personification of an evil bitch, just like in *One Flew Over the Cuckoo's Nest*, but this time Francine was not going to win.

"My name is Nurse Celya, and it's disrespectful not to call me by my name. I know it takes some effort to be civil, but I'll advise you to do so. I'm not immune to the pain of detox, but the upside is that it lasts for a limited time. The downside is that recovery lasts for the rest of the alcoholic's life."

Nurse Celya folded up the blanket at the bottom of the bed. "Anything else you need?" she asked.

"I'm thirsty and freezing. Could I please have more blankets?" Francine closed her eyes in frustration and pain. It was all beginning to happen. She had been through DTs before and recognized the early symptoms. It was clear Nurse Celya was not going to bring her airplane bottles like her last detox when the orderly took care of her alcohol needs during physical therapy. It would be impossible to con Nurse Ratchet into believing that she only drank socially.

Several minutes later, two orderlies arrived with more blankets and piled them on top of her. One of the orderlies gave her water from a cup with a straw while the other orderly pushed her bed away from the wall and held onto the feeding pole. The other orderly pushed the bed into the hallway.

The orderly gave her more water and the other one moved her wrist aside and monitored her heart. She was sipping water when her head slumped.

"Code red!" shouted the orderly monitoring her heart.

The orderly holding her wrist hopped on top of Francine and began to pump her heart. Francine opened one eye.

"You're killing my pelvis," she said with a painful laugh.

"Let's get her to the ICU," said the orderly. "She might go code blue."

As Nurse Celya waited for the hospital bed to roll into the ICU, she smoothed her green hospital uniform and admired her fine figure in a glass pane.

"Looks like Mrs. Freeman has a problem," said Nurse Celya.

"Probably, since she stopped breathing," said the orderly.

"I can hear you all in case you don't know that," said Francine.

Nurse Celya hooked up the hydrating tube, stuck the needle back into the top of her right hand, and tapped it extra firmly. Francine winced and inadvertently raised her arm straight up in the air, barely missing the nurse's eye.

The nurse grabbed Francine's arm with force and threw it down on the bed, causing Francine to grind her teeth.

"I'm going to barf," whispered Francine.

Nurse Celya put a belt around Francine's upper body and put a bedpan close to her head.

"I gather barf is a fourth-grade word for vomit," said Nurse Celya.

"Aren't you the smartest person in the room." Francine vomited a small amount into the pan. "Not bad," said Francine. "This'll be over in a day or two."

"You wish and you hope, but you are dead wrong, Mrs. Freeman."

"I was joking," said Francine. "A little gallows humor never hurt anyone. You ought to get a sense of humor."

Doctor Franklin entered the room with the serious intent of a doctor ready to perform brain surgery. "What have we got here, Francine? How do you feel?"

"Are you guys kidding me? Are you really doctors and nurses? For your information, my heart stopped."

"What happened, Nurse Celya?" asked Doctor Franklin.

"Her heart stopped for a moment," said Nurse Celya.

Doctor Franklin raised his voice, "Didn't stop for long, did it, Mrs. Freeman?"

"I'm not deaf!" yelled Francine back at him. "You don't have to yell."

"In my humble opinion, you like to run the show, but we're in charge now," said Doctor Franklin. "You'll be monitored closely during the next phase of detox. Try to stay calm. Ask for what you need, and we'll be here for you."

"Are you telling me I'm in capable hands, Doctor?"

"I'm sorry but the worst is yet to come," he told her.

"I'm comforted by that thought," said Francine.

"We're here to take care of you," said Nurse Celya. "We are not the enemy."

"It's too early for therapy," said Francine.

"I'll leave you with one thought to retain for the duration of this ordeal," said Nurse Celya. "There is no democracy for the alcoholic."

"Ah, but there must be redemption, Nurse Celya," said Doctor Franklin, "because that's why we are here, working hard to get a patient through detox so we can give her hope of recovery."

"In that case, go out and pray for me, Doctor Franklin. Call on the almighty with force, because good old Francine is nowhere near redemption and never will be."

"Don't you believe in anything, Mrs. Freeman? If not God, then some higher power?"

"Let's not rush things, Doc. I'm not in AA yet."

Francine was relieved to be alone. As her stomach began to cramp and chills overcame her like a pack of wolves, Francine was determined to enjoy detoxing. It was going to be her mission, a mission to satisfy all the other missions that failed. Contrary to her stubborn devilish nature, she strangely wanted the journey to have some value. Inside the deep recesses of her redundant mind, Francine knew this time recovery was going to be a long haul in rehab. She knew they were going to give her disgusting protein drinks, make her wash walls, clean toilets and sinks, bus tables, and keep a daily schedule. But the worst were the AA meetings. It didn't work the first time. Why would recovery work this time?

She worried about her cigarette habit. How was she going to survive without a cigarette for two months? Maybe she could sneak a smoke when she started physical therapy. She'll get Carlos to bring her a pack, or Ida. It was an addiction she wouldn't give up easily. Her father died of lung cancer, but he was in his eighties. That's enough time to live. In the meantime, a job as an aerobics instructor was out of the question.

Francine was going to miss the five o'clock hour when she lit the drinking lamp. Carol Ann's boyfriend told her the funniest damn story about Jack Webb. Her boyfriend was his cameraman on *Dragnet*, and after the daily shooting was completed, Jack turned to Carol's boyfriend and said, "Davey, the drinking lamp is lit." They'd head for the nearest bar off the Universal lot and the party began. She figured if Jack Webb started his drinking at five in the afternoon, so could she. Nothing wrong with that until you fall down the stairs and break your neck.

Nurse Celya came in several times to check on her. Once, without a trace of empathy, she whispered in her ear, "Hold on, you're almost there."

Francine couldn't reply, but if she could, she would have told Nurse Celya that she was lying because the next four days were going to be a nightmare and the next week was going to feel like a disco ball had plunged into her head, spinning like a top, while the Bee Gees played "Stayin' Alive" for two weeks straight.

Sleep was her best friend. Nausea was her worst enemy, second only to sharp abdominal pain that came on sporadically. She was fuzzy about the time she took her last drink. The alcoholic high usually stayed with most drunks for about six hours. Then the effects of alcohol began to taper off. She was going to need a drink soon.

She remembered the torture of her first detox. The beginning hours were an endurance test of the worst hell imaginable—hallucinations, fever, and agitation all mixed up together and shaken like a martini. The experience was traumatic, fixed in her mind so that when she returned to the bottle six months later, she had no thought about ever getting sober again. It seemed Francine miscalculated her future plans.

A month after the first detox, she went into a group drug counseling program. A religious counselor told the recovering alcoholics that they were out of danger, had crossed the Red Sea to the Promised Land, and were all blessed. They had to stay strong and live joyfully among the chosen people. The drug counselor told them to build their tents, grow their food, weave their own clothes, and stay close to loved ones for support. Francine thought that was crap and told the counselor as much. She had the drug counselor flustered as he attempted to boost his righteousness with more biblical references than an evangelical preacher.

Francine countered that life was messy, and it was damn hard to keep the center from falling apart. As a parting shot, she thought, *You can keep your blessed and shove it.*

Chapter 4

In The Throes

"How are you feeling today, Mrs. Freeman?" asked Doctor Franklin on her third day in detox.

"Let's reverse roles," said Francine. "How would you feel?"

Doctor Franklin held her wrist and took her pulse.

"Are you flirting with me?"

Doctor Franklin smiled and carefully placed her wrist down on the bed. "I'm flattered you noticed."

"I knew there was something about you I liked."

"You're looking better today. Not as war-weary. Anything you need at this moment?"

"A bourbon and 7."

"Always with the joke to deflect how you feel," said Doctor Franklin as he studied her chart.

"No, that's how I feel. I want bourbon and 7. It's my wall of shame. You might be surprised to know that I wasn't always like this."

"Yes, you were, Mrs. Freeman," he said. "Another notch in your belt. But don't get ahead of yourself. You're not out of the woods yet."

He checked Francine's pupils, then put one hand on her arm to check for any trembling.

"Cool, moist, and clammy. How are you sleeping? I know you are not eating. Are you still nauseous?"

Francine didn't want to play the assessment game anymore

"The silent treatment won't get you anywhere," said Doctor Franklin.

She felt like vomiting; her stomach was cramping, but Francine would be damned if she would give Doctor Franklin something he wanted.

Left to herself again, unable to sleep, dizzy, and mentally down, Francine stared at the ceiling and began to cry uncontrollably. That damn, wicked Doctor Franklin ripped her mask off. Detoxing was a cover until it wasn't. The problem with detoxing in front of people was the possibility, no, the inevitable probability that once stripped of all dignity, the patient, the person who is hiding from reality, will be brought down, humiliated, and buried under the sins of omission. The beautiful condition of alcoholism was about escaping the present, leaving the gray reality of life behind, being somewhere else that feels right and good. The difficulty of recovering from alcohol dependence is finding a way to use your imagination to ward off what alcohol masked. *There's the rub.*

Nurse Celya entered her room and Francine faked sleep. She had no more fight left in her body.

"I know you're awake, Francine," said Nurse Celya without indicating a false concern. "You've lost the power to resist, and that's a good place to be."

Beads of sweat appeared on Francine's forehead. Nurse Celya placed a damp cloth on her neck, under her chin, around the sides of her face, and moved it slowly to her forehead. It was soothing, but Francine refused to acknowledge the gesture.

Nurse Celya put down the cloth and offered Francine water. She stuck the straw between her lips and waited for Francine to drink. She drank the water but refused to open her eyes.

"Mission accomplished," said Nurse Celya.

Francine slept with the restlessness of a colicky newborn. She awoke with a burning sensation that she had to pee. The pain was agonizing. With strength she did not possess, Francine pushed off from her pillow and sat up. She needed help to get to the bathroom, but she couldn't reach the buzzer. Doubled over and unsteady as a rag doll, Francine crawled along the edges of the bed. Ahead of her was a dresser. If she could reach the dresser, she could make it to the bathroom. She noticed a bottle of pills placed close to the end of the dresser, probably left by an orderly. Thinking it might be a mirage, she grabbed the pill bottle and read the label. If she consumed the bottle, it wouldn't be the worst thing she had ever done. It would be a relief. Maybe Nurse Celya's right. *I have lost the power to resist.*

Francine wet herself and slipped off the bed to the floor with the pills in her hand. She rolled the pill bottle under her bed and waited for help to come.

Rachel sat in the unadorned hospital waiting room, sterile and smelling like old garbage, reading a book on alcoholism. The number of books she had read on addictions could fill a hall closet. She understood the research, preexisting conditions, genetic predispositions, human pain, suffering, guilt, and anecdotal stories in group counseling of children of alcoholics. As she watched her mother mask her pain and disappointment in her own life, Rachel felt helpless against her addiction. Alcohol was the elixir that prevented Francine from releasing her guilt and shame. However, Rachel witnessed a contradiction that gave her some hope that Francine was strong enough and mean enough to face her demons. Rachel never saw her mother drink too much when she was with her family, but she was not around at night when her mother had a drink and then another strong bourbon that replaced her dinner. It was natural she should worry about her mother's weight and suggested several ways to guide her to a healthier life. But Francine held on tightly to her pattern of resistance.

Rachel read that sometimes withdrawal symptoms can worsen and become life-threatening after the first week. She guessed that this must be the scariest time for her mother—as she looks to escape inside a bottle.

During the months that she attended Adult Children of Alcoholics meetings, Rachel tried to reconstruct why she became her mother's protector during her formative years, why she denied and made excuses that her mother had a serious issue with alcohol. Through her brief therapeutic experience in Al-Anon, Rachel understood that she pushed her emotions down deep into her unconscious. Her one focus was to be the good girl: she wanted to save her mother as she saved herself. In her freshman year in high school, she read Philip Roth's *When She Was Good*, a story set in a small town in the Midwest in the 1940s. The father of protagonist, Lucy Nelson, was an alcoholic who was thrown in jail. She couldn't save him, but she tried saving everyone around her, even though it meant destroying herself. Rachel tried to avoid that scenario, conscious of preserving her own identity in school and among her friends. And it worked until it didn't. She was panicked to leave her mother to go to college, so she did not go too far away.

Mark got off the elevator, took a deep breath, and sat down next to Rachel.

"I thought you'd be on the way to the airport by now," said Rachel.

"I want to see how your mom is doing," said Mark. "I'm catching a later plane to St. Paul."

"Are you sure the papers I signed for the intervention are legal? I've got the right to put her in treatment, right?

"We've gone over this. You probably should have intervened the first time she fell, but her lies are part of the disease. This is the right thing to do. And please lay the guilt aside. This is your mother's mess and let her handle it."

"I'd gladly give this job over to someone else," Rachel said. "I'm going to face her criticism and disdain."

"If that happens, you can take it."

"The intervention made me realize that I never took her alcoholism straight on. I made excuses and I lied to myself."

"The good girl always gets lost in the shuffle when trying to live someone else's life. Al-Anon 101. Rach, please don't lose yourself in her recovery. This is Francine's journey, and she has to learn to throw away the crutches. Take some distance."

"You sound like my ACA counselor. She said I would have had a better understanding of our family dynamic if I had stepped away, but I couldn't, I wouldn't, and here I am."

"Don't be so hard on yourself. She and your father got married too young. They weren't old enough to be parents at nineteen. They had nothing to glue the marriage together. It was the time, the mid-sixties, and all the pressure was on getting married. And besides, she was pregnant and Catholic."

"It feels like this journey will never end."

"I'm sorry, honey," said Mark as he kissed her on the forehead. "I've got to take off. You're going to be fine."

Rachel closed her eyes. In her exhausted state, she thought of the night of the living dead, when her parents were fighting and drinking and the house burned down. She heard them arguing about why her mother thought her father was a failure. A failed golf pro. Accusations flew around the living room. Her father called Francine a drunk. He went to bed. She poured another drink, lit a cigarette, and fell asleep. Smoke began to fill the room and her father ran downstairs. The rug in the living room was smoldering. Her father brought Francine to consciousness. Sparks started to fly from the fireplace. Her father ran into her room and carried her out of the house. Francine followed and stayed calm. They all watched as their house burned to the ground.

Poor dad. He didn't know what to do or how to cope. All he had left was to go home to his parents in shame. Out of the blue, Mom stopped drinking again.

Rachel's eyes were still closed when Nurse Celya came into the waiting room. "Mrs. Miller, you can go in now."

They walked down the quiet corridor without speaking. A few feet from the door, Rachel stopped.

"How is she doing?" asked Rachel.

"You'll have to see for yourself. It's early in detox. For every day she feels better, the next day, she'll feel worse. It takes time.

"You sound like you know this journey," Rachel said to her.

"I know this journey very well," replied Nurse Celya as she opened the hospital room door.

"Someone is here to see you, Mrs. Freeman."

"I'm asleep, can't you see that?" said Francine.

"Your eyes are closed, but that doesn't mean you're asleep. Your daughter is here."

Francine opened her eyes as Rachel entered the room with trepidation. "Hi, Mom, how are you doing?"

"Oh, my sweet baby, how do you think I'm doing? Do I look like I'm getting ready for the prom?"

"I'm not going to banter with you, Mom. How are you feeling?"

"What's gotten into you, babe. You used to be my. . ."

"Good girl. I'm still your good girl only in a different way now since I hold the keys to the kingdom of potential freedom. What is new is that you can't bully me or intimidate me. I finally have the upper hand and legal papers that allow me to intervene to admit you to the hospital to detox. It's technically called an intervention."

"Oh, my, aren't we on our high horse."

"I wanted to see how you were doing, and now I see you are your usual self, I can go."

"What are you still doing here?" asked Francine to Nurse Celya. "This is a private conversation."

"May I speak frankly, Mrs. Freeman?" asked Nurse Celya.

"Of course you can," replied Francine. "I live to hear what you might say."

"You were lucky your daughter was generous enough to put you in detox because I suspect that your nine lives are up."

Nurse Celya left the room. Francine pouted in silence.

Rachel walked to the window and watched the snow outside whipping around the side streets with mean fury. "She's right, you know," she said.

"Sobering. No pun intended. Remember I told you a long time ago that I didn't need saving?"

"That's not my intention now. I want you to be comfortable. I'm going to give you space to do your recovery and try like hell to detach from the outcome while I work on my recovery."

"Do I detect a little self-pity?" Francine said with dramatic flair. "Come on. You put yourself in that position. I have nothing to do with your decision to put me in here."

"I don't want to go around with you about this."

"While we're being honest, I resent the hell out of you for putting me in detox," said Francine. "If I'm willing to die, then so be it. I'm not reversing course."

"Who's the martyr now, Mom? You can give it out, but you can't take it. You're going to do all that is required to complete your detox and recovery, and you are going to learn to live sober. And that means group counseling, AA, in and out of the shrink's office, cleaning toilets, and dishing out food. And, you'd just better get this out of your system now, because I'm sick of worrying about you and your falls, your broken bones, and you driving drunk."

"Stop right there, oh, high and mighty, and take a breath," said Francine. "I never, ever, drive drunk and you know that. Don't you remember, I was a member of MADD?"

Rachel almost choked on a laugh. Ironically, her defense against her alcoholism was a two-year stint in Mothers Against Drunk Driving. The height of hypocrisy. Francine could side-step an issue faster than McDonald's could make a hamburger. Rachel was supportive of her mother's work with MADD, yet, she hoped her commitment would translate into a permanent recovery program. Rachel let her mother decide what was best for her. It was a mistake and Rachel made excuses to herself for why she had not encouraged her to go into a recovery program a long time ago.

Francine began to cough. Rachel rushed over to her bed to get her water. She leaned over her body to press the call button for a nurse. Francine angrily shook her head and continued to cough until she drank enough water to end the seizure.

"Don't call that bitch," she whispered.

Rachel sat on the bed and took her mother's hands.

"You're skin and bone, Mom. Is this what you want to look like? Where is your pride?"

"I lost that long ago, babe," Francine said. "My parents couldn't raise a decent, responsible kid even if they had a playbook."

"This is an old story," said Rachel, "and you keep insisting on telling it every chance you get. You're seventy-seven, it's 2018, and it's time to lose it. Tell the story about why you are here in this hospital."

"Here's where I am today. My last husband left me well-off. I earned every penny of the money, and now I can do whatever I want."

"That's over. Tell me your story now. Today. No nostalgia, no pie in the sky fantasies, and skip the hyperboles."

"I'm here in this place you put me in. You have no right to sit in judgment of what's right and wrong in my life. That's my story now."

"You almost killed yourself again," said Rachel. "Alcohol-related accidents can be lethal."

"That's not all that can be lethal. But I'm still here, and I'm probably going to continue to drink no matter the detox or the recovery. That's all I know. That's my story."

"I'm sure you had some happiness along the way."

"With you, yes. With men, no. God, I hope the truck driver is in his grave by now."

"Mom, don't go down that loser road, please."

"Betsy Johnson, my co-worker at the Walker school district administrative office . . ."

"You're going to do this anyway, aren't you?"

"Who can forget my drinking buddy? Sexy Betsy. One day after work, we went to our usual bar, you know it—the Sidebargr in downtown to have a drink—and I literally ran into Gary Richelli, member of the Teamsters Union, owner of a big rig, and an all-around asshole. He played country music, strutted around in brown, dirty cowboy boots, and donned a straw cowboy hat. And I thought his never-completely-shaved face was fascinating."

"I couldn't figure out what you saw in him. He wasn't even sexy," Rachel told her.

"His last name ended in a vowel. That was the gold standard for me. Your grandfather, good old Richard, would shoot his balls off with his World

War II M1 Garand if he ever met an Italian whose last name ended with a vowel."

"How could you not figure out that the truck driver was abusive and disgusting? He smelled of some kind of musky cologne. He was another stray who turned into Frankenstein. What kind of man would be so cruel?"

"Good thing he was away most of the time doing his long haul drives," said Francine.

"You should have done a background check. You were his fifth wife. And he had other families, and he was cheating. There was nothing good about that situation."

"You're right. Let's get off of this putrid story and get to the point because I know what you want, and, I'm telling you, I don't know if I can give you that."

"Full recovery is too much at this stage of your life?"

"Is that it? Those are high stakes. I've been here before, my darling. I mean right here in this bed, in this hospital, in group counseling, in this sterile cuckoo's nest, and I can't do it. I don't want to do it. I want to be left alone. Please, Rachel."

"I can't let that happen. I can't let you will your death."

"I'm not willing it, my baby. It's happening."

Francine knew Rachel didn't understand what she was telling her. Her death was taking its time, but it was happening slowly and painfully. The pain in her abdomen, the coughing. She was on her way out. At least with alcohol, she didn't have to wrestle with real life.

Rachel hugged her mother and kissed her on the forehead. "It's finally my job to leave you alone."

Chapter 5

Rachel

Rachel couldn't stand another minute in her mother's room. She smelled death every time she inhaled. It was all she could do to hold on to her sanity for the rest of the day. Anything that had to do with her mother's illness made her anxious. Her role in Francine's recovery compromised Rachel's nature. Playing offense was a new role for her. She'd rather take a back seat and let someone else support her mother's journey. The big question was still to be resolved: would her mother finally take the responsibility for directing her own life?

Despite how Francine managed to hide her first fall from her family, and despite her infrequent attempts to stop drinking, Rachel felt her mother couldn't keep her promise to quit. Why would she quit now? Are the stakes too high? It was easier for her mother to keep denying her self-inflicted wounds. In her redundant mind, no one would be the wiser.

Six months after the first fall, while talking to her mother on the phone, Rachel heard the slur in her speech and confronted her. She was drinking. She admitted as much. It was five o'clock in the afternoon and that was her time to drink but only wine. Not the hard stuff.

Rachel figured she slept most of the day and drank her dinner. She wondered what had happened to going to AA meetings. Rachel heard the sound of Francine dumping the wine into the sink and listened as she unscrewed a cap to a bottle and poured herself what she supposed was a bourdon and 7.

And then Francine expounded on how AA is overrated—just a bunch of sad loser stories. Francine never considered herself a loser. Just screwed up. Rachel thought she should reconsider going back to meetings, that drinking her way through life didn't make sense.

Francine didn't appreciate her daughter's tone. The conversation ended with her mother dropping the phone into the cradle. What Rachel imagined was her mother taking a sip of her drink, then drinking the rest with her eyes closed. Then all would be right in her mother's world.

∽

Rachel had to get back to work in the city so she could put in a few hours on a marketing project that was due the next day. Queen of Angels Hospital in suburban Zeeland was thirty minutes from downtown Grand Rapids. She dreaded the drive and the afternoon traffic. Since becoming empty nesters, Rachel and Mark had outgrown the need to live in the suburbs. They researched moving to a high-rise condo in the city, and it sounded like a good idea, until the downtown crowds and traffic proved fatal to their psyches, and they decided to stay in Forest Hills and buy another lot to plant a vegetable garden.

After Francine's first fall, Mark considered moving downtown again to put distance between Rachel and her mother. He suggested she focus on her life and work instead of her mother's life. She had never done that before. Most of her life was involved in protecting her mother.

Rachel kept some distance from Mark when it came to discussing her mother's dysfunctional behavior. It took too much energy to elucidate her process. She never told him all the details of Francine's marriage to Peter. He only knew Peter as a nice man who provided for Francine, but he didn't know how that relationship started on a negative note. She never told her husband about her mother's calls to Carol in the middle of the night three months after the wedding, inside a bathroom, screaming that she wanted to put a pillow over his head and kill him. Mark would have been horrified; Rachel was horrified when Francine told her the story. Rachel thought it said volumes about her mother's state of mind at the time of her marriage. Those middle-of-the-night phone calls to Carol saved her mother from doing something disastrous in a fit of angry fury.

Instead of going to the city to work, Rachel drove west to the airport. She needed to connect to another reality, to the house she lived in for most of elementary school, before her mother left Pittsburg. Brighton Heights was once a comfortable middle-class neighborhood in Pittsburg where Francine and Bill lived when they were first married. It made no sense for her to fly to Pittsburg to see the old neighborhood, except that she wanted to be in a familiar place where she could sit and think about a time when her family seemed normal—when she possibly seemed normal. When she could be honest with herself. When she realized she hated being in marketing and advertising. The money was good, but it was a daily grind. A fresh start in another field would be a breath of fresh air. She dreamed of growing farm-to-market vegetables in Caledonia. At least, she still had dreams.

When Rachel turned into the cul-de-sac where her home was located, she did not recognize the surroundings. The house she lived in for first seven years had burned to the ground one fateful night when her parents were drinking too much and arguing about how destructive the marriage had become. After her mother fell asleep on the sofa, a spark from the fireplace landed on the rug and smoldered. Smoke began to fill the house. The fire alarm went off; Bill ran down the stairs screaming at his wife, Rachel in his arms. He pulled Francine off the couch and ran out of the house to find fire trucks on the lawn and the neighbors huddled in a group. It wasn't until later that Rachel understood the machinations of her family that night. Nothing was ever the same between Francine and Bill. He left to live with his parents; she took advantage of her in-laws' generous offer to rent her a house.

Rachel recognized a neighborhood defined by wealth. Each house had been remodeled and looked like a mini-mansion. All vestiges of the sixties middle-class family dwellings were gone. Everything was white and gray on the outside, and probably the same on the inside—no color, no warmth, no remnants of her former life. Gone were the track homes, the Fuller Brush salesmen, the old bikes, and falling down basketball hoops. She knew nostalgia was a waste of time. Only fools reach for the past. Rachel didn't know whether to laugh or cry.

After Francine kicked out her second husband, Gary-the-truck-driver, and put a few more years in the Brighton Heights school district, the best her mother could come up with was to move back to Grand Rapids, the scene of her early childhood where she remembered being happy. Ten years of working was enough.

Rachel was horrified. She had no connection to Grand Rapids. She doubted that her mother could make a living.

Francine was sure she was going to get another job in a school district. Or better yet, her mother said, she'll marry a rich man.

She told her Mom she was not going with her. "I'll be eighteen in two years, and then I can petition the courts and make my own decisions. I don't want to move to Grand Rapids, and I don't have to follow you."

But Rachel did follow her mother. She went along because she loved her mother, despite how Francine's life was turning out. Or maybe she went along because she had been with her mother all her life and she knew no other life. Perhaps her fate in life was to keep the message of hope and renewal alive so that Francine would one day forgive herself for insisting on living her own private existential telenovela.

Rachel wanted desperately to help her mother over the years, but she didn't have the perspective—the long-distance view of being the adult child of an alcoholic. The good girl could only keep vigilance over her mother and try to keep the peace. But being the good girl had a cost—it prevented her from taking down the negative psychic walls that Francine put around herself, walls that barricaded her from consciousness and blocked her from making her own decision to get clean and sober.

Francine had been sleeping for almost the entire day. The orderly had never seen anyone sleep so much. She was a sleeping machine.

"Rise and shine, Mrs. Freeman," said the orderly in a firm voice. "Time to get up and start moving."

Francine did not respond. He suspected it was going to take a crane to get her up.

"If you don't get up now, I'll call for Nurse Celya, and she won't be as nice as I am with you."

Francine opened one eye.

"You see, how easy it will be with me in charge," he said. "We need to get you moving today because your detoxing program is over, and now is your time to go to physical therapy."

"You don't have to be so polite," said Francine, "and by the way, what is your name since we've been up close and personal for two weeks."

"Ricky," he said.

"I'm not going to move, Ricky. I still don't feel well."

"You'll feel better if you move, so please get up. Give me your hand. No more sleep."

Ricky detached all the tubes from her body.

"Wait, I have to jingle," said Francine.

"What's that?" asked Ricky.

"Oh, come on. I have to pee, jingle, go potty."

As Francine tried to stand up, her legs wobbled. Ricky took her in his arms.

"Shall we dance?" asked Francine.

"Are you in pain?" asked Ricky.

"Damn right I am. I've been in bed too long, and I can't walk by myself. We have to do something about this."

Ricky carried Francine in his arms to the bathroom, set her down on the toilet, and patiently waited. "You are light as a feather, mi amor. We need to put real food in you."

Several agonizing moments passed. "I can't jingle now," said Francine. "Oh, God, this is awful. I'm so embarrassed. Please help me up."

Ricky helped her into a wheelchair. He knelt in front of her and held her hands.

"This is hard, Miss. Francine," said Ricky. "I must walk you up and down the halls. You're frail and we must make you stronger. Are you ready?"

Francine looked devotedly at Ricky and started to cry. She wiped her face and showed determination in her eyes.

"You're very good-looking, Ricky," said Francine. "Did you know that? You could be a movie star."

"Some have said that," said Ricky with a wry smile. "So, Miss. Francine, let's get going."

Ricky lifted Francine out of the wheelchair and held her close to him. When he felt she was steady on her legs, they set out on their journey down a long institutional hallway, devoid of anything that resembled humanity. Whitewashed walls, brown and green linoleum floors, no windows or paintings. A few patients were walking with oxygen poles or shuffling to nowhere in particular, while nurses buzzed in and out of rooms, carrying trays of food or medical needs. Francine became confused and began to falter. She clung to her helper.

"Am I going to make it?" asked Francine. "It's a long journey to the end. I'm pathetic in the athletic department. Hard to breathe."

"It's always difficult at the beginning, Miss Francine, but it will get easier as you go along."

"That's what they said the first time I went on this tour."

Walking with Ricky made her bones feel like they were being put through a meat slicer. Every part of her body hurt with a burning sensation.

After the walk, Ricky put her back in bed, refilled her water glass, and pulled the blankets around her cold body. When he left the room, Francine sat up and dangled her legs over the side of the bed. She slid off but held onto the side rails to see if the pills were still there. The bottle had rolled toward the oxygen pole, near the outer edges of the bed, close to the bedside table. Forcing the muscles in her arms to work, she retrieved the bottle, opened it, and counted the pills. Anything over ten pills would do the trick, put her to sleep for good. She held them in her hands and climbed into bed.

That afternoon Ricky packed up the few things Francine had brought to the hospital and moved her to the physical therapy wing of Queen of Angeles Hospital. When she found out Ricky would no longer be by her side, she was heartbroken. Francine brought the pill bottle to her new room. She didn't know why.

Rachel came regularly with food she would eat because if she didn't, her mother would have died of starvation. All she would eat was mac and cheese and mashed potatoes. If anything on her plate was green in color, she wouldn't touch it. The staff gave up on trying to give her a nutritious diet and acquiesced to her peculiar eating habits. Francine liked cheerios and milk, occasionally, she would eat bananas. Color came back to her cheeks.

A few days later, Carlos walked into her hospital room, and she almost leaped out of bed.

"Careful, Francine," he said. "You don't want to hurt yourself."

"I sure don't. But I'm glad to see you. Tell me everything."

"Getting picked up by the cops didn't make sense," he said. "Man, they're hard cases. I told them where the papers were in your house, but they didn't care. But I got my old job back."

"Of course, you did. I talked to Mr. Marshall while you were in jail."

"You're the best, Francine. He's a good guy. I promise I'm not screwing this up."

"I'm not getting out of here for another week, depending on my ability to build up my strength, then I'm off to the Ritz for rehab. Have you seen my daughter?"

"No. There's no reason for her to come by since you're here."

"Then let's get down to business. While I'm still here, I want you to bring me *The Week Magazine* I love so much, carrot cake, and little airplane bottles. Oh, yeah, and a pack of cigarettes."

"Are you crazy? You just detoxed. Why would you want to go and do that after all you've been through?"

"Think about it Carlos, will you," said Francine. "I'm dying for a drink. No one will know because I'm in physical therapy."

"I love you like my mamacita, but I won't be the cause of anything that has to do with losing your life."

"Please get me a pack of cigarettes, Carlos. No harm in that. Now, how are Sasha and Boo Boo? Do they miss me?"

"Of course, they do. You need to get home and give them all your love."

"Do me a favor and call Ida and tell her to visit me since I'm out of detox."

Carlos set down a deck of cards. "I'll see you in a few days and we can play gin. It'll help you take your mind off this place and airplane bottles." Carlos took her hands. "You look better, Francine. Don't scare me again, please. My heart can't take it."

Two days later, Ida visited Francine. "You look good, Francine," she said. "Your eyes are clear. And you've put on a few pounds." She hugged Francine.

Francine smelled liquor on her breath. Her ability to smell was coming back, and it felt good to recognize odors. Alcohol was especially good to smell. It was a trigger.

"Ida, you've had a few today and you're not supposed to drive when you've had a few."

"Carlos told me to visit you," she said. "I wanted to get here as soon as I could. I took care of the dogs while Carlos was in jail, by the way."

"Thank you, and I owe you another dinner at Chez Moi. Minus the bottle of wine. Speaking of which, how would you like to get me those little liquor airplane bottles?"

Ida smiled and Francine recognized her devilish face.

"You have them, don't you?"

Ida took the four bottles out of her purse and held them up for Francine to inspect. She looked at them as if salvation was at hand. "That's my girl, dear Ida. You're always there for me."

"Carlos told me you wanted a pack of cigarettes. I've got them, but where do you want me to put them."

"In my suitcase. Tuck them in the side pockets. You're the best, Ida."

Part Three: Oak Lane

Chapter 6

Recovery

On the first day of May, three weeks after Francine was admitted to Queen of Angels Hospital, Rachel walked Francine to the doors of a modern, three-story building on the outskirts of East Grand Rapids. The limestone and glass facade was pristine in the afternoon sun. Francine, strong and steady on her feet with her neck brace firm around her neck, held her purse close to her body and entered the facility without waiting for Rachel to hold the door open for her. Rachel held the door open for herself and suitcase in hand, walked behind her mother. Francine turned around, looked into her daughter's eyes, and squinted.

"At least I didn't have to push you through the door, Mom," said Rachel. "You made it easy."

"You have a gun to my head, babe," said Francine, "and you didn't give me a choice. I hope you don't have high expectations."

"Look at the positive and be surprised about the outcome."

"What's the name of this place?" asked Francine. "It looks like an insane asylum."

"Oak Lane," Rachel said. "All the other places had bars on the doors."

With trepidation, Francine held herself back and stood behind Rachel as she spoke with Doris, the front desk administrator. Doris was a nondescript woman of indeterminate age, but definitely over sixty. She wore a net around her hair, for what reason Francine couldn't figure out. She wasn't preparing food. Maybe she was a germaphobe. Francine wandered off while Rachel worked with Doris to get her mother checked in.

Francine hummed to herself as she walked around the lobby and scanned pictures and plaques that lined the beige wall opposite the wood and granite front desk. She felt warmth on her back and found the source in the sunlight that shined through a skylight window. A shudder went through her body. She clutched her purse even closer to her chest and looked down at the brownish institutional vinyl flooring. The pattern looked like vomit from a long-ago hamburger.

Francine peeked around the corner of the wall that separated the lobby from the ground floor offices, which were mostly empty. She was surprised that nothing much was going on. Expecting to see the inmates wearing jail clothes, carrying folded sheets and blankets as they marched to their dormitory rooms, Francine was relieved to feel the quiet. Residual headaches and mild stomach pains were reoccurring. Maybe Oak Lane would be a cure for what ails her.

"Ready?" asked Rachel.

"For what? My orange is the new black jumpsuit?"

"Your counselor wants to see you."

Francine peered down the empty corridor unsure of what was expected of her.

"Is the counselor's office down this hallway?"

"Yes, Mom. He'll talk to you for a few minutes, explain the procedures, set you up in your room. I'm afraid you are sharing a room, but I know you'll get along."

"How do you know that?" asked Francine. "I'm a whirling bitch with new people."

"You're stalling and you're scared, and I don't blame you, but, please, let's get this started."

"You have some place to be?" asked Francine.

Rachel took her mother by the arm and led her down the hallway to the third office on the right. The sign on the door read "Doctor Jerry Peterson." She gave Francine a brief hug.

"Doctor Peterson will be your counselor. You'll be fine, Mom. Open up and be yourself and see what you uncover."

As Rachel turned to go, Francine took her arm.

"I don't need to uncover or recover anything from my life," Francine snorted. "I was perfectly fine masking my memories with bourbon."

"That's a good start, Mom. You're getting the hang of it already."

"How do you know this is going to work for me? Do you have a crystal ball?"

"Try not to hate Oak Lane right away. Besides, you can't hate a facility. Hate is directed against content, a person, or a philosophy. A facility is brick and motor or steel and . . ."

"I get the point. What are you now, my shrink? Maybe if I felt better, I'd banter with you, and we'd have fun. But I'm not up to the effort."

Francine took a deep breath and tried to stop the pain in her abdomen. She turned and winced so Rachel wouldn't notice.

"Let the games begin," muttered Francine under her breath as she faced the office door.

A psychologist's office reveals little of the doctor's personality. Doctor Jerry Peterson's office was different—full of life and color and quirky tchotchkes from Africa and Asia and pictures of police chiefs and city officials. There was a woven red rug under a bamboo framed coffee table. It was an eclectic room, fun and warm.

Doctor Jerry Peterson stood up as Francine entered. He had the sweetest smile on his face. He wore beige khakis and a yellow and blue Hawaiian shirt that covered his protruding stomach. As he held out his hand to Francine, his eyes squinted. She thought he smelled like lemons.

"Please sit, Francine. It's good to meet you. You can call me Doctor Jerry. I know you're not settled in yet. Everything you see and feel is new and awkward, but in time you will find the experience to be non-threatening and productive."

"That's pretty positive stuff, Doctor Jerry. Do you give this speech to everyone on the first day?"

"Pretty much," he said with a twinkle in his eye.

Doctor Jerry proceeded to ask her questions, and Francine lied in response to all of them:

How are you feeling after detox?

Fabulous.

How is your energy level?

Superb.

Any issues at the moment?

None.

What do you expect?

Nothing

Francine figured, why tell the truth when it's his job to find out the truth? She didn't want to help the psychologist analyze her issues. After all, Francine Fisher-Reynolds-Richelli-Freeman was a woman of substance, a known unnatural beauty with a Phyllis Diller laugh who sold the most tickets to win the homecoming queen of Bishop Shanahan in a crowd of real beauties. Francine bought the tickets; Francine won the crown. This psychologist-cretin and his cohorts will have to figure out why a smart, self-loathing, self-sabotaging woman like Francine Fisher-Reynolds-Richelli-Freeman insisted on being an alcoholic.

"I'd like to give you a heads up about your roommate. There might be issues that arise. Keep an open mind and try not to be confrontational," Doctor Jerry said.

"That's no fun, Doc," said Francine. "I mean if two people have the same self-loathing issues and antisocial personalities, it's a perfect prescription for bonding, right?"

"It's not that simple, Francine," said Doctor Jerry.

"I think it is. Drunks have a knack for self-sabotaging. It's built into their DNA."

The roommate was a nightmare. Doctor Jerry should have given her the real truth: dirty, ragged, surly, antisocial, and full of self-loathing. By the time Francine settled into her room and insulted her roommate for being disorganized and slothful, she was ready for a drink. She would even drink beer, and she loathed beer.

"What's your name again?" Francine asked her roommate.

"I told you already," she said.

"Well, tell me again, so I can call you something other than pathetic."

"Thanks for the compliment," she said. "My name is Bonnie. Like 'my Bonnie lies over the ocean.' You're not so charming yourself. I forgot your name, too."

"Francine. Do you have a last name?"

"I won't be here long enough for you to remember it," said Bonnie.

"Are you planning on escaping?" asked Francine.

"Maybe. What about you? Are you staying the thirty days?"

"I'm under orders to stay the entire time," said Francine with a burst of enthusiasm. "But the fortune teller doesn't have a clear answer to my dilemma. While I'm here, I'd like to do some decorating in this room. Some colorful pictures would cheer up the space and a woven rug in the center would make it feel cozier."

"You won't be staying," said Bonnie. "Look at the statistics."

"I'd rather be drinking about now. It's five o'clock somewhere in the world, but this place is too damn expensive to screw around, so the odds are that I will do my time. We have a group meeting with Counselor Jerry in a few minutes." Then she rolled her eyes and added, "La di da. Can't wait."

∽

An hour later, Francine entered a cheerless recreation room painted yellow with a bizarre off-white wainscoting that extended about five inches above the floor on every wall. It could have been a baby nursery or a doctor's waiting room for all the care the administration put into making the recovery room comfortable and warm. Maybe the yellow color signified sunshine and happy puppies. Or, maybe they found several leftover gallons of yellow paint in the maintenance room, or someone had cans left over from redecorating a newborn's room when the paint store ran out of pink or blue.

Francine felt like she was losing her mind. She became fixated on the room—there was no thought behind the composition of the room, no relatable art, or interesting chairs, or side tables for literature. Or pictures of a bourbon bottle with a big red X across it signifying alcohol was prohibited on the premises. If the recovery room was meant to help cure addiction, it failed. As if the curse of being an addict was going to vanish with sunshine colors and florescent lighting. By definition, a room in a recovery facility was always going to signify punishing reality and lost lives.

The huddled figures who sat in uncomfortable, bright orange vinyl chairs in a perfect semi-circle knew this truth: addiction was uncompromising, and it would take more than yellow walls to calm their demon lover. That was the one abiding truth in Oak Lane.

Francine found a chair as far away from 'my Bonnie lies over the ocean' as possible and pulled her blanket tighter over her shoulders. The smell of Lysol antiseptic was palpable.

"How are y'all doing today?" the counselor asked, his Texas twang prominent. "In case you might have forgotten my name, I'm Doctor Jerry Peterson, but y'all can call me Doctor Jerry. Welcome."

"It's a meat locker in here," said Francine. "Can you turn the heat up?"

"Would you like to start by introducing yourself, Francine?" asked Doctor Jerry.

"No, Doctor Jerry, I wouldn't," said Francine. "I asked about turning on some heat."

"I'm afraid I can't do much about it. It's controlled elsewhere in the building. We like to keep the temperature on the colder side so that y'all will stay focused and centered with intention. When it's warm, it's tempting to give in to sleep at this very early stage of your recovery."

"Well, that might make sense for you, Doc, but my nipples are about ready to freeze off." Several people in the room snickered. Some looked down into their laps.

"Hang with it, Francine," said Doctor Jerry. "Now let's go around the room and make our introductions."

Francine loathed the group counseling experience with a passion, almost as much as she loathed AA. Having to engage with a group of people who had arrived at the bottom of their lives and felt oh-so-sorry for themselves as they blamed the other guy—husband, wife, lover, loser boyfriend, father, priest, best girlfriend—for their fall into disgrace. They had abdicated personal choice in favor of chemicals that masked their better selves. Francine heard it before, had it all figured out, and she was satisfied by her observations about the state of addiction since they all related to her.

Ironically, if she wanted a way out, if she felt like she had enough, if recovery was too painful, well, then she had a bottle of pills and four adorable mini airline liquor bottles plus a pack of Marlboros. She had a treasure trove of goodies. Amazed she got away with hiding them throughout detox and elated that Oak Lane didn't search her suitcase when she entered rehab, because she guessed she was a distraction with her antics, a sense of independence washed over her. Francine thought she might have the beginnings of some control over her life. It was a new feeling. No more uncertainty.

A very large and imposing man, well over six feet tall, with beady blue eyes and a short white beard looked to be about seventy stood and introduced himself with his crooked smile.

"Hi, my name is Don. Sober forty years and my demon lover caught me when I wasn't paying attention. I stopped working AA."

Rhonda, an African American lady in her fifties looked more like forty. She was a sturdy, muscular woman with beautiful brown skin and perfectly coiffed hair.

"Hi, my name is Rhonda. This is my second time in rehab. I was sober for ten years. I served time and relapsed when I got out. I'm a big believer in AA."

Dean was a thin plain-looking man in his mid-thirties addicted to his fidget spinner. When he twirled the fidget spinner, he was in his comfort zone.

"I'm Dean and I'm nervous. And did I mention insecure? That's why I'm an addict. It's my third time in rehab."

There was Bonnie, the roommate, sullen as ever. She did not respond to the introduction and neither did Ronnie, an executive in his mid-fifties. He was dressed for cocktails and probably thought he was too good to be in rehab as evidenced by his snug three-piece suit on his muscular body. He sat in the corner near the door at the ready to hop into his stretch limo after the group meeting.

"Is this like a self-help group because I don't do that stuff?" asked Ronnie.

Alexa, a chronic nail biter, was a glamour girl in her late-twenties. She looked like she had been drinking since she was ten because her mother left her at the age of thirteen with a seventeen-year-old babysitter almost every night while she partied with the fast crowd at the Rendezvous cocktail lounge in the Amway Grand Plaza Hotel.

"Hi, I'm Alexa. Mine is a typical rich kid's story. No mother or father to speak of. No boundaries. I liked to drink, and I did it to excess. No one was watching."

An African American man in his late-fifties was wearing a long-sleeve shirt that had never seen an iron. He was also in desperate need of shoes.

"I'm Bluzy. I ended up on the streets after the Gulf War, went to prison a few times. Lived in a bottle and can't seem to quit."

Francine was the last of the group to introduce herself.

"Hi, I'm Francine Fisher-Reynolds-Richelli-Freeman. I'm seventy-six, born in 1942, mother of one daughter who put me in this luxurious spa. I live in Zeeland and I'm an alcoholic."

After the introductions, after the awkwardness of the circumstances, Doctor Jerry detailed the way the counseling session worked.

"How many of you have been in AA meetings before?" asked Doctor Jerry.

A few people raised their hands—Don, Rhonda, Alexa, and Francine.

"The way this works in a group counseling session in rehab is that no one person takes center stage. Consider it like a melting pot of people co-mingling insights and emotions. In an AA meeting, there is no cross talk. AA is structured differently. You say the Serenity Prayer, then one or two people volunteer to go to the front and share his or her story. Do not voice opinions or proffer uncalled for comments. There might be another share or a review of one of the Twelve Steps with a discussion. The meeting takes about an hour."

"Sounds super easy," said Alexa. "Nothing should take more than an hour of our time."

Even the Francine of yesteryear registered the intent behind Alexa's callous remark. She was riveted on Doctor Jerry's response.

"But in group counseling, Alexa, we can have freedom to share, compare, comment, express a personal opinion, make an observation about yourself, or support others in their journey if it's appropriate. When in group, keep your resistance level to a minimum, keep your hearts open to others, and above all try to be honest with yourself."

"As I said before," remarked Ronnie, "I don't do self-help group stuff."

"The stuff I'm talking about is learning to improve yourself. Evolve. Learn something new about your addictions, change your perspective, your circumstances, re-direct the negative flow of your existence."

"Truth be told, I'm not an addict," said Ronnie.

Doctor Jerry asked him how he arrived at that conclusion.

"My acute observational skills. One of the lawyers in the firm told the head honcho that I drank too much, and he did that because he's got a hard-on for me."

"We can get that story straightened out in time, Ronnie. For now, let's focus on not resisting the process or making excuses for what happened to you."

After two hours of what Francine thought was a piss poor outcome of counseling, a room full of the walking dead, she had a pounding headache from her neck brace, and the pain in her stomach was ratcheting up the Richter scale. Much like a hangover, but without the booze, she was drifting off, barely attentive, no focus on what Doctor Jerry was saying about the process. If that's what recovery was going to look like moving forward, Francine knew she couldn't do it, couldn't bear it, couldn't be counted among the accountable. A bed awaited in her room. Hopefully, her roommate wouldn't talk.

"Francine," called Doctor Jerry as she was walking out the door.

"I need to get to my room," she said still shaking from the cold. "I'm not up for a chit-chat."

"Okay, I get it," said Doctor Jerry. "But can you please engage me for a moment? Please look at me, Francine. It's okay to be quiet in the early sessions, but remember, you are the only one who counts in your recovery. Don't spend time disparaging others for their unfortunate journeys because that story was showing on your face."

"I don't get anything out of those loser stories. They're depressing, like my first time in AA—all the same, all familiar, and all exhausting. God, I hated AA. What am I supposed to learn from them? It's not my life. And I can't stand sitting in a circle."

"You are not in an AA meeting. This is not a circle. This is group counseling. Maybe in time, you'll see that the sharing process will be beneficial. In the beginning, I understand how these stories can be annoying, maybe even unhelpful, but if you listen and focus, you'll begin to find connections or threads. It's challenging, I know, but it's worth it for your own personal growth."

"I want to scream at you right now. I didn't set this challenge. My daughter is in the driver's seat, and I have a sneaking hunch my recovery is more for her than for me."

"That's not fair, Francine. Your daughter is giving you an opportunity for self-knowledge, and to find the truth of why you have been masking your pain for decades. Besides, what else have you got to do in the glory years of your retirement but to learn more about why you have persisted in your addiction?"

"Let me level with you, Doctor Jerry. I'm not that interested in self-reflection, but it seems my daughter is determined that I examine my sins of omission. My life reads like the lyrics to a country western song. 'My old man left me lying on the linoleum floor without a pulse.' It doesn't take a rocket scientist to figure out why I never had a reason to stop drinking. The deck was stacked against me, given the circumstances of my dysfunctional parentage and a life of bad choices. Life is messy and complicated. If guilt and shame are staring me in the face daily, why not wait for the click in my head to go off and wake up the next day to do it all over again. That's from Tennessee Williams—*Cat On A Hot Tin Roof* in case you needed a reference. That's what Brick did in the play. Waited for the click to go off in his head. After all is said and done, after the false starts and stops with my addiction, there seems no apparent reason for me to embrace lucidity."

"Those are hard judgments about you and your daughter. Lots of anger in that confession. Getting a handle on your anger is the first step. Then the goal here is for you to begin to live courageously with more kindness for yourself and the ability to ask for help when you need it."

"I'm here and I'm staying. That's my response for now. And you're right. I shouldn't be so hard on Rachel. She has a right to be angry at me."

"Rachel has done this intervention so you both can understand and reconnect differently.

We'll leave it at that for now, Francine. I wanted to give you a heads up that next meeting, we'll discuss your duties covering the desk for Doris. You'll have to put on your administrative voice."

"I only have one voice, Doc, and that will have to do."

Chapter 7

Groundhog Day

The bed was cold. Her feet were freezing, and she couldn't find a way to get warm. Residual detox. The effects lasted longer than she remembered from her first effort to get sober. Strange how memory deceives if memory is mixed with imagination. Then memory becomes distorted and tells lies.

Bonnie came into the room, interrupting Francine's thoughts. Francine could hear her breathing heavily and tried to ignore the distraction.

"What do you want?" asked Francine. "I'm trying to rest."

"You had a phone call," Bonnie told her. "Staff couldn't find you."

"How about coming to my room to find me? Where do they think I'd be? Besides, this must be a mistake. I haven't even spent one night in this jail. No one wants to talk to me."

"I don't know about that," said Bonnie, "but you had a call."

She crawled out of bed, put on a thick gray hoodie, and wrapped the threadbare cream-colored blanket from the bed around her body. She imagined she must be standing in a deep freezer. When she opened her mouth to breathe, she could see her breath. She left her neck brace on the bed.

Francine approached the administration desk with seething anger. Doris was on the phone. It sounded like a personal call. A buzzer went off, indicating dinner, but Francine had no clue what was going on until she saw the other inmates walking down the hallway in lockstep toward what Francine believed was the dining hall.

"May I help you?" asked Doris as she clicked off her cell.

"Doris, we met when I came in today. Are you finished on your personal call?"

"What's it look like?" asked Doris.

"I want to know if I got a call, because I was in my room minding my business, and no one came to tell me I had a call. Bonnie, my roommate, heard a rumor that I got a call. If I had a call, I should have been notified. If not, no harm, no foul. So, Doris, was there a call for Francine Freeman?"

Doris looked at her as if she had two heads. It took her a moment to compose herself in front of the disturbed, angry alcoholic in the throes of recovery.

"You don't have to get confrontational, Francine. I know it's your first day and things are new and awkward, so I'm going to forgive your attitude. Yes, there was a call for you, and no one could find you."

"Did anyone bother to check my room?"

"I don't know," said Doris. "The note here says your daughter called. It's best to go to dinner now and deal with the call later."

"No, it's not best. Here's the deal, Doris," said Francine, "I don't want to go to dinner. I'm not hungry. Where can I call my daughter in privacy? I need to talk to my daughter."

"All clients have to attend dinner," said Doris. "It's not just about the food. It's a time for our communal experience. Sometimes we have speakers or an inspirational program."

"We could have a confrontation about this now, but I'm not in fighting condition. I need a drink and a cigarette. I'll be back, and I expect to call my daughter in a private setting."

Francine had lost her composure. Her mind was trapped by fear of the unknown. She was hanging on by the promise of a glass of bourbon in the near future.

She entered the green-tinged dining room and counted about thirty people in various stages of pain and anxiety. They were spread out around five tables, each with a bouquet of generic, half-dead, grocery store flowers. If it was an attempt to give the dinner meal a festive air, it was not working. No one wanted to be there, least of all her. No one was interested in eating. Everyone wanted a drink. For Francine and the rest who were in the early stages of recovery, nothing but a drink could make them feel better. They were angry at having to be in a facility that addressed their addiction and tried to bring them to sobriety. The room was full of dry drunks.

Francine didn't know what it meant to be a dry drunk until her first foray into the detox world. A dry drunk always wanted to drink, but he or she did not take a drink because of a commitment to recovery. A dry drunk might not have had a drink in fifty years, because cravings for alcohol could be set off by triggers—people, places, and things—that reminded the alcoholic either consciously or unconsciously that alcohol masked any pain, any shortcomings, any fear of death. Francine knew the dining room was filled with plenty of dry drunks because she was one. She was on a rampage. The stakes were high.

Francine felt angry every day since she entered the hospital to detox. She was angry from the moment she woke up to the moment she went to sleep. She knew that an addict was never a former addict. An addict was an addict for life. Two detoxes—one failed and one to be determined—taught her that reality.

In place of a drink, Francine would gladly smoke a cigarette. She wanted the pleasure of filling her lungs with nicotine and toxic particles that increased the possibility that emphysema would make a silent entrance into her lungs and she would die of respiratory failure instead of by downing a bottle of pills. Oh, hell, she knew she had COPD. How could she not? Just another life-long addiction. She vowed to search for a hiding place outside the building and sneak a cigarette at least once a day. Ida put the Marlboro box inside the lining of her suitcase.

Francine stood at the back of the dining room and rolled her eyes over the poor creatures who stared at their plates in silence. She noticed the tall, large, balding older man with a white beard named Don, who introduced himself in group that afternoon. He waved at Francine and indicated a vacant seat next to him. Francine stubbornly didn't move toward the table, but the man kept insisting and made a sad face at her, pantomiming that he was crying. She smiled and walked toward Don who began to change his sad face into a happy face. Francine liked his smile.

"I'm Don," he said.

"I know who you are big guy. How tall are you?"

"I'm six feet, five inches," said Don. "We met up in group today, and you're Francine, but I'm pleased to meet you in more comfortable surroundings. I saw you standing at the entrance looking forlorn, and I thought, this young lady needs a seat and a friend."

"Don't get carried away, Don," said Francine. "I'm furious right about now. The dummies that run this jail couldn't find me when I got a call from my daughter. Good old Doris was more interested in talking on the phone instead of sending staff to my room. I need a bourbon and 7 and a well-done steak."

"Don't we all," said Don. "Tonight, we get chewy chicken and mushy vegetables. None of which I like. So, what are you in for?"

"Aren't we all in here for alcohol?" asked Francine. "We're purists and are sticking together."

A server brought Francine her dinner and she waved it away.

"They're out to poison us with these plates," said Francine. "Polystyrene is a compound of carbon and hydrogen."

The server set the plate down and walked away. Francine drank almost a full glass of water and burped.

"Is this even food?" asked Francine. "It smells awful. This place costs a fortune, so we should have gourmet food. If my daughter found out about the lack of amenities and the slop we have to eat, she'd be coming through the door in a New York minute. But I exaggerate."

"Maybe gourmet comes later," said Don. "As in, if we behave ourselves and follow the rules, there is an uptick in quality meals."

"You're funny, Don," said Francine. "Since this isn't your first rodeo in rehab, got any advice?"

"I shouldn't be answering that question. It's part of the code of not discussing therapy outside of therapy. It gets confusing."

"Then save your pearls of wisdom for group talk, Donny boy."

"Where are you from, Francine?"

"Devon, suburb of Philly," Francine said. "You?"

"I'll be darned. Me, too."

"Damn, you might be my new best friend. I might not be as pissed off as I think I am."

"It's good to have a friend in here," said Don. "By the way, where is your neck brace?"

"I flushed it down the toilet."

Francine put her fork down, closed her eyes, and took a deep breath. First night, first flight. Where, oh where, is the bar? She had been dreaming of booze every night for the last week.

"Hey, Francine," said Don. "I'd love to be your best friend on this journey. At least we'll have a sober friend when we get out of here."

"Maybe you'll go through this and make it out with flying colors, dear Donny, but maybe I won't. The jury is still out with me. I'm intentionally resistant. It's my life's work."

"Your life's work is to put some meat on your bones," said Don. "You didn't eat a bite. One of the ways you build up your energy and resolve to move forward is to eat."

"You look like you never miss a meal," said Francine.

"Cute. Let me see if I can change this diet and get a better chef."

Don got up and headed to the kitchen. Francine was lost. He gave her momentary stability. Men gave her that for a time, but it never lasted. When she looked around the table, she witnessed four other people looking at anything but each other. No one talked. No one smiled. They were all dead behind the eyes. Francine didn't want to engage in shop talk.

Before Don got back from bringing her food, Francine hurried to the front desk and envisioned another skirmish with good old Doris. To her relief, Doris was not behind the desk. Instead, there was a young Latino looking as sharp as a model. Alert, smiling, genuine, he resembled a younger version of Carlos, but not jaded by years of failing to find himself because of his resistance to authority, or his inability to listen to instructions and carry them out, which oddly enough sounded like an analysis of what had been going on with her for the last fifty years. Francine had been in lockdown for almost a day, and she had a revelation. *Fancy that.*

"May I help you?" asked the young man.

"Yes, you can. I just wrestled with the worst of prison food. If you were in the Soviet Union, let's say, in the gulag, you might imagine what slop I'm referring to. But, poor boy, you are an innocent bystander to my anger, so, with your permission, let me verbally binge on you. My roommate, Bonnie, told me before dinner that I had a call. When I checked with Doris, she told me they—I'm thinking a staff person—couldn't find me. Incredible. Isn't my room the obvious place to look? But there I was—in my room. I'd like to call my daughter now because she called me hours ago."

"Hi, my name is Tomas. And you are?"

"Francine. Glad to meet you. Can you tell me where there might be a private phone?"

"Nice to meet you, too."

Tomas checked the phone log with diligence. "Yes, Rachel called. And no one went to look for you? Take it up with management. You can go into the office. It's more private."

"Thanks, Tomas," said Francine. "You are a peach. Sorry for my lack of social graces."

Francine went into the office, picked up the phone, and held the receiver in her hand with trepidation. It didn't feel good to call Rachel on her first day. Something was wrong. The plan was for Rachel to pick her up on the last day of rehab. Three weeks on the dot. Things between them weren't perfect now. How could they be with Rachel's exerting her intervention, but they will learn to live with the unlivable and carry on with impunity.

"Missing me already?" asked Francine.

The silence was crushing.

"What is it?" Francine asked. "Rachel, what is it?"

"Your friend, Ida, had an accident," said Rachel. "She . . . was driving."

"Driving . . . no" whispered Francine.

"The police said she was drinking," said Rachel. "She hit a parked car and died instantly."

"Can't be. We have a pact, Ida and me. No driving while drunk. Never, ever drive while drunk. And we promised to come to each other's rescue if we fall, if we are in trouble. That's not possible. Ida would never drive drunk. You have the wrong information."

"Maybe I do," said Rachel. "Maybe I have the wrong information, but she crashed into a parked car at the shopping center a mile from Oak Lane. The police on the scene smelled alcohol on her clothes and in the car, and there was an open bottle. She hit her head on the steering wheel."

"You think she was coming to visit me at Oak Lane?" asked Francine, "But you can't have visitors in here."

"I'm not sure, but she called to ask me where you were, and I told her you were going to be transferred to Oak Lane," Rachel told her. "There were flowers on the front seat. Daisies."

"Coming to see me, then, getting me flowers. That's what Ida would do. Ida would check on me."

Rachel took a long breath. "I'm sorry, Mom. I know she was your best friend."

"Longest friend in Grand Rapids," Francine added. "There's no life without Ida."

Ida. Her Ida. The Ida who saved her after the first fall. But not the second fall. She was too drunk to drive. So she wouldn't drive drunk. That was the pact they made. Ida was coming to see her.

"Was anyone else hurt?"

Francine was proud of herself. Calm at the moment of catastrophe. Ida died.

"No, thank God," said Rachel.

Francine heard Rachel sniffing on the other end of the phone, but she felt nothing. She was bereft. All-consuming grief. Why wasn't she hysterical, carrying on like it was the end of the world?

"I have to go to the funeral," said Francine.

"I'll see what I can do. It should be fine to get a pass for you. I'll call you when arrangements are made. Please take care. Stay strong and pray."

Pray. Right, pray. For what? For whom? She and Ida used to joke that they were doomed—they were heathens and there was no damn redemption. She slumped down into a chair, tightened the blanket around her, and stared at a painting hanging on the wall opposite the desk. It was a nature painting, colorless, uglier than a mud hen. It was a mud hen. How real. Francine wondered who picked the art in this upscale glam rehab. Why couldn't Francine feel anything? This was Ida, for God's sake. Ida in the ground.

"Hey, little girl," said Don as he peeked through the semi-closed office door. "I got us some better food. Come back and give it a try."

Francine didn't move, didn't look up.

"Get out, Don. Get the fuck out."

She began to cry. Don slipped into the office and closed the door. He sat down across from Francine in a chair that was tighter than spandex on a three-hundred-fifty-pound woman. He saw tears cascading down her face.

"What's happened, Francine, can you tell me?"

"I've got to get out of here. I need a fucking drink."

Her face was drained of all color. An imaginary white sheet draped over her head.

"I'm not kidding, Don. I need a fucking drink. Or I'll take my pills."

"Give me the pills," he said. "Give me the damn pills or I'll turn you in."

"Not a prayer in hell. I'll take them first."

"What happened?" pressed Don.

"Ida died. My best friend died."

"I understand. But a bottle of booze isn't going to make it any better. Go to your room or go to the chapel or lock yourself in the bathroom and mourn her death."

Don got up to leave and turned away as Francine unleashed her tears, strong and fierce, and sometimes gentle and pure, so pure that she was reduced to an innocent child. Her body was failing, her heart was breaking, and there would be no consolation in the foreseeable future. Francine went somewhere deep in her soul, in a place that had never been touched.

"You can be sad without guilt or shame. It's healthy to embrace the way you feel. Sit with it. Be with it."

Francine stared at Don as if he had three heads. His intrusion into her pain made her furious.

"What kind of crap is 'Sit with it. Be with it?' Some psychobabble mantra from Guru Raj. I can't talk, and I can't breathe, so you need to leave me the hell alone, or get me a bottle."

She abruptly left the office and went to the chapel. The little chapel was small and semi-dark, but the silence was embracing. She could hear her beleaguered breaths as she took baby steps to the fifth pew from the altar. Francine lowered herself onto the dark wooden bench. It was hard as a rock and her sit bones ached, but she felt an odd comfort sitting alone in a chapel. She was a child again. Waiting for confession. Without looking at the cross, Francine knew that Jesus was watching—watching her resistance to Catholicism, watching her defiance of a God-fearing belief, watching her push back on recovery, and heading into an old, familiar path she knew was not going to bring peace. Ideology was a myth that claimed to be truth. If there was a God, Ida would not have died in a mall parking lot near Oak Lane.

She wanted her pills. She wanted a drink. She wanted someone to put her in solitary confinement because Francine knew she would never escape her pain. She closed her eyes and let out a chilling cry.

Chapter 8

Ida In The Ground

Tomas came into the chapel and sat behind Francine.

"Tie me to this pew so I won't run out, whoever you are."

"It's Tomas, Mrs. Freeman. It's time to go to bed. If you need help, I will get you a wheelchair."

Francine was too tired to respond, to be angry, or to be civil. Ida's death pushed her deeper into darkness. She couldn't tell one emotion from another. Every feeling blended together like she was drunk, far away in another universe where time stood still.

"You're going to feel better," said Tomas. "In the morning, you won't feel so tired."

"I'm never going to feel better. I lost my Ida."

"Sleep is the key to unwinding yourself. Let's get you up in your room."

Don was watching from the back of the chapel as Tomas lifted Francine out of the pew and walked her slowly down the chapel aisle. She was as fragile as a twig in the wind. He had been there before. No one could touch him when he lived in what he called the dark shadows. Don was deeply ashamed of his situation but felt positive he would recover from his fall from grace.

Francine gave him more strength to continue his sobriety. They were at opposite ends of the alcoholic spectrum. She wanted to escape the pain. He wanted to face his pain.

He had seen plenty of pathetic alcoholics and drug addicts in his time on the road—singers, musicians, and roadies of all gender and sexual orientation. But Francine's sadness produced a profound vulnerability that was heartbreaking, and it chilled him to the bone. He had no idea what prompted her tears, but he knew it was crushing her heart and soul.

The next morning, Tomas walked Francine into the dining room and seated her at a table with two other people. She was too weak and exhausted to eat breakfast. Tomas tried to get a few bites of the scrambled eggs into her. He buttered her toast and poured her tea. Francine didn't speak or eat. Tomas knew better than to intrude on her space and offer platitudes, which would make her angry.

Doctor Jerry stood in the back of the dining room. He knew the group was out of bounds for Francine at this moment. She was officially closed off. He left her alone for the next two days. On the third day, Francine disappeared from Oak Lane.

∽

It was a beautiful, sunny summer morning at the cemetery. A small group of people gathered around a burial plot surrounded by lush, green vegetation. Trees provided cover from the penetrating sun. Ida's estranged daughter was there, looking sullen because she had to attend her mother's burial. Ida had tried to reach out to her daughter many times over the years, but all efforts were met with hostility. Even today, Karen was hostile. Ida couldn't understand why her daughter was angry at her all the time. Drink had dulled Ida's memory and her need for reconciliation.

Drink had not dulled Francine's memory. She was crystal clear about why her own daughter put her in detox and recovery. If it weren't for her family, Francine knew for a fact that she would have been Ida in the ground, and her family would be at the funeral, including her beautiful granddaughter, Ari, and handsome grandson Douglas—both in college and doing well, balancing friends and studies. Francine had taken them to the lake house in the early years, the best years of her life, and they loved their summers of boating and water skiing. If Francine was in the ground, she would never again see her family again. Everything was on hold until she was able to pull herself out of the recovery swamp. Never drinking again seemed farther away.

A tall, good-looking middle-aged rabbi dressed in a well-made black light wool suit with a prayer shawl around his neck was reading the Mourner's Kaddish. He was speaking the prayers for the dead in English, but Francine couldn't hear him through the pounding vibrations in her head. The neck brace was her guillotine. There were ten people at the Jewish burial, including Karen, her husband, two adult children, and members of the Jewish congregation that constituted a minyan, the requisite ten mourners to be in attendance for the funeral.

She and Ida had a pact. Francine would die first of emphysema or lung cancer, and a year later, Ida would die in her sleep of heart failure. Neither one had a clue about the state of their livers. Francine considered getting tested, but she hoped she had her father's German constitution. Ida had an irregular heartbeat and was convinced she would have a stroke in bed.

Francine searched for Rachel's hand to give her support. Although they had been less affectionate toward one another in the last few years, funerals often made people more vulnerable, more attuned to the cyclical nature of life. Their hands held the promise of a recognition that sometime in the near future, Francine would be lowered into the ground with Rachel's unconditional love.

With touch, lucidity came back, and Francine wondered what the rest of her life had in store. The thought of the recovery group back at Oak Lane made her feel untethered. She didn't want to reveal secrets, spill her guts to people who were strangers. All that was left when the curtain came down were dull memories of other people's stories. Ida was spared the endurance test of surviving just to feel the pain of a daughter's hard-core disdain. Rachel always loved her unconditionally. Yet, despite the appearance of being in recovery, Francine secretly clung to the last vestiges of addiction declaring her right to inflict damage to herself. After all, Francine still had four small airline liquor bottles and enough pills to contemplate the possibility of joining Ida in the ground.

Karen glanced at Francine. Francine nodded, then felt compelled to say something to Karen, sullen Karen, surrounded by her family, she supposed, but nevertheless requiring some form of acknowledgement from her mother's best friend.

"Karen, I'm so sorry. I loved your mother and I'm going to miss her."

"You have a nerve," said Karen with punitive intent. " You gave my mother an excuse to drink. So you're responsible for her death."

Karen dismissed Francine by walking away from her. Francine was momentarily stunned.

Rachel rushed over to her and put her arm around her.

"I want to go. This neck brace is giving me a headache. Ida's in the ground now."

For a few minutes, they felt connected to each other—mother and daughter finding common ground in grief. Francine walked ahead of her daughter, slowly making a path with sure-footedness back to the car. Her slight limp seemed to have vanished.

Rachel helped her mother into the backseat and got in on the other side. She adjusted her neck brace.

"Is that better, Mom? I loosened it a bit."

"Can you take it off me? The damn thing is like a vise. Now I know what Hannibal Lecter felt like."

Rachel manages to get the neck brace off.

"It could have been me in the ground instead of Ida."

"You and I weren't like Ida and Karen. I'd never stop talking to you. I love you, Mom. You know that."

"You are a wonderful daughter and I love you to the moon."

"We're both working on a new story to tell ourselves—so please don't beat yourself up. You have to stop measuring how valuable you are by the way you were treated."

"You mean disrespected and unsupported growing up?" asked Francine. "That's a big ask."

"You'll learn to let go of the pain."

"If only—but it's something to think about. But right now, today with Ida in the ground, and at my age and state, I'm staring down a waterless well."

When they arrived at Oak Lane neither mother nor daughter moved to open the door.

"What's on your mind?" asked Francine.

"Do you remember my wedding? The Jewish wedding."

"As opposed to the civil ceremony. What have you remembered all of a sudden?"

"When I told you that Mark and I wanted to get married, you said there won't be any damn Catholic wedding. 'Over your dead body,' you said. You remember I had to push myself away from you for a while to reconcile my feelings."

"I remember asking how Mark could allow a Christian ceremony," Francine told her. "He's Jewish for God's sake."

"I was furious with you, but we finally agreed on a Jewish wedding and a civil ceremony and not make an issue of religion. You bought me a beautiful wedding dress and bridal veil. And a random Justice of the Peace performed the ceremony at city hall, and he forgot our names. We both laughed at that."

"As I recall, a month later you were married again. What was the name of that temple?"

"Temple Emanuel. That's what Mark wanted, and you rallied around our decision. I wanted to tell you how proud I was of you that day, just as I'm proud of you today."

"Just so long as you weren't married in the Catholic Church."

"I remember being furious that Grandpa didn't attend my wedding because Mark was Jewish. Ida's Jewish funeral reminded me of that moment. I'm still resentful."

"Don't waste your time thinking about the dead bastard. Hatred was Richard's religion. He wouldn't go anywhere if there was a Jew within ten feet of him, and he held the same disdain and hatred for Italians. I was not allowed to date a boy whose last name ended in a vowel. Of course, those were my favorite boyfriends—popular and sexy, and handsome, and, God, they were full of life. The Nazi even secretly suspected that Carol's mother was Jewish. Her mother hid it well and it didn't come out, except Carol told me she and her Irish Catholic father were not accepted into the snooty Devon country club."

"His behavior was pathological," said Rachel, "and his sickness showed how a man filled with hate can hurt people, even destroy people."

"Payback's a bitch. No one attended his funeral, except your grandmother. She was the flip side of the same coin—only her sin was her piousness. She believed her devotion to the Catholic Church would absolve her from living with a bigot. Rachel, my darling, if you're proud of me, I'm doubly proud of you."

༄

When Francine returned from burying Ida, she found an envelope on the floor of her bedroom. It was probably pushed under the door because it landed halfway into the room. Before she picked it up, she noticed Bonnie had moved out. The room was empty. Bonnie's dolly, Annie, her stuffed dog, and her shredded, faded blue blanket were gone. It took her less than a week to leave. But then, Bonnie left before she arrived because she was determined not to be in recovery. *Sayonara, Bonnie, baby.*

Before Francine opened the letter, she threw her neck brace on the bed, then emptied the four airline liquor bottles and emptied into the sink. She fretted about what to do with the bottles. Maybe on one of her walks, she could bury them in the ground. The pungent smell of booze permeated the room. Francine sprayed perfume around the sink area, then she wrapped the bottles in her underwear. That was as close to taking another drink as she could manage. The fumes would float into her vagina when she wore the panties.

Francine opened the letter with hesitation. She peaked and then she read.

Dear Francine,

The loss of your friend, Ida, was a huge moment for you. I worried about you because it felt like your blues went deep. Your absence indicated that you went to Ida's funeral. I know you are suffering. But Ida's death marks a new beginning for you. Life without Ida. She is resting in peace and so, too, will you need to rest in peace.

I propose that we begin a letter-writing relationship and carry on like teenagers who are best buddies before the invention of the Internet. You don't have a phone anyway, so it won't matter to you. You probably still writes letters.

So, let's do that and have some fun, while we are here enjoying the fruits of our labor, and make our days just a little more secretively meaningful.

See you at dinner. I'll save you a seat.

Your friend,
Donnie Boy in Room 205

It was a game. Kind of corny. Maybe not. Maybe good. Someone cared. That was the problem. Someone cared. A man cared. A man to the rescue. Francine didn't trust it. This was a pattern that Francine followed like a dog pulling on a leash. She must pause and be cautious.

It was almost dinner time. If she didn't go to the dining room on her own, Tomas would come to get her. She didn't want to go through that again. She changed her funeral clothes and put on worn gray sweats and a red-plaid shirt. Her hair was a mess; it needed color and a trim or a wig. She lost her hair too early. Bad luck breaking her neck in between hair appointments. That was always a drag. She and Ida shared hairdressers. Ida. Ida in the ground.

Don to the rescue, Francine thought. There he was sitting at his usual table, all smiles, saving a seat for Francine.

"How are you feeling?" asked Don.

"A little better," she said. "Your note helped. I haven't had time to write you back."

"How have you been sleeping?" he asked.

"If you call drinking dreams sleeping well, then I guess I'm sleeping like a baby."

"I read something once about when your heart hurts, wrap yourself in friendship, shared tears, and in time, that will make us hopeful and happy again."

"I suppose a guru like you would call that a mantra."

"Something like that, but in case that doesn't get you, I've got something else that will cheer you," said Don as he motioned to the server to bring Francine a hamburger fit for a queen.

"This is better than a drink about now. How did you know I was starving?"

"Not difficult to figure that out. When you let go of stress, you find your appetite and some happy sensations."

"Happiness is overrated. It's an expectation that isn't reachable."

"Do you believe in anything, Francine?" he asked.

"Do I look like I do?"

"I'm trying to figure that out."

"During the one semester I attended at Duquesne, before I found out I was pregnant, I took a French philosophy class. I remember a quote from Montaigne. 'The surest sign of wisdom is constant cheerfulness.' I thought that was a reasonable intention. Nothing big, nothing small. Just the right fit. That's what I had in mind each time I married. But it turned out it was just another exercise in self-destruction."

Francine devoured her hamburger and made little happy sounds that got Don laughing.

"I don't believe you are predetermined to fail at happiness. The idea in rehab is all about digging and finding better ways to build your life. Anyway, you probably learned that happiness can't be found outside yourself. Happiness resides inside you."

Francine finished her burger, wiped her mouth, and drank a glass of water.

"I'm not ready yet to build a better life, Don," said Francine. "I need some space to reconsider my options."

"Do you have any left, dear Francine?"

∽

It was late morning when Rachel drove up to her mother's house. She opened the car door and Sasha and Boo Boo ran out to the front yard to do their business. She picked up a hose attached to the outside of the house and began to water a few flower beds.

Carlos saw the dogs come into the garage and got out from under his car. They jumped on his legs.

"I'm Rachel. And you're Carlos. Good to meet you."

"How is your mother doing?"

"As well as can be expected after three days in rehab. I came to tell you that Ida died in a car accident."

"This is out of nowhere. Francine will take this hard."

"I think she is in shock."

"Can I help?" he asked. "Can I take the dogs back? I'm used to taking care of them."

"That would be great. I'll let my mom know they are back with you, and she will be pleased."

"I won't get in trouble again, I promise. My registration and license are current. And your mother got me my job back."

"Of course, she did," said Rachel. "One more thing, Carlos. Can you please remove all alcohol from the house?"

"It's already done."

∽

As Francine entered the counseling room, Doctor Jerry was waxing poetic about changing cognitive behaviors in order to sustain recovery. "It's about the importance of attending AA meetings as the linchpin for alcohol and drug recovery," he said.

"It's good to see you, Francine," said Doctor Jerry.

"Are we allowed to ask what happened to Francine?" asked Rhonda.

"If Francine wants to tell us."

Francine took a seat and glanced across the room. Her imagination created an apparition of Ida sitting in a chair looking serene and happy.

"My best friend died a few days ago, and now I'm in mourning for my life," she said to the apparition of Ida. "She saved my ass more than once. She was my rock. Since Ida died, I was thinking that if I keep looking at myself through the lens of a bottle of booze, I'm going to end my life sooner than I expected. Ida died driving drunk. But we promised each other we wouldn't drive drunk. If I put a mirror up to Ida's death, I know it could have been me. Like they say, no one to save me now, praise the Lord, hallelujah, and all that crap, except myself."

"We're sorry for your loss," said Doctor Jerry.

"She was a first-class enabler, by God. No one left to prop me up. That being said, I want a drink so bad I could blast out of here in a cannon." The apparition of Ida disappeared. "Obviously I'm not ready for prime time. There's no upside to the downside."

This burst of honesty caught the group off guard. Some looked down into their laps, others turned their heads away from Francine. Alexa cried. Dean got out his fidget spinner.

"I guess all I have left is to drink in my dreams," said Francine.

"Where is your pride?" asked Rhonda.

"That's the last thing I care about, babe."

"I'm Rhonda, not babe," said Rhonda.

"That's the way I talk, babe. No harm meant." Francine stood up. "I feel crappy, Doc, so I'm going to my room. Looks like I'm the only occupant since Bonnie baby flew the coop. There's no upside to the downside."

No one moved. Every person in the room was Francine. She united them with her presence, her irony, and her anger.

The room was quiet for several minutes.

"Is Francine okay, Doctor Jerry?" asked Alexa.

"Confidentiality is the rule around here."

"Right. Thought I'd try bending the rules," she replied.

Rhonda swiveled around in her chair and uttered a disgruntled sound.

"What is it, Rhonda?" asked Doctor Jerry.

"Why not? She is one of us. All for one and one for all. Maybe we can help."

"Only Francine can help Francine, Rhonda," said Doctor Jerry.

"We're supposed to be open with each other," said Rhonda. "Isn't that the reason why we're in group? Aren't we here to help others?"

"Yes and no," said Doctor Jerry in his Texas cadence. "This is a process of personal discovery, and it's a process that can take a lifetime. That's why we don't judge. Judging damages your mental and physical health, to say nothing of your recovery. You want to get to know yourself with openness. Get rid of the cobwebs. Get rid of the self-pity. Get rid of the blame. Get rid of the shame. Get rid of the self-important opinions. Francine will be open with us when she's ready, and then we can support her."

"Sounds like a good rap but is she coming back?" persisted Rhonda.

"As far as I know, Francine will be back," he said.

∽

The next morning, halfway through group counseling, Doctor Jerry waxed poetic about changing cognitive behaviors in order to sustain recovery.

"I'm sorry I'm late everyone," said Francine as she entered the room. "It took a little time to wake up."

"Please come in and take a seat. I'm talking about the importance of attending AA meetings as the linchpin for alcohol and drug recovery," he said. "I know you have some strong feelings about AA, Francine, so I'd like to hear you start this off if you are up to it."

"I'll dive in. I'll admit I gave it my all in AA the first time around. I went to meetings for months and tried to do the 90/90 program, but, and I don't mean to offend anybody, I got tired of listening to the tragic stories about alcoholics falling off the wagon. Six months later, I quit."

"Consistent attendance is the key. Once you stop going, you start drinking. Statistics bear this out."

"My daughter told me I'd be the star of AA meetings. She said I had humor and honesty. It didn't happen that way in the meetings. No one appreciated irony. It was grim. I don't like grim. I figured they were all losers, and I am not a loser."

"I don't like that word—loser," said Doctor Jerry.

"I'm not a loser, Francine," said Rhonda. "Don't judge us."

"It's not about winning or losing," said Doctor Jerry. "It's about changing your life, with consciousness while making good choices and sustaining good habits. This will be who you become."

"Amen to that," said Rhonda. "I stopped going to meetings and here I am. There is wisdom in what Doctor Jerry says. AA is a journey into habitual consciousness. That's why we all listen to those stories. They reflect the human condition."

The group was quiet. No one else was ready to jump in and acknowledge the wisdom of Doctor Jerry's words or Rhonda's observations. No one cared at this stage of recovery.

"Question to y'all. What was the moment that you were most proud of yourself?"

"I did two years of sobriety in a women's detention center," said Rhonda. "When I got out, I realized that ex-cons have no preparation to live in the real world once you leave jail. You're out there rolling around like a boat in a thunderstorm. No skills. No routine. No job. No support. So I'm back a second time. And coming back to recovery was the proudest day I've ever had."

"I never had one of those days," said Bluzy.

"Everyone has a proud moment, Bluzy," said Doctor Jerry. "I'll get back to you on this. What about you, Alexa?"

"Me? I'm most proud of walking out of my mother's house and never returning. I realized what a narcissist is capable of."

"I don't have that kind of moment," said Dean. "You can get back to me, too."

"Graduating at the top of my class at Wharton School of Business at Penn," said Ronnie.

"Recovery is the center of my life," said Don. "The first time was righteous and the second time after being sober for forty years was a true blessing. All I ever care about is my sobriety.

"The first time I got sober was because of my ex-wife. What a pistol. What a drunk. The two of us, me and Ivy, tore up the world making music and filling the nights with alcohol-fueled orgies. Together we thought we ruled our universe. Until I didn't. I woke up one morning after a night of boozing and realized I had blacked out after laying hands on Ivy. Two things in the lexicon of my drinking bouts: never drink to blackout and never lay hands on another person. I never drank in bars, and that took the problem of public fighting off the table. But expect the unexpected behind closed doors. My head was throbbing, my body was several degrees removed from crippling agony. Ivy, the beautiful; Ivy, the child; Ivy, the love I couldn't endure any longer, was passed out on the floor—mouth open, bruises on her arms. She would sleep until evening. Until darkness took her away again into the bowels of the bottle.

"I took a Vicodin and left the Malibu house that hung by a thread at the edge of the cliff overlooking the Pacific Ocean. I drove along the Pacific Coast Highway to an AA meeting. Every drunk knew about the AA meetings in the iconic Presbyterian Church north of where I lived. The meetings were legendary for Hollywood celebrities who attended. No judgments. No labels. They didn't have to hide among their own. It was the nearest hope for salvation. As all AA enclaves, I would be anonymous in the Malibu movie star community, keeping its secrets from the executives in the entertainment business. Until death or drink do us part.

"I got up and left the meeting, packed my bags, got in my car, and left the scene of the crime. Ivy was still on the floor, bloodied. I was off to Northern California, to the mountains of Mount Tamalpais, not San Francisco where temptation was everywhere, became a DJ, honed my guitar skills, and joined a band. And another band. And another band. And I never took another drink for the next forty years."

"What made you fall off the wagon after forty years?" asked Rhonda.

"Another woman. What else?"

"That was quite a ride, Don," said Doctor Jerry. "Anybody need to take a break?"

No one responded, but the breathing was audible in the room.

"Let's keep going," said Bluzy.

"Francine?" asked Doctor Jerry.

"I'm not capable of giving a short answer, as you might guess, so I'll expound. At Bishop Shanahan High School, I was one of the six most popular girls to be nominated as a homecoming princess. I felt like I'd be queen for a day for the rest of my life. But that was only the beginning. Tradition was that each princess was given a booklet of tickets to sell to raise money for the high school. Whoever sold the most tickets became the homecoming queen. My mother announced that she would sell my tickets and buy me my crown. She worked in an insurance office, and everyone would buy them. I told her she wasn't buying me the crown. I told her I was perfectly capable of doing my own selling. And I told her to stay out of it.

"My mother slapped me across the face and told me never to talk to her like that. I brought my hand to my face—it was hot and stinging—and I said, 'Don't you ever slap me again. I'm eighteen and you have about as much control over me as the gray hair creeping out of your scalp.' My mother's back went rigid because she had no more control over me at that moment. I watched her wring her hands—guilt-ridden martyr that she was. That was the proudest day of my life, second only to selling the most tickets and becoming the homecoming queen of the class of 1960."

Don, Bluzy, Ronnie, and Dean started to clap. Rhonda joined them reluctantly.

"You set the bar high, Francine," said Doctor Jerry.

"That was nothing compared to what my father did to me. My mother told him what I said, and he came after me with his favorite belt. I was eighteen, remember, and fully grown, and hard to believe, but somewhat athletic. He grabbed that belt and raised his arm, and I moved so fast that he ended up falling into the staircase, hitting his head on the banister. He was drunk. It was all broken, never to be fixed. Nothing could be fixed."

"Why do you say that, Francine," asked Doctor Jerry.

"Because we were never coming out of that moment. My first semester in college, I took an art history class and learned about the concept of bas-relief—like you see in Greek and Roman cathedrals and buildings—carved figures into stonework, like decorative pictures, more like sculpted elements, people, or animals attached to a solid background of the same material. That's what my family resembled. That was who we were for eternity—buried in our backgrounds.

"After it was over, after cheerleading for the homecoming football game, after the senior ball, and buying champagne from a local Chinese liquor store to celebrate, I told my mother that I wasn't a failure, no matter what she thought, and I told her that she can never take away my happiness."

"What did your mother say, Francine?" asked Doctor Jerry.

"She told me it was a sick thing to say because she wanted me to be happy. And I told her that was a lie, that she couldn't find happiness herself, so she took it out on me. No matter how many rosaries my mother said, she would never change. And I'll always be who I am."

"That's not quite accurate, Francine," said Doctor Jerry. "The possibility to grow and change and recognize the truth of who we are is right in front of us."

"I'm living proof of that," said Don. "I was a lifer in AA for forty years, and when I stopped going, I gave in to my habit. Forty years in, and it took three months to fall in love again. But I created space to grow and change once again and push the boulder up the steep hill."

"What happened, Don?" asked Dean overworking his fidget spinner.

Doctor Jerry indicated to Dean to put his fidget spinner away.

"I discovered how vulnerable I was despite sobriety. Sobriety felt like a ruse. My higher power was illusive. If my higher power was real, I wouldn't have taken that first drink, then consumed the entire bottle of Johnny Walker. Anyone's higher power is only good when self-belief is present. It's my personal theory of recovery. Self-belief leads to belief in a higher power. Which comes first? Are they the same? I wrestle with this existential state daily."

"What's that like, Don?" asked Bluzy.

"I remember one sleepless night when all defenses were buried deep inside me, and I fell into a self-sabotaging trance. There was no possibility of escaping the vise on my limbic mind. Without conscious thought, I embraced my demon lover. Johnny Walker was my comfort. That beautiful limbic brain began to run the 'Don Show.' I couldn't stop the relentless thoughts of wanting to drink, how it would taste, how he would feel, euphoric and not angry anymore. My chest felt as if a steel band was tightening around my heart, my ears were ringing, my mouth was dry, and my head banging so hard I felt it was coming apart at the seams. In a split second, I left all I knew about sobriety behind me."

"It's difficult to hear the negative stories," said Doctor Jerry, "but that's how you build your learning curve. It's always a tenuous relationship at best at any stage of your recovery, so as long as you know that your unconscious is complicit in your disease, that your pain-pleasure center will always want to rise to the forefront of your conscious mind, it's crucial that you commit daily to acknowledging consciousness. Practice awareness and take it one day at a time. What do you think, Ronnie?"

"I think I'm an impatient man," said Ronnie. "I don't want it to take too long."

"Recovery is a matter of self-esteem," said Rhonda. "Why are you living on this Earth? What will people remember about you other than you're a drunk?"

"We'll take that question in our next session. Let's break now. And please pick up a list of duties for the next couple of weeks."

Francine returned to her room in a state of confusion. She didn't understand what happened in group. She went deep and dark. She needed to write to Don. She found a pen and paper and prepared her thoughts without distraction—you always have to come back to the present. Time lasts forever until it doesn't. Ida is in the ground.

Dear Don,

I was blown away by your share today. Your journey went deep. Thank you for your honesty. It meant a lot to us all.

This is a good idea to write letters to you because you might have a clue about what I'm feeling. I thought I could last in group today, but it wasn't going well with me and Ida.

Ida told me she didn't want to stick around, and I told her it was fine if she left the room.

I've been through this AA maze once before, tried to meditate and take care of myself, but it never worked. I always came back to my worst self. What's your secret?

You did it for 40 years, so how did you convince yourself that it was worth giving up your demon lover? Alcohol is all I've got and all that I'll ever have to soothe the savage beast.

Do you think I'm on a death march? I sound a bit over-dramatic, shades of melodrama or smell-o-drama, but I've been drinking most of my life to get to the end zone. Like Ida, but she got there sooner than later.

Save me a seat for lunch, babe.

Fran in 210

Chapter 9

And So It Went And So It Goes

Francine was used to being front and center in her life. Quite impulsively, suddenly, Don was beginning to intrude in the recesses of her redundant mind. She was used to life unfolding one drink at a time. Nothing ever proceeded by leaps and bounds, except maybe her impulsive move back to Grand Rapids.

Life was good when examined through the lens of a bottle—even better if it was accompanied by a man who enabled her drinking. If she ever recognized a moment of self-reflection, she took to her bed to sleep away the gnawing sensations of insecurity. But with the introduction of Don into her life, she began to recognize that she could feel without alcohol. That was some kind of revelation.

Surprised she cared for someone for the first time in decades, Francine didn't know what to do with that feeling. She wanted to tell Don that she liked what he was proposing with their exchange of letters and knew it was a form of therapy in its own way, which made it an outlier in a traditional therapy setting. It was strictly forbidden to fraternize with other inmates. Journaling was a better process. But Don was different. He had forty years of sobriety, and his experience counted for something in this alcoholic madness. His falling into sin after four decades was a gift to her. Other people had weaknesses and gave in to them. She wasn't the only freak show. Rehab gave the addicts the ability to recognize those weaknesses and be mindful that at any minute anyone can fall into the grip of addiction.

"All that matters is trust," said Don to Francine as they walked down the hallway to group therapy the following week.

"I trust you, but I don't know why," said Francine. "And I'm surprised at myself."

"First rule: trust in yourself. Trust is possible when you let go of your distress about where you are and not worry about the months ahead," said Don. "This is Oak Lane, for God's sake, not an insane asylum or a jail."

"It's a better bargain than being stuck in three bad marriages."

"And you made a new friend in the middle of it all."

"You're not like Ida, but I can talk to you."

Francine had a whiff that change was coming—good or bad—she felt she might have a chance to live straight. She couldn't imagine what that was like, but maybe this is what Rachel meant years ago when she told Francine how to make decisions.

"My daughter told me to use my third eye when I am about to make a decision," said Francine to Don as they continued to walk. "She practices yoga, and they tell her the third eye is the eye that really sees."

"Where is it located?" asked Don.

"In the middle of the brow," she said pointing her index finger between her brows and laughing out loud as she remembered the first time she tried to use the third eye with Peter, and he turned into a toad.

"What's so funny?" he asked.

"A memory of my third husband turning into a toad."

"I third eyed you," said Don. "The minute I saw you, it was all about the third eye."

Francine wanted to believe her connection with Don could be real inside Oak Lane. She wanted to believe in the promise of hope. And maybe she'd have a laugh or two along the way. And maybe she'd feel some happiness, which she always felt was unattainable. Or maybe Francine could simply be cheerful because happiness was an illusion unfit for polite society.

The counseling room was quiet as Francine and Don entered. Doctor Jerry was sitting in a chair inside a circle of chairs. He had rearranged the room and made it more intimate instead of the straggling arrangement it had become.

"Nice," said Alexa. "We're up close and personal."

"Good morning y'all. I'd like y'all to tell each other about where you're from, how you arrived in Grand Rapids, and why. Who wants to begin?"

"What the hell. Looks like I'm getting the hang of sharing in group," said Francine. "I was full force on moving to Grand Rapids decades ago because it was the scene of my early childhood, and I remembered I was happy, or at least I thought I was. I was unreasonably nostalgic about the city—I lived here from kindergarten to seventh grade—and I held a firm belief that moving here would change my life for the better, or at least give me a good start."

"Do you remember when this was?" asked Doctor Jerry.

"It'll be thirty-seven years ago this summer that I moved from Pennsylvania. I had Rachel with me, and I felt peaceful for the first time in years. No judging from my mother, no pointing fingers from loser men. Rachel rebelled at the move, but she had no choice. I needed a new life and a few good possibilities."

"Exactly, how was it peaceful?" asked Doctor Jerry.

"When I left Devon—if you haven't heard of it, it is a little burg outside Philadelphia—for Michigan, I put the worst of my memories with my parents and two ex-husbands behind me. My mind slowed down along the drive, and I felt my breathing accelerate. The anger receded as I saw the beautiful, green, dense terrain, the blue skies, and open spaces driving into western Michigan. And then I saw Lake Michigan and I knew I was home for good."

"What were your goals in college?"

"Besides finding a husband? Doc, it was 1960 and women went to college to get married. And I didn't need a college degree for that. I had no other interests. Obviously, I had no imagination. I guess the truth is that I returned to Grand Rapids to connect to something that was missing in my life."

"And did you ever find out what that was?" asked Rhonda.

"I was looking for myself and never did find her."

"Maybe you were looking for pieces of you that you lost along the path—pieces that didn't fit with your choices at that time. Your true nature was buried under resistance to being who you wanted to be."

"If I had found my true nature, I wouldn't have gotten pregnant before the first college semester was over. According to my mother, my life was over because I had a best friend who was everything that I was supposed to be. Carol had ambition and discipline. You know the kind that gets into Penn, or maybe had the option of a highfalutin women's college. She became somebody despite the fact that she married too young and ended up divorced with two kids. But she never made my mistakes like drinking and men."

"Some women or even men don't need or want that commitment," said Ronnie.

"My marriages weren't good for my mental or emotional health," said Francine.

"That's because you married the wrong men for the wrong reasons," said Rhonda.

"You got that right. My mother always said my first husband was a man with barely an idea of a career floating in his straw brain. Of all the men on campus, I picked someone who had a golf scholarship. When I told Carol that, she laughed her ass off. It is kind of funny."

"What about a medical student or a lawyer?" asked Alexa. "Think big is what I say."

"His family had money," Francine said, "and my mother thought that was his only appeal."

"Besides pleasing your mother, what did you want?" asked Doctor Jerry.

"You mean besides getting out from under two despicable parents?" asked Francine. "I never pleased my mother, and my father was a first-class bigot who thought the Nazis should have won the war. He would have joined the German army if he could have arranged a prisoner exchange—he was an anti-Semite, hard-core to the right of Attila the Hun. Nobody asked me what I wanted, and my guilt is that I gave up before I entered adulthood."

"Your parents weren't there for you, Francine," said Dr. Jerry. "You were vulnerable and you got lost, and as a result, you couldn't grow up with strong enough values to make good decisions."

"They didn't know how to be parents. We couldn't find a nurturing connection—and we all lived in our own private Idaho."

"What did you do to make a living when you came to Grand Rapids?" Dean asked as he fumbled to put his fidget spinner away in his front pocket.

"After I rented a house in Walker, I sent out letters to school districts looking for work. I landed an administrative position in the substitute teacher's office in Kentville. I was good at my job and life was easier. My memory was always sharp. My boss in the Devon school district coveted my memory. Doctor Adams called me a goddamn savant. It was my claim to fame. He'd say 'this woman, this here woman is a freak of nature, a savant, by God, by golly. She knows the name of every substitute teacher in my school district and every subject they teach. She knows my schedule better than my secretary. And what's more, Francine remembers telephone numbers. She's a goddamn phone book.' I guess I was the happiest I had ever been since I was homecoming queen."

"Did you stop drinking?" asked Bluzy.

"I didn't drink as much. No blackouts. No fuzzy brain in the morning. Best of all, no men. I loved not having a man."

Doctor Jerry smiled. "That's an interesting observation."

"One that I never made before out loud," said Francine. "During the first couple of years in Grand Rapids, I was breathing a sigh of relief."

"Kind of like you are right now, Francine," said Doctor Jerry. "Your face has lost its stress. You're in a good space."

Francine was not completely honest. She didn't want to confess her original sin—the sin of how she met and pursued Peter, her third and last husband. Her life's choices were beginning to sound redundant, with no end to her penchant for self-sabotaging. The group didn't need to know every detail.

After counseling, Doris caught up with Francine in the corridor outside the group room.

"You've got a phone call, Francine," she said. "It isn't your daughter. It's a man."

"Thanks, Doris for finding me."

"You can take it into that little office room."

Doris led Francine into the office and Francine picked up the phone.

"Hello. Who is this?

"It's Carlos. I know you don't have a lot of time, but I had to tell you that I took Sasha to the vet. She kind of stopped eating."

"Oh, no. Not like Sasha. What did the vet say?"

"I'm sorry, Francine, she wasn't doing well. Her heart was fading. He had to put her down."

Francine was not going to lose her composure. Not now. She looked across from her and saw the apparition of Ida. She wasn't in the ground. Ida was with her across the room. Ida wasn't crying and she loved Sasha, too. Francine held on.

"Who has her little body?" Francine asked.

"I have it in an urn. I'll save it for you for when you come home."

"Carlos, don't worry. I'll be fine. If you want, call Rachel. If not, you and I will take care of this. I'm thankful for you once again for all your help. You're the best."

"I'll wait for you to come home, Francine. We'll bury her together in the backyard. I'll make a plot for Sasha."

Francine hung up and began to breathe deeply. Tears ran down her face. In Francine's other life, the death of Sasha would have put her in a drinking spiral. Instead, she needed a walk. She took her neck brace off and headed to the outside door to a backyard garden.

Don caught her arm as she was walking outside. "What's going on?"

"One of my dogs died. And although I'm bereft, I'm mostly fine. It's progress."

They walked on a nature path surrounding a manicured lawn. Don led her to one of the Red Adirondack chairs.

"This is a treat," said Francine. "I feel like I can breathe."

"I hope I'm not intruding. Do you want to talk about the dog and what the death . . ."

"Stop, Don. It hurts. I loved her madly. Dogs and people die. As you would say, it is the existential state. My life is so boring with sadness and chaos. I'm really sorry. It feels like my past will never end."

"Is this where you use your third eye theory?" asked Don.

"No, it's used to decide whether or not you want to engage with someone. Do you feel that person is connecting with you, lying to you, exposing you, or just screwing with you?"

"Like what I did to you the first time I saw you in the dining room. Got you to come over to me."

"Yes. That was using the third eye and I connected with it. But it can go wrong, too, like when I thought I used my third eye with my last husband. Mind you, I wasn't out hunting for a man. When I worked at the school district, after work on Friday afternoons, one of my co-workers at the school district, Rita Woodhouse, and I would drive into Grand Rapids and have happy hour at the Davenport Hotel. Rita was cool and elusive and a good foil for me. We both spotted Peter in a three-piece suit looking like he stepped out of *GQ*, gray-flecked hair mid-fifties with a body in decent shape. The race was on. I thought I would engage Rachel's third eye theory to see if it had legs.

"Peter spotted us at the bar and bought us drinks. After an hour's worth of conversation, it was clear he had money and brains and was a first-rate financial advisor for Paine Webber. The man was accomplished, a recent widower, and had a beautiful house in a classy Grand Rapids suburb. It was obvious that Peter was the anthesis of my usual choice in men. I thought my life might be turning around. I let Rita pour on her charm and I kept third eying him. He didn't turn his head toward me for maybe half an hour. Then he did, and then he called me to go out."

"Sounds like the beginning of a beautiful romance," he said.

"This ain't *Casablanca*, Donny, this was *Nightmare on Elm Street*. Be careful what you wish for—the point is, I could not reflect on the man other than his executive trappings and my third eye took me on a journey I should have avoided."

"I was holding a good thought for a moment."

"Living a decent life was no match for a loveless relationship, which became yet another alcoholic tar pit. I drank so I wouldn't kill him. He drank so he could die before me, and he almost did the night he lit himself on fire."

"What the hell," said Don.

"We had a summer house on Elk Lake, and I used to bartend at a restaurant on the lake to get out of the house and away from Peter. One night, I came home to find that Peter, as usual, hooked up to the oxygen pole—he had emphysema—smoking a cigarette, and the God-damn oxygen bag had just caught fire. He was panicked and screaming for help. Thank God, I had a fire extinguisher on the wall. Something told me I would need it one day. I put out the damn fire and told him that was the end of everything."

"How fast did it take you to find an assisted living facility?" Don asked.

"Three months. I was on my sixth interview and desperate, and I bribed and begged the last facility in Kentwood to take him in. I cried buckets and told them it had become too difficult for me to manage him anymore. I called Carol, told her what happened, and she told me my job was done. I earned every bit of Peter's money. I saved his life and found a place to care for him in his last miserable three years."

"I think you have a talent you overlooked, Mrs. Freeman. You can tell a hell of a story. Even though you carried the pain of your family secrets, you hobbled together your ability to develop resilience."

"Could be, but I sucked at self-esteem," she said.

"But not at humor."

"Oh, babe, I used humor to cover for the pain of my dysfunctional life. And as you might have noticed, humor didn't get the job done."

Don gave her a big bear hug, and they stood together in stillness until the dinner bell rang. "I've got to say something, Francine. It's a confession of sorts. Please don't judge me."

"I'm pretty tuned into you, babe, so I'm not going to be too surprised."

"I'm getting too close to you. This is good and not good."

"Right. Double-edged sword. I read that for at least the first year, to keep distance from other alcoholics and addicts."

"I may have already crossed that line. The letters . . ."

"Let's go back inside. We have to sort this out in another place."

"It's going to be painful when we're over. Just saying . . . we can't be together. This is our only moment. Going through rehab together is our gift."

"You go on in, Don. I'll be in a few minutes. I've got something to do."

Francine looked up at the second-floor balcony—she wanted a way to get upstairs. There seemed to be no staircase from the outside to the second floor. It was probably for the best since she couldn't make the climb. There was no other way but to use the elevator.

Chapter 10

War Is Hell

Two days passed and a letter came from Don. Francine didn't have time to respond or know what to write back. He waxed poetically about some Sufi poet.

They met in group and Doctor Jerry proffered his PTSD scale.

Doctor Jerry was a Vietnam vet. In fact, he was a Medal of Honor Vietnam veteran. He didn't come across as a dandy in the Air Force, or a pretty boy sailor on a missile battleship. Doctor Jerry fought a war in the Viet Cong jungles and had some near-death situations that scarred him for life. That's why he preferred to counsel alcoholics and drug addicts. He knew why the grunts smoked pot all day as a way to relieve fear and anxiety while they watched death all around them, maybe losing a best friend or two. Who doesn't know that drugs and alcohol made you feel better?

When Doctor Jerry smiled, his eyes squinted almost to full closure. Francine fixated on those eyes, and she wondered what they would look like wide open. Maybe they didn't open all the way. But they were sweet eyes and full of hope. He told the group that most of the guys who made it out of Nam suffered from some form of PTSD. Even Doctor Jerry himself.

"Sure, I smoked pot all day and night. It was the only way to cope with the cruelty of war. When someone died next to you, maybe your buddy, you felt like the bottom of your stomach dropped into the dirt. My best friend died and I still can't get it out of my mind. You live with it. You live with the suffering of loss. After a time, the alcohol or drugs bring no comfort. No one can console you except your own embrace of the memory and the challenge to keep your buddy alive within yourself, close to the heart."

The sound was sucked out of the room. Each member of the group retired to his or her own heart and soul. Ten minutes must have gone by. During that time, Francine thought of Ida—keeping her alive and close to her heart.

"That's what's called a meditation, y'all," said Doctor Jerry.

"I served three tours in Iraq, and I had those feelings, like you," said Bluzy.

"Not quite, Bluzy," said Doctor Jerry. "I came home and stopped what I was doing because I wanted to feel my loss. I wanted to understand I did right when I disobeyed orders from my commanding officer when he ordered my platoon to get into a senseless battle that would kill us all. I had reasons to disobey orders because I was on the ground, and he was miles away. I was informed, and he knew nothing about the situation, so I took my own counsel."

"Guts ball," said Bluzy.

"You some kind of hero?" asked Rhonda.

"Probably to the guys whose lives I saved," said Doctor Jerry. "No one in my platoon lost his life. The day I was assigned to my platoon, I told my men that no one was ever going to lose his life under my command, and that was a promise I was able to keep."

"How did you do that?" asked Francine. "Everyone was dying all around you, or they were close to death."

"My commanding officer thought he was a hotshot, and it was his army or no one's army. He didn't see the enemy, and he never questioned me about whether I thought his harebrained strategy would work with my troops. It was never going to work. I would have sent my men into slaughter if I had followed his orders."

"You ignored the order?" asked Don.

"I could have been court-martialed, but I didn't care because my men needed to stay alive. I made them that promise. I smoked a joint and thought about it for a few minutes. Life's about making great decisions in the moment. I felt empowered because of the idiocy of one ignorant prick."

"What happened?" asked Bluzy.

"I thought about how I would feel if I followed my commanding officer's orders, and I put it on a scale of one to ten, one being the lowest and ten the highest. I knew I would feel ten in my bones if I followed my own counsel because I loved those sons of bitches in my platoon more than anything in the world. I countermanded my superior's orders and was willing to pay the consequences because I felt like a fucking ten."

"Is that how you make decisions about your life, Doc?" asked Francine.

"Fucking A," said Don.

"Try it, and see if it works," said Doctor Jerry. "Before you decide to drink or use, stop and ask yourself—how will you feel if you don't drink or use and how would you rate yourself for not following through. What would you rate that decision on the scale of one to ten? Will you be a five or seven or ten? Then suppose you decide to drink or use, what numeric number will you assign to your condition after that—two, four, eight? Can you live with that number? If not, next time you drink or use, remember the way you feel about your decision. This is the way you can get distance from your decisions—good or bad—before you make them."

Don recited, "'Take one step away from yourself—and lo! behold!—the Path!' Sufi poet, Abu Said."

Francine shot a look at Don. That's what he wrote in his letter to her before group.

"Why do you like that quote from Abu Said, Don?" asked Doctor Jerry.

"We get all wrapped up in our thoughts, in our self-important opinions, and we don't know bupkis about who we are inside ourselves. We label, judge others, and have no gravitas in the universe. Judging others is fatal to the development of our souls."

"How do you know this stuff, Don?" asked Rhonda. "I mean are you some kind of guru? Are you that 'think you know-it-all' kind of guy?"

"I know nothing, dear Rhonda," said Don. "I surf life."

"You didn't answer my questions, Guru Don," said Rhonda.

"I don't have to answer your question, Rhonda. It's an existential state. Life is life. It exists until it doesn't."

"It sounds like a Buddhist mantra," said Ronnie.

"It has elements of Buddhism," said Don. "Still your mind. Stay in the presence of your existence."

"What do you think, Doctor Jerry?" asked Rhonda.

"In the presence of stillness, anything is possible. You are able to listen to your fears and move closer to your dreams. You will acquire the freedom to move away from the negative thoughts and closer to forgiving yourself."

"Do you stop thinking?" asked Rhonda.

"You let go of thoughts, the negative experiences, and cultivate light, thereby increasing the positive aspects of living."

"Sounds like goals for rehab," said Francine.

"In what way?" prompted Doctor Jerry.

"Get rid of our old stories and reimagine our life now. Like what's going on now instead of brooding on the past. Get rid of the same old story we always used to tell."

"Francine, what's the same old story?" asked Doctor Jerry.

"Parental messages. Shitty decisions. They bring up old wounds. Old attachments. Old hates," said Francine as she stood. "Are we done yet?"

"I think y'all should take a break and have lunch," Doctor Jerry proffered.

∽

Francine and Don walked into the dining room. They were in no mood to talk. Every food selection that Francine walked by made her sick. She hadn't been able to eat a decent meal except for scrambled eggs for the last two weeks. Prison life was daunting. Eggs were soft and made her stomach feel warm and comfy. Francine skipped the hot food and picked up two pieces of dry white toast. She scooped up the strawberry jam and a cup of tea.

"Is that it?" asked Don. "That's all you're going to eat? Come on,

Francine, this can't keep a bird alive. You're disappearing faster than a musician on crack."

"I got triggered in group just now. Nothing specific but in general. Like I distanced myself and see my life at a glance, at a distance, carved in stone in bas-relief. And I got angry."

"If I could get into your brain, Francine, what would I find?" said Don. "I'll get you a hamburger."

Francine had not always been in retreat from food. She loved to eat but, of course, that was then, before alcohol and sleeping most of the day, and wandering around at night, and breaking her neck twice. There was a time she cooked breakfast every day, mostly eggs and toast, but that was so far in the past she had no emotional recall. Her taste buds were shot.

Luckily, she could still smell. It didn't matter. Her body was sick, and nothing was going to heal years of the devastating effects of smoking and drinking.

Don returned and put a hamburger on her plate.

"No cheese."

Don pulled the cheese off. "I'm not going to interfere in this process you're going through, but maybe step back a little."

"You have no idea how I hate that know-it-all attitude, Donny. It puts me off. Don't ever tell me what to do."

"Shades of your mother? If so, cross her out of the pictures. She's dead and gone. Get a new perspective on life."

"Everyone in my life thinks they can tell me what to do. Even my grandchildren. Douglas thinks I swear too much and Ali thinks I should wear a wig. And you think I don't eat enough to keep a squirrel alive." Francine stared at the hamburger like it was a lump of coal. "The smell reminds me of my high school cafeteria. Closer to my mother's kitchen when she overcooked broccoli."

"It's your choice what you decide to eat and not eat."

"Right, it's my choice. At this point, I could care less what I look like or how healthy I am. I'm up for being the poster lady for end-of-life osteoporosis." Francine thought it was more like liver failure.

"I should talk. I eat a lot of junk food. Truth be told, I could live off a diet of French fries smothered with Velveeta cheese."

"That'll fatten up your arteries," she told him with a laugh.

The waddle of skin under his chin was getting its jollies as he chewed. His eyes glazed over with orgasmic elation. She watched Don's Adam's apple and was fascinated by the outline of his tongue moving around his mouth. It was strangely erotic, thrilling almost to be thinking of sex again. Francine reckoned that her last orgasm occurred the same day Sheriff Jeff died.

"What are you musing about, Francine?" asked Don. "You've got that far-off look in your eyes, mellow and sexy."

"I'm thinking inappropriate thoughts about Jeff Grady. Glorious Jeff Grady and lingering sexual desires."

"Want to tell me about it?"

"When don't I want to tell you. You know part of the story—Peter and I were at each other's throats near the end. It was an alcohol freefall. I was driving him crazy prowling around the house looking for something to do besides smoke. He wasn't so pleasant to be around either. I knew the bar at the Resort was looking for someone to bartend because the last few times I was in the bar, the bartender on duty asked me if I knew of anyone who might want the job. I was orgasmic and leaped at the chance to put my name in. The Resort was a great place to hang out at night, and it was only twenty minutes away by boat from the lake house. I liked the feel of the oak bar and the low mellow music from the nineteen fifties."

"How did the old man feel about that?" asked Don.

"I told him I'd get to the bar when it's still light and go home when it's dark, and he told me I will do no such thing. And I told him to screw off because he was the one who wanted me out of the house. I told him I'd work weekends and substitute when they needed me. Those were the days I met Jeff Grady and began a relationship that would last for the next five years. It started before Peter almost blew himself up. When that happened, I had to quit bartending because I couldn't find Peter an assisted living home, but I continued to time spent with Sheriff Jeff. He gave me some sanity . . . and lots of sex."

"What happened to good old Jeff?" asked Don.

"One Saturday night, I was making him his steak and when I asked him how he wanted it cooked, he didn't answer. I went out on the deck and there he was not moving, drink still in his hand, cigarette burned to the end, head falling to the right. He died right then and there. Heart attack."

"Brutal," Don said.

"I'm leaving you with that thought. I've got to run an errand. Would you mind taking this neck brace off?"

Don unhinged the neck brace, took it off and handed it to Francine.

"See you later."

Francine entered an elevator next to the dining room and got off on the second floor. There were no offices or administrative services, but there was a balcony that looked over the backyard. Francine leaned out over the balcony, closed her eyes, and dropped her neck brace. Hell was over.

Chapter 11

Carol

On a Wednesday of the second week of counseling, the group was in an energetic mood. There were smiles and an exchange of jokes and funny tidbits of life in rehab.

"Who was the most important person in your life?" asked Dr. Jerry.

"You tell us yours, and we'll tell you ours," said Rhonda.

"That's not the way it works," Doctor Jerry said. "This should be easy for y'all. Think about it as an exercise—talking about someone you admire, the whys and wherefores. Sometimes we think about important people in our lives, but we don't verbalize the reasons they have left an impression on us. You don't have to analyze the relationship—don't judge. Keep it at a distance."

"My mother," said Rhonda. "She was kind and good and supportive and I loved her to the moon."

"What happened to her?" asked Don.

"She died when I was thirteen and my world collapsed. That's the way it goes when you lose a parent, especially a mother. I heard once that when your mother dies, you can finally become a woman, able to assume responsibility for yourself. I didn't do that."

"Because of drugs or something like that?" asked Dean.

"Something like that," she replied.

"My most important person was my dog, Pete," said Dean. "He was the best friend anyone could have because he listened all the time."

"You didn't have to engage your dog in conversation, right, Dean?" asked Doctor Jerry. "He or she was there to listen."

"No judgment," Dean said.

"I never had a most important person," Bluzy said. "I wanted one, but I couldn't find one."

"Maybe you didn't want to get too close to any one person," responded Doctor Jerry. "It might be something you could work on after recovery."

"There were too many important people to count," said Don, "but if I had to name one it was my brother, Chris. He wasn't a blood brother, but he was the brother of the woman I loved, the woman I destroyed, who destroyed me as well."

"Francine," said Doctor Jerry. "Where are you right now?"

"No worries, Doc, I'm here in this room thinking about Carol, my most important person even though my mother liked her more than me."

"What about Ida?" asked Rhonda. "I thought she was your best friend."

"Ida was my best friend from when I moved to Grand Rapids. Ida was my co-enabler. That's a different kind of friendship. We bonded to keep us safe from the dangers of alcohol; we watched out for each other; we told lies and secrets to each other about navigating our lives with alcohol; we thought we were saving each other by closing a curtain around our friendship. The curtain was to cover up our addiction. But we never said the word addiction. We never told that truth.

"Carol was different—Carol and I had a relationship based on my admiration for her and Carol loved my humor and quick wit. I met the first day she entered St. Norbert's grammar school in the eighth grade, and we were together every day for the next five years—all the way through high school. We double-dated, spent summers together, had overnights, mostly at her house because mine was a house of horrors—and planned our slumber parties with our clique of friends. We shared fantasies and desires that no one else would ever hear, and we trusted each other to hold our secrets forever."

"That's a big statement," Doctor Jerry said.

"Carol saw all my wounds up close—how my parents treated me, my mother's regular rant about how I would never amount to anything. She saw how my mother was super strict when I wouldn't bend to her dictates. She witnessed how Colleen used sarcasm and anger like a bazooka gun to control my mind. And she counted my scars as I got older, the husbands, the depression, the inability to find a pathway to self-respect. We were friends too long not to share the best and the worst of our natures. 'In good times and in bad times'—like the song lyrics in Sondheim's musical *Follies*—'And we're still here.' Carol had a high tolerance for all the craziness going on in my redundant mind—but she never judged me, never uttered a negative word against me, always stuck up for me even though she knew that my fatal flaw was my resistance to making good choices because I didn't think enough of myself—and that I masked difficult choices with alcohol. I loved her, but I didn't understand her choices either, so different we were—Carol in the arts and taking risky adventures—being somebody. Me hiding."

"What happened to her?" asked Alexis

"Carol moved away from Grand Rapids after graduating from college. Her dream was to settle in New York and try her hand at acting. She took risks, grew, stretched, even when it didn't work out. She had common sense in spades—and she kept landing on her feet. She was my rock. At my wedding reception, I dragged her in the bathroom and told her I made a mistake marrying Peter. She said, '*Peter is your job. You married him for the money. You don't have to love him or even like him. This is the last and final marriage of Francine Fisher-Reynolds-Richelli-Freeman. Forget white picket fences and unrequited love. What's love got to do with it, as your mother and Tina Turner used to say.* Carol was right. Peter died and I saw it through."

"Take a breath, Francine," said Doctor Jerry. "Let's everyone take a breath. If you need a bathroom break, do it now."

Francine left the room and headed for the restroom.

Don walked into the ladies room and saw Francine doubled over in pain.

"Are you all right, Francine?" he asked.

"I'm fine," she said as she splashed water on her face. "Just too hot is all."

"You had a breakthrough," whispered Don.

"Is that what it was? It felt like a high colonic."

"There's more to that story, I'm sure," he said

"It's insane to think we don't know anything about ourselves. But I'm not making up my life—I'm not doing improvisation in rehab. Get this: the wedding reception was a disaster. He was barely finished grieving his wife's death, and there were pictures all over the house of her and his kids. All her little knick-knacks were in place. Nothing had changed or moved. It smelled of her presence. I'm surprised I didn't uncover a sarcophagus in the basement. It took me a full year to get him to move to Zeeland. And then he bought an RV, and we went on the senior tour to nowhere and lived so many places my head split open."

"Widowers are lonely creatures," said Don. "The minute they meet a young woman who is attractive and smart, they want to get married again."

"How many wives did you have?" Francine asked.

"Two. The last one broke my back and sent me to hell. Marriage is a made-up construct, or a trap, or call it unnatural. Pick your favorite description. It works until it doesn't, so why get married? It's simple: people are in love or not in love. Two people don't need a piece of paper, a priest, or a judge to sanctify a committed relationship. Unless, of course, the marriage is about money."

"My last was about money, but it was also about the lack of sex. He was a prig. An incompetent. An imbecile. Want more adjectives? You know what happened when I tried to have sex with him the day we got engaged?"

"You didn't get laid before you got engaged?"

"You make that sound like I committed a crime."

"I'm fascinated by how you think, Francine. You're wound up so tight."

"He had to get a little tipsy before sex. Then, after he got off, I asked him, 'Did you know that women have orgasms, too, Peter?'"

"Can't wait to hear this," laughed Don.

"He said, 'Oh, for Christ's sake, where did you ever hear that?' I answered with my best snark that I read it in the bible."

"I'm going to say something I'm not supposed to say," said Don. "No wonder you drank. You know, I'm not serious, but your misguided bullshit detector was not working, and you paid a price. Like all of us drunks."

"After the first year of marriage when the RV debacle was over, we didn't talk for two months. I lived in purgatory. We moved four times. What finally soothed my soul was Peter's purchase of a second house on Elk Lake in Northern Michigan. I was finally at peace—at least, for a time. Elk Lake was heaven—a mile-and-a-half wide, nine miles long piece of paradise. There was a boat dock at the end of the four-bedroom green and white house. Peter had even thought to buy a ski boat to complete the perfect scene."

"Were you happy? Or was this another wet dream?"

Francine pulled a cigarette out of a pack in her purse and started to light it.

"Are you crazy, lady?" said Don. "Put that away. You'll have the cops on us before you take the first drag."

Francine stuffed the cigarette back in the box and closed her purse.

Rhonda entered the restroom.

"Sorry I was just leaving," Don said to no none in particular and ran out.

"If you got something going on with Don, you'd better rethink your situation," said Rhonda as Francine slipped out the door.

Don was in a hallway off the corridor to the group counseling room trying to control himself. He was laughing so hard he was crying from the embarrassment of encountering Rhonda in the restroom.

"What in hell are you doing out here? We have to get back to counseling." Francine handed him a Kleenex from her purse. "What's so damn funny?"

"I would love to have had a torrid affair with you," said Don. "And please forget I ever said that. It's clear you trigger me."

"The last torrid affair I had was with my old fuck buddy, Steven Shay, who worked my old school district in Devon. That's not to say Sheriff Jeff wasn't a slouch in that department."

"When did you have time for a torrid affair?" asked Don.

"You always have time for a torrid affair. How can you not? Best-sex-ever Steven Shay. Too bad he was married. I saw him at least once a month, and he kept me sane for a while."

"Sex is supposed to drive you crazy, Francine, not keep you sane. Sometimes I think you're crazier than a raving gorilla. Somewhere along the way, you committed to making wrong choices and those unhealthy decisions rewired you for emotional isolation with alcohol. I bet you never thought of getting sober."

"Hell, no. It got worse. Steven asked me to divorce Peter and live with him in Hudsonville. He wanted to take care of me, and I wouldn't have to work as Peter's house-frau. Can you imagine? Free at last."

"That's not freedom. That's another form of bondage. Besides, you would have lost your place in the money line and then what would you end up with? Years of misery and no money. Bad move. I bet you Carol talked you out of it."

"She told me that Peter's daughters were going to get barracuda lawyers to keep their portion of the money. But Peter's daughters couldn't get anywhere. I had Peter redo his will with ironclad clauses preserving my money and the lake house."

"Then you did your job well," Don told her. "Let's get out of here. Doctor Jerry probably has the police after us by now and Rhonda is reading the class their rights."

∽

Francine didn't return to group. Instead, she saw Alexa walking down the corridor to group and bribed her to use her cell phone to make a call to Carol.

"I love it when I think I'm getting away with something," she said to Francine. "My lips are sealed."

Francine returned to the backyard and crouched down around a dark corner. The ground was damp and filled with old leaves, but the debris from the spring foliage was shimmering under the colors of the setting sun.

"How are you? What's going on?" Carol hadn't spoken to Francine in over a year. Her life had changed—she was by then an empty-nester, a freelance writer, and working with her partner, David, on remodeling houses in Seattle.

"I called to tell you I'm in rehab," whispered Francine.

"What the hell does that mean?" asked Carol. "Are you in jail? Christ, Francine, I haven't talked to you in years, and you call because you're in jail? Do you need bail?"

"No, babe." Francine dropped the whisper in favor of a deep gravel sound. "I'm in recovery. I detoxed a month ago. You'd be proud of me. I'm doing it."

"I'm always proud of you. You're my bestie."

There was a long silence on the phone. Carol could hear Francine breathing.

"What happened?" asked Carol.

"Don't get your panties in a knot. I took another fall, same stairs, different day. But I'm fine. Better than fine." Francine experienced a sharp pain in her stomach and took some deep breaths. "Who knows what state I'm in, but I'm detoxed and in counseling. I suppose the next stop is the dreaded AA."

"I'm glad for your recovery and more than relieved you called. What happened to Peter?"

"My job is done with Peter Freeman. I put that pain in the ass into assisted living years ago, got him to codify his will, and made sure I got the house in Zeeland and the lake house and a comfortable salary that I can live on for the rest of my miserable dog-shit life, provided I don't live past eighty."

"What's going on with you, Francine Fisher," said Carol. "I know there is more to this story."

"Way before I got rid of Peter, I was having a torrid affair with Sheriff Jeff who hung out at the bar in the lodge. I'd known him for years, and I was crazy about him. While old Peter was blowing himself up, I was having gut-wrenching orgasms. Oh, God, babe, he was a hunk, and it was a party every day."

"You're using the past tense, Francine. Not a good sign because you had no luck with men, even when things looked like love was blooming."

Francine was choking up and Carol could hear the beginnings of a cry.

"One night about two years ago, I was preparing a summer dinner in the kitchen while Jeff lounged on a deck chair, smoking, and drinking bourbon and 7. I saw him take a deep inhale from his cigarette and a sip of bourbon, then lean back into the deck chair and close his eyes. It was a heart attack."

"Why didn't you call me?"

Francine lit a cigarette and Carol heard it through the phone. She inhaled deeply. "I didn't know what to do. I mean, he went and died on me, and I fell apart. Besides, you didn't need to hear one more story of the man that died or got away. I'm assuming you haven't stored up enough empathy in your life so far to give a damn."

"Point taken," said Carol. "This isn't the end of your life. You're in rehab and you probably have miles left in you to get yourself together and find a life that will make you happy."

"No, I don't have miles left, and no, I won't find happiness again, and there is no need to be condescending." Francine heard the lack of feeling in Carol's voice.

"No, Francine, listen," said Carol. "I do truly feel horrible that Jeff died."

"You're not even sympathetic. Forget compassion."

"I feel terrible," said Carol. "Francine, please, I'm not being dismissive of Jeff Grady's life, because I know you loved him with all your heart and soul."

Carol's pleas fell on deaf ears. Her words only cheapened Jeff's death and sullied Francine's romantic illusions. Francine was angry and hung up. She took a long drag off her cigarette and noticed Don standing next to her.

"I could smell the smoke," said Don. "Subtly is not your suit."

"I just wrote off my oldest best friend, my most important person."

"Take a breath, Francine. Stand back and detach a minute. Having a fight with an old friend isn't huge stuff right now. That's why we don't go outside our therapy. Let's get back inside and take it one step at a time."

Chapter 12

And The Beat Goes On

Francine closed the door to her room, tucked her notebook under her arm, and walked down a corridor. Rhonda appeared behind her. She looked like the spy who came in from the cold—furtive eyes and serious demeanor.

"What you got under your arm, Miss Francine?" asked Rhonda.

"Don't you look spiffy, Miss Rhonda. All dressed up and nowhere to go."

"Oh, I got a place to go, for sure," Rhonda said. "Group with Doctor Jerry. We girlfriends can walk together."

"I have to make a stop first, but I'll be right along babe," said Francine. "Oh, I forgot. Sorry, I called you babe, as in, I've got you, babe."

"I love Cher, so I'll forgive you," said Rhonda. "It's growing on me."

Rhonda turned to go and headed to the top of the stairs, lingering, waiting for Francine to join her.

When Francine reached Don's room, she opened the journal, pulled out a folded piece of paper, and slid it under the door. With difficulty, she pulled herself up the wall to a standing position and turned to go. Rhonda was directly in front of her path.

"I don't think this is your room, girl, is it?" asked Rhonda. "Are you up to something? You got some kind of naughty-girl look on your face."

"None of your damn business," said Francine as she turned to walk down the hallway.

Inside his room, Don saw the letter slide under the door. After he heard soft footsteps retreating, he picked up the letter and read.

Dear Donny Boy,

> *You are my best friend in this walk of shame. You've been a rock star this last month. First, because you shared with me your fall from grace, and in the aftermath, you have faced your demon lover with grace. I wish I could have grace. I used to say it's over-rated, but you proved it isn't.*
>
> *I face my alcoholism with a certain amount of false bravado and with an intention not to pursue my deplorable choices but soldier on with clarity. For most of my life, the world looked bleak unless I was staring at the bottom of a bottle of bourbon where I hid my persistent self-loathing, fulfilling my promise to myself not to amount to anything.*
>
> *The reality is that most of my life is over. Scary thought. At my age, real-life reveals itself as something other than effort, other than accomplishments.*
>
> *I'm not very deep. I wonder rather than pursue. All I have left is the long reach of my own foolish life.*

Francine in 210

―

Don entered the group room, but Francine didn't acknowledge his presence.

"I'm aware that some of you are not ready to leave the sanctity of Oak Lane," said Doctor Jerry. "Three weeks is not enough time to implement the necessary resources and skills to enter the outside with all its distractions and temptations. Minimum recovery period is ninety days."

Those in the room stared at Doctor Jerry as if he spoke a foreign language.

"Are y'all with me this morning?" Doctor Jerry asked. "Does anyone need a cup of coffee?"

"I do," said Ronnie. "I didn't get my second cup at breakfast."

"Go ahead and get another cup," said Doctor Jerry.

"Where is everyone?" asked Rhonda. "We've got a few people missing. Head count is low. Alexa is not here."

"Group counseling can be a cocoon for addicts," said Doctor Jerry. "It's a sure thing, a constant. But it also can inflict daily pain, insecurity, and more than a dose of anxiety."

"Is that what happened to Alexa?" asked Bluzy.

"I don't know," said Doctor Jerry. "Only Alexa knows. But it is common that a few of you will head for the nearest liquor store the moment your month is over. Don't be shocked if that happens. It's the most natural reaction to recovery. But let's say you don't do that because, if you've learned anything during rehab, you'll want to seek additional support. Preferably not family members because they are waiting in the wings to become your best enablers. They don't like to see you suffer."

"Are you sure, Doc?" asked Francine.

"Why do you ask?"

"Because my daughter is an adult child of an alcoholic," said Francine.

"Your daughter intervened out of love," said Rhonda.

"Rachel has her own path to travel, and because she intervened, she is learning to take care of herself first and separately support you," Doctor Jerry said. "At the same time, you've been learning to re-learn and to develop a new way of thinking and experiencing. Think of it as separate and equal personal responsibility for both of you."

"I guess I'm afraid that I won't have her with me in the same way as I once did, and selfishly I'll miss her—the way she was with me. But we both have to live differently now."

"It wasn't good for either of you," said Doctor Jerry. "Rachel could never tell you how she truly felt about your situation, and you were hiding your emotions in the bottle. Right now, it's crucial that you don't look to your family for support. What is true is that family help in the recovery process will be about as effective as taking up the mantle of sobriety alone. Don't do it. This is why AA exists. You've been to meetings, and you know what they're like. It's designed to make sure you will never be alone in your sobriety. I want to encourage you to do ninety and ninety: ninety days, ninety meetings, and then find yourself a sponsor. Talk to other people in recovery, have a phone near you at all times, journal every day how you are feeling because you will feel the need to use every day.

"Those are the facts. We also have a list of engaging activities that might interest you in the area of volunteering. When you have a regular scheduled place to go weekly, it's easier to stay inside the lines. Besides, it's good therapy to keep yourself busy and help others along the way. And lastly, remember my one-to-ten chart. How will it feel if you take that drink, drive down that familiar freeway off-ramp, go with a friend to happy hour, and think you are really going to drink a Diet Coke? Be mindfully aware of everything you do. Don't go unconscious because going unconscious is the definition of drug and alcohol addiction."

"It'll take another ninety days to get my head wrapped around all you said," said Dean,

"What about you, Don?" Rhonda asked, her eyes drifting to Francine.

Francine shot a dirty look at Rhonda and stood up abruptly.

"Please sit down, Francine," said Doctor Jerry. "No need to be reactive."

Thinking better of provoking Rhonda into a confrontation, Francine sat down. Her heart was pounding. She stood up again.

"Since we are all about honesty in this group, I'd like to clear the air about what my new best friend, Rhonda, is asking Don about."

"It's up to Don to tell his story," said Doctor Jerry.

Francine moved close to Don's chair and stood as still as a statue in a museum.

"Maybe it is and maybe it isn't. It doesn't matter. Rhonda is referring to my relationship with Don. He's my friend. He makes me laugh and makes me feel good about myself. We write letters to each other. It makes us feel connected. We slip the letters under each other's door, and to be honest, I don't know whether I would have made it through the first day in rehab without Don. And I don't even know his last name. And if that's against the rules, suck it up."

"McDonald," Don said.

"There it is. The full freaking Monty."

The avalanche of Francine's pain was suffocating the room. She took a deep breath, returned to her seat, and closed her eyes.

It felt like a lifetime before the energy in the room returned to a semblance of balance. Still, no one spoke. A fear of contagion hung in the air.

"Honesty requires the ability to still the mind, have patience, and release anticipation," Doctor Jerry said.

Ronnie returned to the group room with a steaming cup of coffee. No one looked up.

"I have pills," Francine spoke into her lap. "I wanted to take them. Because, you know, I should be dead by now. I didn't. I haven't." She lifted her eyes to Doctor Jerry. "I'm flushing them down the toilet after group."

After everyone had left the room, Francine was left to stare at the uncheerful yellow wainscoting. She thought healing should take place in comfortable and warm surroundings, like the luxury spa she once experienced in Cancun decades ago that offered massages, facials, hot steam, lounge chairs. Like those rarified recovery places in Malibu or Mexico. Thirty days of being pampered, rubbed down with Egyptian oils, scrubbed with luffa sponges while inhaling eucalyptus tincture, and having a hot guy bring you to orgasm.

She longed to feel embraced by her environment, like Don was holding her firmly in his arms and telling her all will be well, and that he would always be there for her, no matter where they ended up. It was a lie. It was an illusion. It was a fraud.

Don popped his head into the room. Francine mouthed, I'm sorry. He smiled.

Don held the door for her as she passed to the hallway.

"I'm not going to miss this place," Francine said. "But I'm not ready to leave."

"I'm going to miss us," said Don. "We were a good team in here. I hope the walls keep our secrets."

"I haven't made a friend in a long time, Donny boy," said Francine. "You broke me down and then embraced me."

"I'd say that's a pretty good definition of friendship."

"Thanks for your nice note," whispered Don. "I liked your honesty. You're deeper than you think. What you did in there, in front of the group was amazing. Man, it was like you were at the crap table and it was the moment to roll the dice and up the stakes. And you damn well won."

"I never told anyone that much about myself. It came out flowing, like an avalanche."

"It works like that sometimes," said Don.

"All well and good, but what am I supposed to do after rehab?"

"Talk to Rhonda. She's got resources."

"What does that mean?" asked Francine.

"Volunteer gigs. You know, stay busy and involved. Have purpose, a goal. Rhonda knows about this stuff."

"That's a new way of looking at my future, don't you think?"

"Only if you're serious," cautioned Don.

"I think I am, Donny boy. As serious as I've ever been."

Chapter 18

Beginnings

After lunch, Don was left with a pit in his stomach. More so than after reading the letter Francine had slid under his door. Then came her honesty in group. The avalanche of truth. He shouldn't have participated in the catharsis. He knew the rules against fraternizing with the opposite sex in recovery. Mixing genders was fraught with more internal conflicts than might be anticipated in the outside, a world populated by so-called "normal people." The recovery process was the primary focus. The male/female relationship between two alcoholics was considered a negative dynamic and created a detour that could sabotage the best intentions of recovery. Don had a rule: no relationships between two addicts. He violated his own dictum.

Through years of sobriety, Don learned that an addict is addicted to two or more substances or behaviors at the same time. Crack and sex. Alcohol and sex. Alcohol and coke. And sex. Dope and sex. Heroin is a downer and usually doesn't pair with sex, only other opioids. No matter what the addiction, stay out of the way of a fellow traveler.

Don still mourned not following his own advice years ago.

As he sat in his quiet room alone with his thoughts, he reworked several scenarios about how to tell Francine they couldn't do the dance anymore under the Oak Lane roof. And if they decided to meet and commune in the AA vernacular anywhere in the world, they must be prepared to have an attitude of professionalism. Leave neediness and warm bodies aside, sit down in a café with coffee, and do not dialogue about personal concerns related to their addiction. They are not each other's sponsors.

Don entered Dr. Jerry's office and waited for the doctor to enter.

"What's on your mind," said Doctor Jerry as he sat across from Don.

"I want to say that I like Francine more than I should. She is funny and smart, and she makes me laugh. That's a rarity today. Sure, she loves an audience. She comes alive telling a story. With her history, I can't figure out how she still has that sharp wit and intelligence."

"You got too close. What's your plan?"

"We've already discussed getting too close. We're aware. She understands the pattern she has with men, just as my pattern with women was a fool's errand."

"Why don't you write all this in your journal, all the temptations and wrong choices, and get some distance between you and your past. You're a writer, even if it is writing songs. You'll get distance from Francine with this exercise. Then you'll be able to decide how best to handle your good-bye."

"Good idea, Doc. That's helpful. Always gratitude for the process."

Don went to his room and began once again to tell his story and find his center. He took his journal out of his backpack and began to take a bumpy ride.

LAST WILL AND TESTAMENT

Being in the music business and tramping around the L.A. music scene in the sixties made me crazier than a hyena hunting his prey. Writing a song, fronting for a band, hanging with the Wrecking Crew. Those L.A. studio musicians gave me status. They were the best of the best musicians in the country, playing for every famous sixties and seventies group and solo artist on the top of the charts. I knew I was good at what I did, including singing backup and playing decent guitar. But damn those women kept coming around and getting me in trouble. With no impulse control due to alcohol, I had no way of stopping myself from undressing a girl with my eyes and falling in lust with every part of their anatomy. They say the bottle is the demon lover, but I knew damn well, a woman was hiding inside.

I was married before I was twenty-five to a beautiful Amazon of a woman, divorced before I was twenty-seven, and lost to alcohol before I was thirty. Lila was a ball-buster of the first order. Of course, my drinking didn't help the state of my marriage, and her addiction to gambling at the twenty-one tables in Las Vegas or the Indian reservations classified her as an addict as well. The marriage self-destructed in the Mai Thai Bar at the Stardust Hotel two years into the marriage, and never the twain met again. I sure loved that woman.

A year later, in a radio station where I was working, the program director told me to get to AA or I'd be out of a job. I hated the guy from the day I was hired to do a DJ stint in the late afternoons, but I was conscious enough to know I had become irrational and outspoken with fellow musicians and was asked to leave a gig on several occasions. I couldn't stop the erratic behavior that consumed me. If I wanted to continue in music, I'd have to go kicking and screaming into an AA program.

There was no job to return to when I got out of AA in Long Beach. A month later, everything changed. I headed to Miami, sober. I didn't have to start over again in the music scene because my ex-brother-in-law had a half-ass salsa band gigging around Miami. I played bongos and was a half-good backup singer.

Doing ninety-and-ninety in AA and making friends, I started to like myself again. I was a dude with keen instincts and some talent with no desire to take a detour to the dark side again. Miami was a shining light, and besides, the seventies were in full swing. When I felt like I was stable enough to head for New York, I made sure I searched out a daily AA meeting.

New York was a drugged-up, fucked-up monster of a scene. I couldn't figure out how anything got done. Musicians with little discipline staggered on stage and performed songs that hit the sweet spot of their audiences. It was uncanny, like the collective unconscious of mankind erupted with volcanic energy and tore through the fabric of normalcy. I tried to find a niche. Most of the time, I stayed safe in my closet of a room and wrote songs and tried to peddle them to producers. It didn't work. After six months of lingering in a sub-set of hell, I bought a train ticket back to Hollywood and got into the movies.

I was a natural character actor. Better yet, I was agile for my height and size, and sometimes fit the bill for the odd sidekick directors were looking for. I still wrote music and peddled my tunes, some better than others. It was all a game, and I took it with a grain of salt and a sense of humor. I rode the highs and the lows as I tried to stay away from beautiful women, or get dragged into a relationship by another addict. My salvation was that I was never lucky in love. When the lust died, I moved on.

Decades later, I met the one lady that caught my heart and sent me to hell. For the last month at Oak Lane, I have been climbing out of my fall from grace.

Rhonda was packing her clothes in a suitcase that almost took up the entire bed when Francine walked into her room. Francine noticed that she didn't have enough to fill half the suitcase.

"Rhonda," said Francine. "I need to talk to you."

"So, I'm useful to you now? What is it?"

"I get it. We got off to a bad start, or not a start at all, but let's put it behind us and move forward."

"Where are you going with this?" asked Rhonda.

"Resources. Don said you've got resources."

Rhonda stopped packing, turned on Francine. "In the emotional sense, you are not a friend, so why would I offer to help you?"

"Because, this is the beginning of our recovery and I want to start out right, and because I'm asking you to start all over with me and you," said Francine. "This shouldn't be difficult if you understand the twelve steps. Remember forgiveness? You know, making amends. What other steps might you be familiar with?"

"I get the point," said Rhonda. "What can I help you with?"

"I want to volunteer, and Don said you might suggest some places where I can sign up," said Francine. "He said you had resources."

"A few. Go on."

"What part of volunteering don't you get?" asked Francine.

"Volunteering is a means to an end, as in staying out of bars and your personal liquor cabinet."

"I'm not getting this. Maybe I should start again, like, what are you going to do after rehab? I mean, are you going back to work right away? Or taking time off?"

"I need to get a job," said Rhonda. "But in the meantime, I'm volunteering at a women's correctional facility. Maybe I'll get a job as a guard and then move up the ladder. I've got some managerial skills I'm working on."

"Really? Jail?"

"It's a women's correctional facility, Francine," said Rhonda. "A place where women do time for a variety of crimes, mostly drugs and forgery. Didn't you ever see *Orange is the New Black*?"

"I heard about it. What's that got to do with me?"

"It takes place in a women's correctional facility. Where've you been?"

"In a bottle. I'll have to catch up."

"It might help you get the lay of the land," said Rhonda. "Want to go to jail with me?"

"Oh, babe, I thought we already did that together."

"This isn't going to be easy, girl."

∽

The day before Francine was to leave, she asked to see Doctor Jerry in his office. He was a stranger, and yet, they had shared secrets for the last three weeks. The answer was on the wall.

Doctor Jerry was the real deal. She read the plaques of congratulations from the city, the state, the Lion's Club, and Rotary. There were lots of photos of Doctor Jerry and Michigan officials.

"What's on your mind, Francine?" he asked as he escorted her into his office.

"I want to volunteer at the women's correctional facility with Rhonda. She recommended that I watch *Orange is the New Black* to prepare myself."

"That's an interesting choice," said Doctor Jerry. "You'll get an orientation from the facility and be assigned your responsibilities, then you can decide if it's for you. It's not exactly a piece of cake for your first volunteer gig, but I'm not going to dissuade you from it."

Francine had doubts about volunteering in the women's facility. She didn't think she was ready to be let out in the wild.

"I want to caution you to stay away from relationships, all relationships, including Don and especially your daughter. You both need distance to process how your new mind is learning how to function."

"Can I say goodbye to Rachel?" asked Francine.

"It's not goodbye so much as it is creating distance from your past life and re-imagining your future. You've got a steel trap for a memory, Francine. I've never met anyone in my life that can quote chapter and verse of a past event. Your memory is both a positive and a negative. It's good because using the memory muscle will keep your mind strong; it's bad because it doesn't allow you to move forward. It tethers you to everything that triggers your base instincts. It's time to let go of self-sabotaging everything good about you, and when you do that, you'll start to be more aware and conscious of your choices."

"You're saying I have to unlearn before I learn."

"The way you unlearn impulse behavior and find reason is to question what you think will be your decision, look for consequences, and use the one-to-ten scale."

"I went out in six months last time. I can do better this time. I want to show Ida that I can do it."

"You have to want sobriety for yourself, Francine, and not for Ida," said Doctor Jerry. "Do you know why you started drinking at five in the afternoon after you relapsed?"

"So, I wouldn't drink all day?"

"Your brain's reward system unconsciously demanded it. That's the limbic brain—your pain-pleasure center or the monkey brain. You had no intention of making a drastic change in your life after your first fall, so you chose to defend your position to drink at the expense of becoming clear-headed. You rewarded yourself by going back to the bottle, and you refused—you resisted disconnecting from your attachment to that bottle. A drastic change to your behavior was out of the question."

"Three weeks is not enough time to process what's going on with me," said Francine. "It's easy to slip and slide."

"Is it possible not to be attached to your thoughts and emotions?" asked Doctor Jerry.

"That's rhetorical, right?" asked Francine.

"When you entered rehab, you clung to them like they were your lifeboat. After you entered rehab—your parents' negative messages, your insistence on being your mother's self-fulfilling prophecy, and your self-flagellation for making bad decisions—have been receding and the emotional yoke is fraying. Any thought of the past reduces the chances of never experiencing personal success."

"Do I care about personal success?" asked Francine.

"I don't know. Better question is do you want to change your story?"

"Rachel has asked me the same question," said Francine.

"Your old story doesn't exist anymore. If you want to move forward and raise your self-awareness, stay in the present. I'll support you, recommend you, but you must believe in you and support and recommend yourself."

Francine opened her hand and gave Doctor Jerry her bottle of pills.

"I've been carrying these around since the first day of detox. I don't feel like dying anymore."

"You were going to flush them down the toilet," he said.

"I wanted to give you a present. And I want to thank you for everything you've taught us. I'm learning to acknowledge my gratitude."

"I'm grateful to have known you," he said. "Come back any time to talk."

Francine left Doctor Jerry's office pulling her rollaway bag behind her and headed to the administrator's desk.

Rachel was at the front desk talking to Doris when Francine came around the corner.

"Doris was just going to call you, Mom," said Rachel.

"Well, I'm here. Warts and all."

Francine walked up to the administrator's desk.

"Thank you, Doris, for everything. And please tell Tomas that I appreciated his kindness. And your kindness, too. I know I was a bitch when I came here, and I'm still a bitch, but I'm a nicer bitch."

"You were never a bitch, Francine," said Doris. "You were angry and scared and that's being human. Good luck on your next journey."

Francine marched out of Oak Lane through the double doors as Rachel followed behind.

She drove her mother home and parked at the curb.

Carlos opened the front door and waited.

"Rachel, I'm going to do two things. The first thing I'm going to do is distance myself from you because you don't have to save me anymore. I'm an alcoholic and I know it. It's my work to follow the path toward recovery. It's one day at a time. When I'm feeling stronger, we'll get back on track. Second thing. I'm going to volunteer at the Ebsen Women's Correctional Facility. I'm not asking for your permission because this is my idea. And I have one request. Please do not ask about my sobriety."

Francine got out of the front seat and pulled her bag out of the back. Carlos left the front porch to help, but Francine waved him away. Rachel was crying.

"Don't cry," said Francine. "You should be happy. I'll regularly call Douglas and Ari to see how they are doing. Thank you for the ride. And thank you for hanging in with me, loving me, and always taking care of me. I love you."

Rachel watched her mother roll her bag into the house as Carlos and Boo Boo followed.

As she entered the house, Francine realized that Sasha was gone. It was a shock and she started to cry. She picked up Boo Boo for comfort. Carlos put on the kettle.

"Are you glad to be home?" asked Carlos.

"This is not the way I wanted to come home, but I'll get it under control. Everything looks great. You've kept the place spotless, and it feels inviting."

Francine pulled letter from her purse and sat down at the kitchen table to read it.

At a generic downtown Starbucks, Francine stirred a cup of hot tea. She was forthright and engrossed in the task of cooling off the drink when Don entered and made a beeline toward her. Francine stood, and they hugged.

"Hey, you look great," said Don.

"It's only been a few days. Glad to get to the hairdresser."

"I'm glad you called," said Don. "I didn't know if you would accept my invitation to coffee. We didn't have a proper goodbye."

"I read your note, and it's better to see each other out of the building, anyway, babe, because we have privacy. I'm sorry for my outburst in group about our friendship; that was uncomfortable, but I'm glad I said it. I felt good, but you suffered guilt. Not fair."

Don and Francine squeezed each other's hands.

"I'm going to jail, you know."

"Rhonda told me on her way out," said Don. "In fact, she was excited to have someone she knows going with her. She said you guys had a good conversation. Making friends. Bravo."

"What are you going to do with yourself now?"

"I'm going back to LA for a while. I've got a brother there. And my son is moving from Austin to LA, and I want to be there for him."

"What does that mean for us?" asked Francine.

"We were there for each other when it was right. But today, there is no us. We don't owe anything to each other. We owe everything to ourselves. That's what works in life-long recovery. Depend on your meetings, get a sponsor, volunteer, make new friends, discover more about who you are becoming. We'll always be in each other's hearts. But two drunks can never be together. You know that now."

"The rules were set before we started rehab. We didn't have a chance."

"The addiction sets the rules," Don said. "I'm apologizing, Francine. Writing letters was a mistake. I was selfish, and I was wrong. This moment would have been easier if I hadn't gone outside the boundaries, but I am not the role model for the perfect AA specimen."

"I don't want to get angry, but I am," said Francine. "It's my old song of resistance to the rules of life."

"Don't go down that road. Tell me what you've done differently so far."

"Do you care anymore? I mean, you're out of this relationship."

"We can't have a relationship, but we can have a friendship. You're angry, Francine. Anger triggers a relapse."

"I'm damn angry, babe, but there is nothing I can do about where we are. The only thing you need to know is that I'm keeping to my program and starting to distance from my daughter as Doctor Jerry suggested."

"Get a cell phone and it will be much easier to connect. Do you have a sponsor yet?"

"I want to tell you to screw yourself, Donny boy, but I can't. I'm too sad."

"Keep your grace, Francine. You'll be fine."

"That's it? Keep your grace, Francine?"

"I deserve that. And you deserve more."

Francine watched Don leave. She was angry and sad and wanted to act out, do something terribly destructive. A few minutes later, she walked outside of Starbucks and lit a cigarette. Don was nowhere in sight. She was on her own. She knew there was a liquor store a few blocks south from where she was standing. As she watched the people passing in front of her, going to jobs, the normalcy made her stop. Take one step away from yourself, and lo, behold the path.

The path led her to the entrance of the liquor store. She looked into the window and saw gleaming bottles of alcohol. She entered the store and walked down the aisles, glancing over the bottles of Jack Daniels. A young man walked up to her.

"Hi, Francine," said Steve. "How can I help?"

"Hi, Steve," said Francine. "Just checking out the bourbon. To buy or not to buy. That is the question."

Doctor Jerry was by her side with his scale of one to ten. If she decided to buy a bottle of bourbon, what number on Doctor Jerry's chart would she choose? And if she didn't buy a bottle, what number would she be comfortable with? Francine chose the number ten.

"Strangest damn thing is I don't want to drink. Nothing cries out drinking at this moment in the middle of a liquor store. But thank you for your help."

"No problem," said Steve.

Part Four:

Lock Down

Chapter 14

Mother Teresa

"You must be off your rocker, Francine," said Carlos. "The penal system is tough. I know a thing or two about lockups. You have to have thick skin and loads of confidence to walk around hallways."

"Rhonda said it was a minimum security facility. I should be fine."

"Please try something else," said Carlos. "How about the Goodwill store. It's always a good place to start."

"I don't want to hang clothes in a Goodwill store."

"Please try it. What about Catholic Charities?"

Carlos might not be the brightest bulb in the light fixture, but he paid attention to Francine sufficiently enough to hang on to his place in her universe. He wanted to help her in sobriety, and she wanted to make him part of the process even though he was on the fringe.

The next morning Francine drove to Goodwill on Riley Street in Zeeland. She usually dropped off her old clothes there. At ten sharp the doors opened. She put out her cigarette and got out of the car. The store windows were dirty, and the door looked like someone had broken in the night before. A few people were setting up at the cash register and reception counter for the day.

She entered tentatively and walked down the scuffed linoleum aisles while she checked out the merchandise. The air smelled stale and musty, and the store's maintenance was less than clean. Francine approached a woman counting money on the check-out counter.

"Hi," said Francine. "How do I volunteer?"

"You have to fill out papers," she said as she pulled a clipboard and gave it to Francine.

"Thank you," Francine replied as she looked over the questions. "You have to commit to twenty hours a week?"

"That's what it says."

Francine tried to look interested in the form.

"Thanks, again," said Francine as she laid the clipboard on the counter. "I may be back."

Francine pushed through the front door and lit a cigarette. Maybe it was too early in her sobriety to volunteer. She didn't have her sea legs. A liquor store was located three doors down in the small strip mall. She took three more puffs off her cigarette, stamped it out, and walked inside. There was no distinct smell. Nothing to knock her over and make her salivate for booze. She strolled down the aisle full of bourbon bottles, switched to the wine aisle, then back to the bourbon aisle. It was a sight to behold. Her feet wouldn't move.

"May I help you?" asked the man. "Looking for something special?"

"It's all special," she said. "Thanks for asking."

With everything Francine understood about recovery, with the number ten floating around her head, Francine moved her feet toward the door and left.

Because Carlos was disturbed by her volunteering at Ebsen Correctional Facility, she drove to the suburb of Holland and found a Catholic Charities thrift shop on Century Lane. The front entrance was clean with sparkling windows and an inviting sign offering drug counseling. Sitting in her car in the parking lot, Francine studied the happy people who entered, carrying bags, excited to shop. It was Christmas every day at the thrift store.

She rarely shopped, and when she did, she would never think of buying used clothes. Somebody else wore those clothes. Old stuff was not her thing.

Grateful she didn't have to shop second-hand. Francine closed her eyes, leaned her head back into the seat, and breathed deeply. Several moments later, she felt a sharp pain in her abdomen and winced. She took it as a sign that volunteering in retail thrift stores might not be in her future.

Because Francine didn't have a smartphone, she got out of the car and bought a local paper from the convenience store next to Catholic Charities and checked for an AA meeting.

The AA meeting was housed in an old community center that was stuck in the middle of a residential neighborhood on the outskirts of Grand Rapids that hadn't been completely gentrified. The center needed a coat of paint. There was no garden or greenery on the outside and the inside needed a facelift. Cold, dark, and dreary. She poured herself a cup of coffee and sat in an empty row of aluminum chairs. The seat was hard as a rock.

The meeting was getting started with the Serenity Prayer.

God, grant me the serenity to accept the things I cannot change, courage to change the things I can, and Wisdom to know the difference.

A young man of about forty began speaking.

"Good Evening ladies and gentlemen. This is the regular meeting of the South Grand Rapids Group of Alcoholics Anonymous. My name is Frank, and I am an alcoholic and your Secretary. Alcoholics Anonymous is a fellowship of men and women who share their experience, strength, and hope with each other that they may solve their common problem and help others to recover from alcoholism. The only requirement for membership is to stop drinking. There are no dues or fees for AA membership; we are self-supporting through our own contributions. AA is not allied with any sect, denomination, politics, organization, or institution; the organization does not wish to engage in any controversy; neither endorses nor opposes any causes. Our primary purpose is to stay sober and help other alcoholics to achieve sobriety. My sobriety was tested this morning. I wanted to say hello to my old bar, The Dog Yard, but I got out of the way of my temptation and took another route here. I feel grateful about that decision. And today I'm working on making amends. Anyone else want to speak?"

Francine shifted in her seat and looked around the room. She again felt a stabbing pain in her abdominal region. It passed and Frank continued.

"I'd like to ask any new member to introduce himself or herself. I see a few new faces."

Francine froze.

"Are you sure? Don't be shy." He paused. "Maybe next time." A woman went up to the front of the room to tell her story.

Francine left before the woman began to speak. She lit a cigarette and waited—for what she didn't know.

At the end of the meeting, Frank came out and spotted Francine putting out the butt of her cigarette near her car.

"Hi, I'm Frank."

"I know. Are you trying to recruit me to come back inside because I can't right now."

"That's fine, but I hope you'll come back."

∽

Rhonda drove too fast into the women's correctional facility parking lot. She had to slam on her brakes to stop the car from going beyond the guest parking. Francine clutched her purse. Rhonda parked and got out.

"Are you coming?" Rhonda asked as she began to walk to the front entrance.

Francine got out of the car and peered at the dilapidated building.

"Sounded like a good idea at the time," Francine said under her breath.

"I heard that," said Rhonda. "It's not the Taj Mahal, but it's clean."

"Oh, that's a good recommendation. I'll put it on Yelp. 'Jail is clean. Come on down and join us.'"

"Hold your judgment until you get in and see how it plays out," said Rhonda. "I know the warden. She's a cool lady."

"Wait a minute. You know the warden? How'd that come about?"

"I served time in this place," said Rhonda.

That was all Francine needed. Another ex-con. She seemed to be collecting not just strays, but strays who served time behind bars.

"I don't know why that surprises me. Were you an alcoholic when you were in jail?"

"No," said Rhonda. "I was dry for a long time before I went to jail. I sold some marijuana to an undercover cop. By today's standards, I might never have served time, but that was then and this is now. I began to drink after I got out. You get lost when you leave prison. That's why I want to help women who have been incarcerated transition to real life. I don't think it's fair that once we get back on the streets, we have no chance of getting a job because we have a record. Society expects its citizens to be productive. That's a joke. You'll find out how you want to help after you check out the scene. There are also AA meetings inside. This way, you don't have to go to the same meeting every day in Hudsonville, or Zeeland, or wherever. Gives you a little variety."

"That's comforting," said Francine. "Why didn't you share this observation in group?"

"Don't be Francine, Francine," said Rhonda. "I shared what I wanted to share just as you did. Let's get back to business. Have an open mind. You might learn something."

Rhonda and Francine entered Ebsen. signed in at the front desk. The institutional odor was a combination of Lysol and Febreze. To the left of the entrance was a check in station with a woman behind plexiglass.

"Hi, Lucy," said Rhonda. "Good to see you. Meet my friend, Francine. She's going to volunteer."

"Welcome Francine. I hope you like our little village," said Lucy.

"Let's hope, Lucy."

Several minutes later, two female guards escorted them through gates that separated the prison from the waiting room.

"Why are we being followed by guards?" asked Francine. "It's creepy. And who's Charlotte Ebsen, and how did she get her name on this fabulous place?"

"You can't enter the facility without a guard."

"It's not like we're going to break out the prisoners."

"Charlotte was a former ice skater. Married well. Wanted to give back, so she built a correctional facility for women that wouldn't have an institutional feeling."

"A jail without an institutional feeling is an oxymoron," snarked Francine.

"Funny," said Rhonda. "Don't let me get tired of you before your orientation. Let's get back to work on being human. And I fully know you have a Tonya Harding joke up your sleeve, so don't get cute."

On the way to the warden's office, with the female guard close behind, Francine and Rhonda passed a man in a white doctor's jacket wearing a black cowboy hat. His green eyes looked straight ahead. Not a muscle moved on his face. He reminded Francine of the cowboy-bartender who worked weekdays at a resort on Elk Lake. He'd stare straight at her with only a glint in his eyes when he served her bourbon and 7. Before she encountered the laconic bartender, she never experienced *glint*. Like *Clint*. All of a sudden, she wanted a drink. On the scale of one to ten, Francine ranked it a two.

The man in the white coat opened the green Dutch door of the pharmacy and walked inside. She hoped she wouldn't fall in love.

"Why is the paint color in these institutions always yellow or green?" she asked Rhonda as they sat in the warden's waiting room. "Total lack of imagination. A few strategically placed colorful landscape paintings would help. I think my next career move will be decorating prisons and recovery centers."

"Do you blab just to hear yourself talk?" asked Rhonda. "Focus on what you want to tell Doctor Stein in the meeting."

"I'm not blabbing about it. Canary yellow triggers me."

"You're full of it, Francine. Where do you come from, anyway?"

Doctor Stein was ready to see them, and they stood and entered her office. She was sitting calmly behind her modern glass desk. Francine looked at her legs, clearly visible under the table. She wore black three-inch heels. Her skirt was deep purple, pencil-thin, as was her body. She wore a white sheer, long-sleeved blouse with a bow that tied at the nape of the neck.

Lipstick with lip-liner was perfectly applied, eyebrows plucked, mascara and eyeliner to match her auburn hair.

"Hello, Rhonda, it's nice to see you."

Without waiting to be introduced, Francine spoke first. "I'm Francine Freeman, ma'am. I met Rhonda in rehab. Oak Lane."

Since Francine was still standing, Doctor Stein rose from her plush leather, ultra-modern chair and asked Francine to take a seat.

Francine was uncharacteristically calm as she sat down in a dark taupe chair with a comfy cushion.

"Rhonda suggested that I might be interested in hearing about what's involved in volunteering at Ebsen."

"Do you have an idea about what you are interested in doing in a volunteer capacity?" said Doctor Stein. "Has Rhonda told you what's available?"

"I don't know yet, but I'd like to look around the facility."

"Rhonda will give you the tour, then. And when you are ready, let's talk more about possibilities."

Francine was trying to be on her best behavior. Even though she felt claustrophobic, she was fully conscious.

"Thank you, Doctor Stein," said Francine, wobbling to her feet. "I might be back."

∽

The next day, Rachel stopped in front of her mother's house in Zeeland. The front yard looked exceptionally beautiful. Carlos was working hard to keep the house in good shape. In fact, it looked brand new. He may have put a coat of paint on the exterior. Rachel remembered that Peter resisted purchasing the house for his new wife, but Francine was going to get her way no matter what he thought. She wore him down with everything she had in her arsenal—logic, price, comfort, beauty, curse words until he signed the contract. Along with the Elk Lake house, her mother had every comfort and wanted for nothing. It was Peter's gift to his wife in death.

The late afternoon fall sun was setting. Silky clouds covered the last vestiges of what had been a pleasant day. Rachel was hoping to talk to Carlos about how her mother was doing—that old co-enabling need had been kicking in lately.

His 2001 Chevy was in the driveway. Tools and rubber tire peelings were scattered over the ground. The mess underneath the hood looked like a bomb had exploded inside the vehicle. Carlos' face was spotted with dirt, and his clothes needed a good wash. His hair looked like he was plugged into an electrical socket. The stray cat was rubbing against his jeans.

Rachel watched Carlos feeling confident that he was aware of her presence. Her original intent after learning that Carlos might be a permanent house guest was to make a fuss and try to get him out of her mother's life. After meeting Carlos and watching him take care of her mother and her property, Rachel had second thoughts. Then she watched him more closely after using her third eye, and she was sure his energy was good and his heart in the right place. Carlos knew she was parked, but he was focused on his work.

The car door felt like a heavy boulder as Rachel pushed it open.

"Hi, Rachel," he said to Rachel.

"How are you, Carlos?"

"I'm good. Work is good. But this car is a pain. I can't keep up with repairs."

Rachel heard Boo Boo bark from inside the house. "Can I let him out? He must be lonely without Sasha."

"He is missing her best friend, and with your mother not home much, he has stressful moments. He'll be glad to see you."

Rachel opened the front door and Boo Boo ran out jumping on her, eager to be petted.

"I know this is none of my business, but how is my mom doing at Ebsen?"

"She doesn't talk much. It's new and she's trying to figure out what to do."

"I wish I knew a little more about how things are going in general."

"She is starting to go to AA meetings," he said. "I know you're worried about her, and I intend to keep up with her schedule. Not too much, though, because she is fiercely independent."

"That's for sure, even when she was drinking, she ran the show."

"One more thing, Carlos. I know my mother is sick. It's obvious and I wanted to know if you have any details. She never went for her tests."

"She's handled her illness for quite a while; in fact, for as long as I've been living here. There is no way anyone can interfere with her journey now."

Rachel knelt and played with Boo Boo and cried. Carlos went back to the business of fixing a tire tread. She felt sure that Carlos was dedicated to caring for her mother—maybe she was a little jealous. She was no longer the designated person taking care of her mother. Letting go of co-enabling was harder than she thought. She was always there for her through pain and joy—and now she had to let go of that expectation. Her mother was distancing from her, and maybe this was a sign that a stronger Francine would emerge. Volunteering was the next step—Francine's natural inclination was to be kind and charitable to others. Makes sense. There was nothing new in that. It was drinking that got in her way and stole her power, sending her into the throes of unconsciousness. No matter where Francine was going, Rachel felt hope.

Chapter 18

The Monkey Chased The Weasel

On the second visit to Ebsen Correctional Facilities, Rhonda and Francine went through the same routine. A guard was assigned to them as the inside gates opened.

"We have a new guard," said Francine as they explored the activity rooms and the library. "It's for our own good. Doesn't matter who it is because they keep the volunteers safe. Let's focus on some of the activities that might interest you. You can facilitate activity time, teach reading, or sewing, or play cards with them and prompt meaningful conversation, or even lead AA meetings."

"You're just showing me places, Rhonda," said Francine. "And these places are dull and lifeless, except maybe the library and that is your territory. I want to come here two or three times a week and interact. I don't do toilets or windows. I do the interaction stuff."

"Look, girlfriend," said Rhonda. "You've got attitude, and this won't work. Maybe you should try another way to use your skill set."

"Maybe I can teach a class. Like a poetry class."

"What, girl? What are you talking about? You write poetry?"

"Wonders never cease. I can also teach how to write an essay. I can do both narrative and poetry. Maybe we can read some fiction. Or start with a memoir."

"Is that all?" asked Rhonda with a smile. "Don't you do anything else?"

"No. I smoke and drink and read."

One of Rhonda's inmate friends, Camille, came up behind her and gave her a bear hug, but the guard intervened and reminded Camille to step back. Her sweet round face turned into disappointment. Camille needed reassurance and a hug.

They did their private language exchange, asked about other inmates, and caught up on who got fired, who got hired, and what was up with the silent cowboy.

"You look good, girl, if I do say so," said Camille. "You're damn right skinny."

"You look good, too, girl. I want you to meet Francine. Camille is my good friend in this victimless crime unit."

"Nice to meet you, Francine," said Camille. "You volunteering like Rhonda?"

"I hope to," said Francine. "What's up with the silent cowboy I saw in the corridor? Who is he?"

"He's our resident pharmacist. The doctor who dispenses the drugs," said Camille. "He always wears a black cowboy hat, a black t-shirt, and black jeans under his lab coat, and he barely talks. But when he smiles, the girls melt. Those two lucky bitches who work with him in the dispensary would crawl to hell and back for him. But, the one who took your place, Rhonda, is ugly, girl. He doesn't have your beauty around him no more."

"Those were the days," said Rhonda laughing as Doc Gallardo walked up behind her.

"Hi, Rhonda, good to see you," said Doc Gallardo.

"Hi, Doc," said Rhonda. "You surprised me."

Doc Gallardo tipped his black hat back on his forehead.

"Francine, this is Doc Gallardo."

"Nice to meet you," said Francine.

"You got a smoker's voice, lady," he said with a slight Texas twang. "If you think you might want to quit, let me know. I have patches."

"Did my low voice give me away?" asked Francine.

"If you're clean and sober, you might want to finish the job and kick the last addiction."

"I've got too many to count, but I'll hold that thought."

"Nice to meet you, ma'am."

The three women watched him walk away in silence. His presence was like a soft summer breeze passing through the corridor; it carried the scent of orange blossoms. As Doc Gallardo walked away, he took the energy of the group with him.

"Whew! Damn that man oozes sex," said Camille smoothing out her long, thick, dark hair.

"That's more than I ever heard him speak in the three years I worked with him," said Rhonda.

"What did you do to make him talk, Miss Francine?" asked Camille.

"I have no idea," said Francine, still dazed.

"He has that effect," said Rhonda. "Sometimes he can look into your soul. But let's face it. You have a deep smoker's voice. Doesn't take a genius to figure that out."

"That's some talent," Francine said.

Right then and there, Francine decided to teach essay writing, letter writing, and poetry. The problem was that she had never done it before. She had never given up smoking before either, but now was a good time to start. New places, new faces.

After Rhonda showed Francine around, she escorted her back to Doctor Stein's office and waited with the guard.

Francine sat in front of Doctor Amy Stein once again. Rhonda had gone off to talk to a group of women who were several months away from leaving. It occurred to Francine that Rhonda and she might have some compatibility with their workshops. It amazed Francine how clear her mind was when not floating in a haze of alcohol.

"What did you decide, Francine?" asked Doctor Stein.

"I want to offer writing courses. First thing is to teach them to write an essay—then how to write a good letter, then journaling, and a memoir piece, and some poetry."

"Sounds great. Have you ever taught?"

"I worked in a school district for over twelve years in the substitute teaching department. I was always writing reports and letters to teachers." Francine was only fibbing a little. She never wrote letters, but she could if asked. "I have a fairly good Catholic school education and a great vocabulary."

"That's not teaching per se," said Doctor Stein. "Anything else?"

"So, that's a no."

"I have to think about it."

Francine stood up, gathered her purse, and put on her sunglasses. "Thanks for your time," she said.

"Can you give a few workshops on how and why you got sober?" asked Doctor Stein. "And how to stay sober?"

"If I wanted to share that information, I could do it in my AA meetings. It's not relevant."

"It's relevant to anyone who wants to listen and learn," said Doctor Stein. "You came to sobriety late in life."

"Yeah, I'm almost dead."

"Why did you get sober if you're almost dead?" asked Doctor Stein.

"To paraphrase Voltaire, 'The world, my friend, is one great shipwreck so save yourself if you can.' Something like that."

"Impressive. What was going on in your life before you hit rock bottom?"

"Who says I hit rock bottom? Maybe I've got another rung of hell to explore."

"You obviously have life-long coping skills."

"I tap dance through life," she told Doctor Stein. "It's no great mystery. I'm a master of deflection. I turned my back on my addiction, and I did it with humor, sarcasm, irony, and huge amounts of pent-up anger."

"What brought you to sobriety?" asked Doctor Stein.

"It was the second fall that got me in treatment again, or more specifically, my daughter put me in detox. She overcame her resistance to my resistance."

"And you went kicking and screaming, I suppose."

"Good guess."

"Did you learn anything in treatment?" asked Doctor Stein.

"I learned that I'm an alcoholic, and I have no power over my addiction. I'm always working on my first step."

"What motivated you to get out of bed today?" asked Doctor Stein.

"Rhonda asked me to come, and I said yes," Francine said.

"I'm sure there is much you can teach these women, although you probably don't believe you can. I want you to lead several AA meetings a week, structure some talks, be a counselor to women who have personal questions. You're older and that means you're a role model."

Francine was about to protest, but Doctor Stein continued before she could interrupt. "I know you don't want to be a role model, but it is precisely that state of mind that can influence some of these women. And you can do it with humor and self-deprecation, which are your gifts. Do that, and then, maybe we'll see about the rest of your agenda. See you back here in two days. Ten in the morning. You're a morning person, right? I'll schedule a room. You can lead the meeting."

Doctor Stein took a sheet of paper from her desk drawer.

"It's a cheat sheet for AA. Use it to conduct the meetings. And ask my secretary to make copies of the Twelve Steps paper and you give them to the group."

"By the way, Dr. Stein, why would you think I know how to stay sober?"

Francine walked out of Doctor Stein's office to tell Rhonda she was leaving and not coming back, but instead, she went straight to the pharmacy window. The guard had to skip some steps to keep up with her.

The silent cowboy was working in silence. His two young helpers, both in their late twenties, were diligently focused on their work, measuring pills into bottles and writing notes on files. They didn't want to make a mistake or lose their focus. If they had to communicate with each other, they did so with their eyes, a smile, or a nod of the head. They looked like mimes. The atmosphere felt like an ashram with a spiritual vibe.

Without looking at Francine, Doc Gallardo spoke to her. "What is it, ma'am?"

"Please, don't call me *ma'am*."

"What should I call you?"

"Francine."

"What is it, Francine?" he asked. "Looking for a patch?"

"You're busy. I'll come back."

"I break every day at two," Doc Gallardo said.

"I'm supposed to be coming here in the morning a few times a week, but I don't know how long I'll stay," said Francine.

Francine walked away, eyes straight ahead, guard following in lockstep. Her determination to get out of prison was consuming her at the moment. She looked in every doorway for Rhonda, and listened for a voice she could recognize.

From a distance, around another corridor, Francine heard Rhonda laugh. She waited outside the door for her to finish making introductory remarks about her topic: how to adjust to the outside world, what to expect, and skills to develop to stay mentally healthy. "Above all, go to your AA meetings."

That was Francine's cue. She stepped inside the classroom and all eyes turned on her. Francine wanted a drink and a cigarette more than anything. She'd kill for either one.

"Ladies, this is Francine Freeman," Rhonda began, "and she will be volunteering at Ebsen. What is your new assignment?"

Francine knew this was going to be the moment when she could let Rhonda go as a friend and supporter, or go her own way alone without backup.

"I'm going to guide AA meetings a few times a week. And I'm grateful to be here."

"Great to have you here, Francine," said Rhonda. "Okay, everyone, please bring a pen and notebook to the next class. It's important to keep journals."

The air outside was corrosively warm. The afternoon autumn sun had a way of entering the body like a dull knife. By the time Francine and Rhonda walked to the car, they were depleted of energy.

Rhonda settled into the driver's side and waited for Francine to get comfortable. They both sighed with relief that the morning's visit was over. Prison visits could be ordeals, stressful at times, and emotional. Francine wanted to wash clean, have a drink, and smoke. She started to take out the e-cigarette but stopped when Rhonda swiveled her head like Linda Blair in "Poltergeist" to admonish her.

"Jesus, babe, that's a little punitive," said Francine. "Don't you think I deserve a treat?"

"Not in my car."

Rhonda drove in silence. Francine stuck her hand inside her purse and fiddled with the e-cigarette. As they pulled up to Rhonda's house, the chill in the car was palpable.

"There's a Starbucks," said Francine. "A sure sign of gentrification."

"What's your point?" asked Rhonda.

"The neighborhood will be worth more in time, that's all. It's a good location on the edge of the city limits."

"Have you taken up real estate recently?" asked Rhonda.

"I've been busy doing other things, like getting sober, but I do know a bit about the housing market, so you don't have to get snarky."

"This is your car, right?" asked Rhonda as she stopped at the side of Francine's car.

"You know damn well it is," said Francine. "What exactly is your problem?"

"I'm moody."

"I did my best in that place. First time I'd been in prison. What did you expect? Cartwheels?"

"Don't go all Francine on me," said Rhonda. "Can't you just still your mind?"

"Are you kidding me?" asked Francine. "I just got out of rehab. My head is exploding."

"Don't exaggerate," said Rhonda. The car continued to idle.

"Why don't you park instead of trying to get us killed," said Francine.

Rhonda parked in front of a house in need of paint and a new roof.

"This is about as much fun as attending a Rotary Club luncheon in downtown Grand Rapids," said Francine.

"Look, people in recovery are suffering from whatever it is that makes them drink," said Rhonda. "It's different for everyone. For me, it's my self-esteem. For others, it's childhood trauma. I know I'm smart, but sometimes I resist believing in my power. It's my curse."

"Your curse is someone else's gift," said Francine. "At least, you know something about why you picked up the bottle. That's progress, isn't it?"

"It's no excuse," said Rhonda. "And excuses don't lead to sobriety. Awareness leads to sobriety. Clear thinking leads to sobriety."

"You're way ahead of me. I know low self-esteem when I see it. I have it, too, but acknowledging that I have it in spades is another level of commitment to sobriety that I don't have right now."

"Slow down, girl, that's too dark for me," said Rhonda.

"Not as dark as the bottom of a bottle," said Francine. "You know what drinking was about for me? It was about waiting for the click to go off in my head. That was the moment I lost the ability to think rationally or sustain consciousness and all was right in my world."

"Don't demean your life," said Rhonda. "You raised a successful daughter, were involved in your grandchildren's lives, and survived three bad marriages. That's something."

"But I never did anything for myself," said Francine.

"You've still got time."

"Not enough."

"You keep thinking and talking like this and you'll find yourself at the bottom of a bottle again," said Rhonda. "You have to realize that the more negative you are, the more you drag yourself down. Try sprinkling some positive affirmations in your conversations; otherwise, I'm not going to hang out with you because right now you are not good for me."

Francine got out of Rhonda's car and walked around to the driver's side. She lit a cigarette and blew the smoke away from Rhonda.

"You probably don't want to volunteer at Ebsen, right?" asked Rhonda.

"It's a lot on my plate. New situation, new people, an assignment to lead AA meetings, which is not my thing. "

"You don't have to do this gig, Francine. You can walk away, or put the idea in your back pocket, or slow down and come back later. It's your call."

"If I do, I'll call you. I'm sorry I bummed you out. The old Francine can be resistant and off-putting. I'll get over it. Time to go to an AA meeting. Thanks, my friend."

Chapter 16

Real Life is Hard

Francine sat in her car in front of her house and thought about the conversation with Rhonda. It was depressing and frightening because Francine didn't want to undo the last two months. She learned in group that to be sober meant living consciously in the present. Easy to say, but damn hard to do.

As she walked to the garage, the cat walked seductively to Francine and grazed her legs with his gray fur. She melted and stroked the stray cat with love.

Carlos walked into the garage from the house. "How's it going, Francine?"

"Just ducky," Francine said as she entered the house. "I hope you're feeding the cat, Carlos," Francine said as she entered the house.

"Don't I always?"

Francine sat on the bed and looked at her watch. It was the bewitching hour. The drinking lamp was lit. Five o'clock. She wanted to smoke but didn't. She wanted to drink but didn't. Instead, she stood up, changed her clothes, went downstairs, and poured herself a large glass of water from the tap.

Carlos came into the kitchen.

"I'll get dinner after I clean up," said Carlos.

"Don't bother," said Francine. "I'm going to a meeting."

"You can microwave it when you get home."

~

Francine drove to a Baptist church in an older section of West Main Avenue in Zeeland. The white wooden façade lit up the driveway like a movie set. That kind of sexy golden light that makes everyone look beautiful. The air smelled of musky dew. She could still feel the remnants of the day's humidity on her body.

Three steps to the landing, two steps to the door, and she heard the group reciting the Serenity Prayer—*God grant me the serenity to accept the things I cannot change*. Francine never experienced serenity.

The interior of the church was a surprise—it wasn't dreary as Francine thought it might be, not just because this was a well-dressed, upscale collection of alcoholics in attendance, but the church felt like a cozy cottage that held the promise of a hip and cool party about to happen. The ceiling was painted a soft driftwood color; the lighting grid gave the space a modern feel and the smell of evening jasmine was intoxicating.

Two rows of light brown, well-worn pews filled the center of the church. Coffee was brewing in a large electric pot on a distressed gray table in the back. Front and center was a podium and mic set up for the speaker, bookended by two large white charts which displayed the Twelve Steps and the Twelve Traditions. A smattering of AA literature was scattered on a small table to the left of the speaker's podium.

She entered a vacant pew and focused on a man speaking behind the podium. He looked to be in his mid-sixties, tanned, sparkling blue eyes, gray, close-cropped hair, and a sturdy and energetic frame. He referred to himself as Ed. The audience was attentive as Ed told his story of how alcohol affected his life, unraveling different scenarios, different aspects of despair many times over, with his different voices depending on where he was incarcerated, in tents under bridges, but without shame and guilt. Ten years living on the streets, eating out of dumpsters, daily fighting over a bottle of wine, getting stabbed, going to jail several times, only to be thrown back out on the streets to do the dance all over again.

In time, he re-entered humanity with heaps of gratitude that took him out from the bottom rung of hell and toward another, more coherent path. The Vets, good friends from high school, and a sweet woman named Rosemary brought him home. He used to be a plumber before the fall; he used to ride a Harley before the fall. He brought his passions back into his life and began his recovery.

Ed was intelligent and a good motivational speaker. His story encapsulated the AA journey. Lost years and tragic stories triggered her dislike for the concept of Alcoholics Anonymous. She revolted at being reminded of what alcoholism represented, even though she was undoubtedly its poster child, like Ed, like everyone in the room. Her first foray into AA overwhelmed her; she was completely resistant to the core values of the program—surrender, honesty, and authenticity. She was convinced the bottle cured all. Besides, she was still alive and kicking, so why not keep drinking.

But despite her adversity with sharing stories, that night at the church and the honesty in Ed's story, Francine realized that life didn't have to have any purpose other than staying present and having gratitude. It sounded simple to do, but it was difficult to accomplish. She was used to going unconscious. It was easier than making good choices.

After the meeting, Ed came up to Francine, sat beside her, and handed her a booklet.

"Hi there," Ed said, "I'm Ed."

"I know. I'm Francine. Good retelling of your journey. It hit the spot."

"I hope I added something new to your journey."

"You've got a great smile."

"And my message?"

Francine knew the AA speak. She had been around the block too many times not to pick up the buzz words.

"Gratitude is good. I like the take-away," said Francine. "But so far, it doesn't get me through the day."

"You're a newbie, Francine, and it takes time to adjust to a new way of thinking. Try a mantra. Keep it simple, say, 'Thanks for the day.' Give yourself a pat on the back for random acts of kindness. Smile more. Smiles are infectious—they change your attitude, start your motor."

"I could strangle your skinny neck about now," said Francine. "I'm grinning. Can you see it?"

"Sure can. That works. One more thing. Get out of the way of yourself so you can see your path."

"Someone else said that to me in rehab. Is that an AA thing?"

"If you ever need support, or want a sponsor, let me know."

"How would that work?" asked Francine.

"Meet with me, talk to me about anything, everything. You know where to find me."

As Francine walked down the stairs of the church, she wanted to pull out what was left of her hair. Her old SUV looked particularly pathetic and uninviting, which discouraged her from opening the door and driving away. Home was not her destination.

"Hey, Ed," Francine bellowed as she turned around. "Does this mean you're my sponsor officially?"

"If you want it, you've got it," he said as he walked into the church.

"Have you got a phone number and all that good stuff?"

"It's on the program I gave you," he said without turning around.

Instead of driving home, Francine wanted distance from people and familiar places. It was hard for her to breathe after the long day. Without thinking, she headed to the entrance of the Ebsen Correctional Facility and stopped in front of the gate. A bright canopy of LED lights sat atop tall, sturdy concrete poles placed generously around the prison grounds. Several guard shacks dotted the stark landscape. The place could use some greenery. Maybe Mrs. Ebsen ran out of money after she had her name put up on the building. The headlights on her car turned off automatically. She thought it would be nice to start a garden with the inmates. She loved her tomato garden.

Francine slumped against the seat, exhausted, and thought about Ed—tonight's AA knight in shining armor. His peaceful disposition was infectious.

It came from within himself. Francine never had that peaceful feeling. Ed was right about one thing: Francine made it her business to be in her own way. It was confounding her at that moment.

A light near one of the guard huts was twitching. A correctional officer came out and watched the blinking light for at least five minutes before the light went out. And so did she.

∽

The stray cat was cleaning himself by the garage as Francine drove up. When she got out of the car and bent down to pet the cat, she noticed the dew was still on the lawn from the night's low temperatures. She tried to stand and found it difficult.

Carlos came out with Boo Boo and helped her inside. Boo Boo jumped up and down her legs. Francine tried to pet her dog but could not bend down again.

"Hello, my baby. Did you miss me?"

"Where were you?" he asked. "I was about to call the police. You scared me to death."

"I took a detour. Help me up the stairs. I need sleep."

Carlos took her arm and helped Francine into the house. She was so weak that he almost had to carry her up the stairs. He laid her on the bed and put an old, faded baby blue quilt over her frail body. Boo Boo jumped up and folded into Francine's side. She was out like a light.

The doorbell rang and Carlos dashed downstairs. Rhonda stood razer straight in front of him. She bore into his dark brown eyes and asked, "And you are?"

"Carlos. Are you from AA or the prison?"

"Both. I saw Francine at the correctional facility early this morning. She was driving away as I pulled up. Is she all right?"

"She was tired and went to bed. Want to come in?"

The La-Z-Boy couch in the living room was enveloping and comfortable with a sweet floral pattern of blue and white flowers dotted with dark navy throw pillows. It was the definition of shabby chic. Rhonda had no idea that

Francine might have a talent for decorating. She heard her babbling on about the colors in the recovery room and throughout the facility and thought she was just batty. But from the occasional chairs covered in light shades of café latte, to the antique coffee table, Rhonda found a new respect for Francine. She could decorate a space with style, but she couldn't dress for shit.

"Do you live here with Francine?" asked Rhonda.

"Yes. And I help out."

"I see."

Rhonda didn't see, but she was not that interested, or curious enough about Carlos to pursue information about him. Their relationship was not her business.

"You have no clue why Francine was at Ebsen after dark?"

"That's where she's volunteering."

"You know the place?" asked Rhonda.

"Somewhat."

"You did time somewhere?"

"Yes."

Rhonda stood up to leave. "Tell her I dropped by, and I'll see her at Ebsen the day after tomorrow."

As soon as the door closed, Francine came down the stairs. She entered the kitchen and methodically filled a glass full of ice and chilled lemonade. As an afterthought, she added a splash of lemon La Croix.

"You met Ronda?" asked Francine.

"She's nice. I think."

"She is my jailer. Not in the real sense, but she is keeping me on the righteous path."

"I'm going to work, and after that, I'm locking up at the church."

Sometimes she longed to be alone and wished that Carlos would find his own life. And sometimes she was happy he was there to take care of things. Carlos had become a fixture, part of the fabric of her life, a choice she made consciously.

The next morning, Carlos was waiting for Francine at the kitchen table. He was holding the morning newspaper rolled up tight.

"You're up early," he said. "I've got a present for you."

Francine took the newspaper and unrolled it. Inside was a mobile phone.

"I'll teach you how to work it when I come home from work."

"My life is now fulfilled. I'm connected to the world even if I don't want to be."

Carlos kissed her on her forehead and opened the door to the garage. The cat ran inside to find Francine's warm hands.

Chapter 17

Love is My Religion

Two days later, Francine dragged herself into Ebsen Correctional Facility's administrative office at eight-thirty. She was sleep-deprived and barely functional, but she managed to sign in at the office and shuffle along the corridor with her female guard who looked like she played basketball.

"Don't you ever get tired of walking with me?" she asked.

"It's my job, ma'am," said the guard.

"You should put on a little weight," said Francine.

"You should talk," said the guard.

Rhonda was reading an old *Time* magazine on a bench outside Doctor Stein's office.

"Hangover?"

"Funny."

"Let's get going," said Rhonda. "You have an AA meeting to lead at nine."

"Can't. Not well."

"If you can walk, you can sit in a chair and lead a group meeting. One of the women will start with the Serenity Prayer, then introduce you, and you'll start off by sharing. Why can't you do it?" asked Rhonda.

"I'm not well. How many times do I have to tell you?"

"I forgot how old you are," said Rhonda. "You look like you're homeless."

"I think I'm a little depressed. Isn't that normal?"

"It's common," said Rhonda. "I'm sorry, but let's see if you can make it through the meeting. You've got some kind of grit, so let's see you put it to good use."

Francine dropped her head and followed her down the hallway, guard in toe.

"Wait up," said Francine.

Rhonda stopped in front of Room 222.

"This is it, Francine. Do your best."

The linoleum floor in Room 222 was chipped and spotted with ingrained stains that were never going to come out. Twenty women sat in chairs scattered about. They were tired, bored, and clearly unmotivated to be at an AA meeting. All heads turned to Francine as she entered the room.

"Where's the woman who leads our group," asked a woman who sat in the front row.

Francine needed a starting point.

"First thing we're doing is some housekeeping. All twenty of you, move your chairs in a circle in the middle of the room. If you choose not to move your chairs and participate in the meeting, then you're not ready to attend an AA meeting. That means someone forced you to be here, or you don't want to stay sober, or keep off drugs, or you are rude and lazy, or you need somewhere to put your sorry asses for the next hour."

A few heads looked up. Some of the women opened their eyes. A few sat up straight. One or two smiled to themselves.

"Truth be told, I'd rather be having my first drink of the day," said Francine without a trace of humor.

The women moved their chairs in a circle. Francine dragged the chair from behind the desk into the circle and tried to remember how Doctor Jerry positioned himself within the group—next to the most vulnerable, or most silent, or most verbal, or most resistant. That's everyone in the room.

She sat next to the woman who laughed at her joke about wanting a drink.

"This isn't exactly the way an AA meeting starts, but I'm going to go against protocol and start with your names. And if you think I won't remember your names, you are mistaken. I have a memory like an elephant, and I will remember each and every one of you until the day I leave."

Every woman in the room gave Francine her name.

"Let's stand and recite the Serenity Prayer."

"God, grant me the serenity to accept the things I cannot change, courage to change the things I can, and wisdom to know the difference."

"Everyone be seated, please," said Francine with a tinge of nervousness. "I'm Francine, and I'm an alcoholic."

"Aren't you too old to be a volunteer?" asked a young, petite Hispanic woman with dark eyes and long curly hair.

"I'm old. But today I'm sober. Is everyone here sober?"

The group nodded.

"The question should be: is anyone here on drugs," said a woman in her sixties, weathered, and skinny as a rail. Her eyes were watery, and her teeth were loose.

"Right. It's probably difficult to get alcohol in jail. Easier to get drugs. But if you are an alcoholic, you'll take drugs as a substitute to get high, so we'll keep both in our vocabulary for these meetings."

Most of the women fidgeted as Francine read the AA paper that Doctor Stein had given her. It occurred to Francine that they heard it all before.

"The idea is to share your story. We may have time for two. That about takes up the hour. But the first order of business: Any new people in the group today? If so, raise your hands."

Three ladies raised their hands. Francine read from her paper.

"Tell me your names, please, ladies," requested Francine. Tina, Marsha, Louisa.

"Thank you all for coming. I know you all know this but I'm going to review the official definition of Alcoholics Anonymous so we're all on the same page. AA is a fellowship of men and women who share their experience, strength, and hope with each other that they may solve their common problem and help others to recover from alcoholism. The only requirement for membership is a desire to stop drinking. There are no dues or fees for AA membership; we are self-supporting through our own contributions. AA is not allied with any sect, denomination, politics, organization, or institution; does not wish to engage in any controversy; neither endorses nor opposes any causes. Our primary purpose is to stay sober and help other alcoholics to achieve sobriety.

"So how it works is this. We either study and talk about one of the Twelve Steps, or a few of you will be speakers, but there is no cross discussion of stories, or responses, or opinions about what is being said. In other words, no judging."

Linda raised her hand to speak.

"Miss Francine, why don't you start. You are the leader. And you need to set an example."

"There are no leaders in AA. I'm just a person trying to be sober one day at a time. I've been to two AA meetings since I got out of rehab, but I haven't told my story before, not even when I went to AA meetings the first time I got sober. I was one of those embarrassed alcoholics and didn't get to rehab after detox. No one asked me to go or told me to go. And I didn't want to go because of how I ended up in the hospital."

The room was silent. The women were listening intently, focused on Francine, riveted by her honesty and her presence.

"I'm seventy-six, and I always drank bourbon. I've never been sober longer than six months. I just finished two months and a few days this time around."

Francine took a deep breath to steady her nerves.

"I fell down the stairs in my house because I was drunk. I fell backward and broke my neck. And nothing happened, except a sore neck."

There was a collective and audible inhale in the room.

"And then, about a year later, I fell down the same stairs, and again I broke my neck. This fall was more serious."

"But you're not paralyzed," said Charla, the withered woman in her sixties. "What's the matter with you? Don't you break?"

"I wear a neck brace, but I took it off because it gives me a headache. I try to put it back on when I remember. The second time I broke my neck, my daughter intervened and put me in the hospital to detox and for physical therapy. Then I went to rehab for another three weeks."

"That don't mean anything," said Nell.

"It means I'm in step one," said Francine. "I'm powerless over alcohol. Truth is that I want to have a drink about five times a day. I didn't know I felt shame and guilt about my drinking until I got sober. I was good at using my defense mechanisms as an excuse to drink. And that's because I carried around a high level of resistance to anyone who told me what to do, especially my mother when she was alive. And even though she died years ago, once in a while, I can hear her telling me I would never amount to anything."

"I feel that way, too," said Tina, one of the new attendees.

"Do you want to tell us your story, Tina?" asked Francine.

"I started drinking early in high school. No one was home after school, and I was bored, so I broke into the liquor cabinet and the rest is history. I used to hang out with the guys who drank, and then I dropped out of school and got involved with drugs and ended in jail."

"Thanks for sharing, Tina," said Francine. "We're all a work in progress."

"I have a question," said Linda. "Do you think you are a dry drunk?"

"What do you think, Linda?" asked Francine.

"I think we're all dry drunks," said Linda. "We can't drink again and that makes us angry. We don't always show the anger, but my boyfriend can tell that I'm angry over nothing and that's when the dry drunk comes out."

"You have to go to AA meetings," said Billie. "AA helps us deal with our anger and helps us stay on the path to sobriety."

"Well said, Billie," said Francine. "We are all a work in progress. I'm grateful for you guys today."

"Thanks for sharing," said Linda.

"And I'm sorry that I took up most of the hour. But if we all want to follow the rules of an AA meeting, we had a little too much cross talk today, but we'll get better. For sure, your comments are appreciated, and you should all have the opportunity to speak, as well as to talk about the twelve steps and which one you are working on.

"Let's close with an intention to practice one of the steps in the next few days and be prepared to talk about what happened to you as a result of your being intentional. Please take a copy of the steps I have for you on the desk. Carry them with you. If you would like to close with a prayer, please do so. I'm not much on prayers. Or just think about your higher power, your conscious awareness, in all things related to your life."

Francine gathered her purse and clutched it to her chest as she tried to gauge the positive energy in the room.

"Thanks, everyone. See you in two days."

Outside the classroom door, Francine wanted to cry, but the guard was hovering over her, and she tried not to embarrass herself by breaking down.

"I don't know how I did that," Francine said to the guard. "I didn't know I knew the words. I was channeling Doctor Jerry."

"You are doing what comes natural," said the guard.

Ed was right. Francine got out of the way of herself. She promised to call him after work to tell him about her first AA meeting in the prison. She knew it went well.

Doc Gallardo was in his cubbyhole, and so were his two silent assistants, doing everything to suck up to their boss.

"Hi, Doc," said Francine. "Still interested in giving me some of those anti-smoking patches? I'm thinking of quitting."

"Thinking or doing?"

"What the hell does that mean?"

"Doesn't help to think. Patches only help when you commit. You have to have an intention, not some half-ass attempt because someone told you to."

"Right. I'm ready."

"Go home and let's try this again tomorrow," said Doctor Gallardo as he turned his back to fill a prescription. "And please don't call me Doc."

"I thought all pharmacists are doctors."

"Technically, you're right. But I haven't finished my doctorate."

"Mr. Gallardo doesn't suit you,"

He turned around and faced Francine with a stern look and then handed her a box of anti-smoking patches.

She read the label. "So, you believe I can do this?"

"I don't believe you can do it, but why don't you surprise me?" he said with his crooked smile.

"I have a hundred questions to ask you," said Francine.

"We have time. You and I aren't going anywhere right now."

Francine didn't want to use the patches. It was her way of getting to know Doc Gallardo, trying to extend the conversation, and plying him with questions he wouldn't answer. She wondered if she could get close enough to him to get his story.

The boxes of patches disappeared into her purse as she stepped outside the front entrance, leaving the guard behind.

Rachel was waiting in her car outside the correctional facility. As soon as she saw her mother, she opened the door.

"What? No hug?" asked Francine. "Never mind. I'm fine. Even got the smoking patches to prove it. And I held my first AA meeting."

Rachel hugged her mother. "How did it go?" asked Rachel.

"A little rough around the edges. I'm usually funnier."

"I stopped by the house and saw Carlos and Boo Boo. I wanted to see how they were both doing."

"He's not leaving, and you can take that to the bank."

"I get that. I have confidence that he is going to do the right thing by you."

"You don't have to worry or get involved. Let it go and we will be fine. I have you to thank for forcing me into recovery. I'm now reasonably in charge of my life."

"You were always in charge of your life, Mom. It was the direction of your life that got off track."

Rachel hugged her mother again and fought back her tears as she got back into her car. Her daughter reached out to squeeze her mother's hand, then drove out of the parking lot.

Francine started her car engine, rolled down the windows, and rested her forehead on the steering wheel. She took three deep breaths as she squeezed her eyes closed. Real-life is hard.

"Who was that?" asked Doctor Gallardo as he stooped down to put his elbows on the edge of the driver's side window of Francine's car.

Francine looked up. "I thought I heard a familiar voice. That's my daughter. Rachel put me into detox. She's having a hard time letting me go. I guess I feel the same."

"You said you have a hundred questions," said Doc Gallardo. "What's the first?"

"You want to have a chat now?" she asked. "I'm flattered you care, but I'm beat."

Doctor Gallardo pushed himself off the car and walked around to the passenger side.

"Mind if I get in?" he asked

"Mi casa, su casa"

"Smells of cigarettes," Doc Gallardo said as he got in the car.

"I've got air freshener, babe; and, besides, it's none of your business."

"It is my business since I technically gave you a drug. Ask me your question."

"Pushy, aren't you?"

She tried to attach the patch to her arm, fumbled, and let out an exasperating sound—like a goat bleating. Doc Gallardo helped her complete the task.

"It takes time, and you'll cheat, but don't beat yourself up."

"You don't fit the pharmacist type," said Francine.

"What type is that?" he asked.

"Not nerdy enough."

"When I was younger, I was a rodeo man. In my mind, I still am, but I'm too old now."

"I cannot grasp that concept. You shock me. It's funny, not like I want to laugh, but funny in an ironic kind of way. You dress like a cowboy but don't have a horse."

"I used to have horses, but you don't need to own a horse to be a cowboy. It's about the rodeo. You might want to discuss this for a while, but I still have work to do. Let me know if you need anything else. I'll take those questions later."

"I'll keep that in mind. Thanks for the drugs."

Chapter 18

The Devil You Know

Fall had turned into winter before Francine was aware. Time was elusive. She guided AA meetings at the Ebsen Women's Correctional Facility three days a week. Her meeting attendance grew. Maybe she was just a sideshow at the facility, or maybe the women were beginning to feel normal and comfortable when she was around.

The older ladies called her Phyllis Diller, and the younger inmates loved her laugh. She was iconoclastic, sarcastic, and ironic, and even though they didn't know what those words meant, they understood the way Francine parsed a phrase, or expressed an opinion, or called them on their defenses. She was a master of defenses—she had them all in her arsenal. The meetings became her recovery and her recovery lived inside her meetings. Francine thought that guiding AA meetings as a form of recovery might not be the correct way to proceed. It got complicated.

Even though Ed was Francine's sponsor, and he was a rock in her life with his perceptive, guidance, and spiritual musings, she decided it was time to take a field trip to see Doctor Jerry.

She called and asked the receptionist for the first available appointment.

Francine drove to Oak Lane, parked, and got out of her SUV. It was a sunny fall afternoon, the same kind of afternoon when she first arrived with Rachel. Two days later Ida died. Memories of Ida's funeral clouded her mind. She almost forgot why she was standing in front of the entrance.

Doris was at the front desk. A fixture.

"Good morning, Doris. I'm here to see Doctor Jerry."

"Sure thing. He's expecting you."

Francine walked to Doctor Jerry's office. She wasn't in the mood for chit-chat.

"I'm glad you called, Francine," said Doctor Jerry. "I was thinking of you the other day."

"I wanted to talk to you because I need some advice about going to AA meetings outside of Ebsen as opposed to leading AA meetings inside Ebsen."

"You understand that the meetings you guide at Ebsen are not substitutes for your attendance at regular AA meetings?" asked Doctor Jerry.

"I understand that in theory. But it's hard not to cross the line of the strict AA meeting guidelines with the women because their inclination is to move into something like our counseling group in rehab. The ladies want to talk and exchange stories, and when I try to stay the course, I sound like a sergeant in the Army. I try not to intrude when others speak. I've explained the rule, given them sheets of information, but I am not effective all the time."

"I don't think you are doing anything wrong, Francine. Your ladies are excited to talk and exchange information and learn. Just so long as they take time to listen, you'll be fine."

"It feels like sometimes I cross boundaries. Maybe I speak too much. Maybe they talk too much. It's hard to tell."

"Do you think they are becoming more conscious, more aware of their choices? If you happen to refer to changing cognitive behaviors, that's not a bad thing. If it feels the conversation is giving them insight, proceed. Protocol is not the end result. Nothing is incorrect about what you are doing. As long as the ladies are listening and processing and reflecting on the stories, you can't go wrong. Remember, stories are just bundles of interchangeable details. It's what's behind the stories that you need to hear. What's going on inside that person who is telling the stories? That's what you want to discover."

"Everything is about shame and guilt, guilt and shame," said Francine. "Do those evil twins ever leave us alone?"

"They go away and come back from time to time. Finding the balance between guilt and shame is one of the keys to staying sober."

"I'm running out of time," she said.

Doctor Jerry reached out and held her folded hands.

"What does that mean? You have nothing but time."

"I get sharp pains," said Francine. "And I can't gain weight. I have very little appetite. Sometimes none at all."

"Have you seen a doctor?"

"What's the point? Alcohol and cigarettes will kill me one way or another. I don't need a diagnosis."

"Let's continue on the path, Francine," said Doctor Jerry. "You've beaten the odds so far, so let's make this next leg of the journey meaningful. The important life lesson in the stories you hear is that at some point, the person telling the story decided not to do the dance with their demon lover anymore. That's the beginning of recovery, and recovery is the process that keeps an addict conscious. It reminds you to be who you were meant to be."

Francine listened and then stopped listening. She was feeling adrift and disconnected from all the reasons why life had to continue.

"Can I call Don?" she asked. "I want to talk to Don."

"You and Don had an emotional connection, and it's best to let him go. Don gave you strength, just as he gave everyone in recovery strength for his insights about sobriety."

Francine left Oak Lane and drove to the Baptist Church on West Main Avenue. She didn't expect to find Ed. The meeting didn't start until seven. But she had a head of steam to connect with him. Dreams of drinking invaded her unconscious, and that hadn't happened for months. Francine was curious as to why her drinking dreams started again. When she woke after a dream, she felt like she wanted a drink, but once she reached consciousness, she knew she didn't have the slightest desire to taste alcohol.

Ed was in the back of the church setting up for the meeting.

"Hey, Francine, good to see you," said Ed. "You're early."

"I know, but I decided that I wanted to talk to you about my drinking dreams."

"Anything different about them lately?" he asked.

"They're confusing. I never know where I am or who the people in the dreams are supposed to be."

"Dreams are about your unconscious. Even though there are other people in the dream, they are all facets of you. Dreams are part of your unconscious mind. Some are your demon lovers, those who want you to drink; others are your angels, the more conscious parts of who you are, which includes desires and needs. I'm sure when you awake in the morning, you think you want to drink, and then when fully awake, you don't. It's normal. You've entered the present and that's your reality. If you didn't have dreams, I'd worry. It would mean you are not processing sobriety in your unconscious. The unconscious is there to remind you about your true journey."

"This is kind of fascinating. Where did you learn this?"

"A Jungian therapist. Jungians specialize in dream analysis. Sometimes the dreams can be triggering, but if you have an awareness of their place in your recovery, your recovery will be easier to manage. Think of it as self-awareness."

"You may have missed your calling, Ed," said Francine. "You know a hell of a lot about other levels of recovery."

"This is my calling," said Ed. "Why don't you set up the literature and I'll take care of the bulletin boards."

Francine took off her coat and picked the information material and AA books and arranged them neatly on the table. She felt an incredible lightness within herself. No fear. No panic. Only pleasure.

The meeting began promptly at seven. The church was only half full, and it felt cozy. Ed started the meeting with the Serenity Prayer and asked who would like to start. He looked directly at Francine. She stood under the gaze of his eyes and walked up to the front of the room.

"This is my first time sharing my story at an AA meeting. Second time sober. It's a relief to finally share. I've listened to your stories, felt a connection, and also disdain. That's me, I'm afraid. But today I feel comfortable and with me, comfort goes a long way toward healing. I can't remember when drinking was not a daily part of my life. It started during my first marriage, I guess. You see I married too young and he was an alcoholic and I didn't know it. But I drank with him and continued to drink to avoid the pain of the bad decisions I made during my life. I never believed in myself. It didn't help that my parents never believed in me either. Although I was conditioned to blame them for everything bad that happened to me, getting sober taught me that they weren't the cause of my failures. I drank and I made choices that took me to dark places. That's what alcohol does, and that's why I'm up here today to remind us all that we are worth living a life of dignity and joy.

Some days, Francine didn't want to leave the correctional facility. She'd shoot the breeze with Doc Gallardo or Patricia, the other pharmacy assistant who was sweet and shy and looked like she was twelve. She became friends with Camille, Rhonda's friend who had been incarcerated long enough to warrant a parole board hearing for release.

Six months into volunteering, Francine saw Camille come out of Doctor Stein's office.

"How did it go?" asked Francine. "Are you on your way out?"

"It went really well. Rhonda prepared me."

"So happy for you, Camille," said Francine. "New beginnings or something like that."

"Thanks, Francine. You made it happen for a lot of us. We all want to be in the driver's seat and guide our course. I'm going to make the most of this. Oh, almost forgot, Doctor Stein asked me to find you. If you have time, she wants to see you."

Francine had a pit in her stomach. She was afraid Doctor Stein was going to take away her AA meetings. For the first time, she was feeling a strong connection to her sobriety. She had to call Don.

The guard followed her outside the front entrance to the prison. She gave the guard a dirty look before she dialed Don's number.

"Babe, it's me. Francine. I kept your number all these months."

"Wonders never cease," said Don. "You have a cell phone. How are you doing?"

"I'm in the big time now, Don. But more importantly, I'm still pissed at you. You left me high and dry. Doctor Jerry didn't think I should phone you. I won't talk long. Just needed to make amends for my anger and that crappy feeling of abandonment I have. And I want to wish you an early Merry Christmas."

"I'm the one who has to make amends. I'm the one who broke the rules. Let's put it behind us. I'm hanging with my brother in LA and headed to Austin to enjoy the music. You know, meeting up with the Texas ladies."

Francine remembered a song lyric that Doc Gallardo taught her—from a Guy Clarke country song—"Don't take all the pieces of my life away."

"Humidity's got to be a killer," she said.

"What about going to meetings?" he asked.

"Good luck, Don," she said ignoring his question. "Happy hunting."

"Call whenever you want."

"Doctor Jerry says you're rarefied."

"I beg to differ, my one and only Francine. I'm more like a bird on a wire."

Don the man, the honest truth-teller was gone. Hold on for dear life, Francine Fisher-Reynolds-Richelli-Freeman.

∽

Francine stuck her head around Doctor Stein's office door. The guard was not far behind.

"Come in, Francine," said Doctor Amy Stein.

"Am I in trouble?" asked Francine.

"Do you want to be in trouble?" asked Doctor Stein.

"Hell no. I mean no," Francine said without protest.

"You're good. Your meetings are more than good. But the rules of the facility encourage the warden to move the volunteer schedule around. It's time for you to relinquish your good work and let another volunteer take over the meetings."

"I get it," said Francine. "I was getting attached to the women, and I had no focus on matters regarding my own recovery. I know part of the recovery process deals with change, and this will be good, I think."

"It's good to change. We wouldn't want to stand still in life. The world outside these walls is full of options and possibilities, to say nothing of opportunities, and we want to try to replicate some of the issues and feelings our inmates will encounter later on."

"I have a request, Doctor Stein. Can I work in the pharmacy? I'm just an alcoholic, not a pill popper. No temptation in that part of the facility. And I've got a memory like an elephant. My boss at the Walker School District used to say I was more useful than a phone book."

"I don't doubt that. Doctor Gallardo just lost an assistant, and he has an opening. You two will get along fine."

Doctor Stein walked Francine to the door. "You're still skin and bone, but your eyes sparkle and you are smiling."

It was a long shot getting a volunteer position in the pharmacy with Doc Gallardo.

Francine figured it was easier to ask for what she wanted rather than be given a job she didn't enjoy. Honing in on your next move took chutzpah, but lately, Francine was up for taking the bull by the horns.

She would have been happy staying inside the warm cocoon of the AA meetings, but Francine figured it could not last forever. Nothing does, but she did a good job, awakened the troops, and carried on in her strange way. She made a few friends, and, more importantly, she was conscious of her life moving forward and never thought of standing in her own way. It was time to visit the silent cowboy.

Chapter 19

Tis The Season

Francine sidled up to the pharmacy window, knocked on the Dutch door, and put her elbows on the counter. She had a grin on her face a mile wide.

Doc Gallardo didn't turn around to acknowledge Francine. "What's up, Francine?" he asked. "I'm busy. I lost one of my volunteers."

"If you turn around, you'll find a replacement."

"I requested you."

"You asked for me?" asked Francine. "Why?"

"I can teach you what to do. You're perfectly capable of learning a new skill."

"I have a cracker-jack memory, and I can do the work of two people," Francine said. "How did you talk Doctor Amy into placing me here?"

"She trusts me. Now you have to trust me."

Francine opened the Dutch door and stood her ground.

Doc Gallardo opened a binder and located the patient medication page. "Fill this list."

"At your service," said Francine.

God, grant me the serenity to accept the things I cannot change,

Courage to change the things I can, and Wisdom to know the difference.

"Good morning," said Ed, "and welcome to the First Baptist AA meeting. Are there any new people at the meeting?"

No hands came up. There was a slight rustle in the room as if a ghost had passed through. Francine put the collar up on her coat.

"We have the privilege this morning of giving the sixth month chip to Francine Freeman on this beautiful Christmas morning. Please come up and receive your chip, Francine."

Francine walked to the front. Ed gave her the chip and she wrapped her fingers around the memento. Francine whispered "thank you" as she went back to her seat, proud and pleased that she didn't make a smart remark about putting it on a chain and wearing it for jewelry. Receiving her chip was more meaningful to her than she thought it would be.

"I'm grateful for my six-month chip," said Francine. "Thank you all for your support."

On her way out of the meeting, she met up with Ed.

"I'm proud of you, young lady," he said.

"I'm proud of me, too, Ed."

"Remember when I told you to trust yourself, believe in your higher power, and you laughed at me because you thought it was about religion."

"It didn't make sense to me then. Religion or spiritual sentiment doesn't sit well with me. My belief is that there's nothing in this damn universe except stars and moons and planets and galaxies. Ashes to ashes, dust to dust."

"Some people think that's a strange way to go through life, sort of a non-philosophy-philosophy of living and experiencing," replied Ed.

"It's pragmatic. Religion and higher power stuff are based on faith, and I don't have faith. I still believe life is about fate, and then it's over. But I liked the part about how we are our own higher power."

"That's perfectly fine, Francine," said Ed.

"I'm sorry because I'm probably offending you. I guess I'm an equal opportunity offender."

"Don't worry about me," said Ed. "I can duck your darts. I'm not firm on thinking there is anyone or any entity pulling the strings in my life. I've made some bad choices, and all of them are on me."

"I'm in the same tribe," she said. "But AA has taught me something I can believe in. I've got power, and I own my power—lock, stock, and smoking barrel. No one can take it away from me, not even some kind of god/king/buddha, in sickness and in health, until death do I part. That's my dance."

"You don't have to believe in God or identify God as a gender," said Ed. "I don't have an ideology. I'm doing my dance as you call it. The dance of sobriety."

"Have a Merry Christmas with your family, Ed."

"And you, too, and I hope the day is peaceful."

"I'm serving dinner at Ebsen and my daughter is not happy with me for not going to her dinner."

"You can do both, Francine. It's a milestone this Christmas, and you can celebrate with gratitude."

"I guess I can make a few amends, too."

"You go and do that, and I'll see you later," said Ed.

"I'm glad you said yes to being my sponsor," said Francine.

"You didn't call me much the last couple of weeks. Everything all right?"

"I know you are around. It makes me feel hopeful. You are near when I need you."

"I hope you will always be around, Francine," said Ed.

"I wish I could, but it may not be so," said Francine.

Francine drove to Ebsen to celebrate. All she wanted to do was smoke, but Doc Gallardo kept an eye on her and her itchy patches. So far, she couldn't figure out how to sneak a cigarette or two during the day. And Carlos was like a warden at home, monitoring her movements and getting in her face, so she didn't have the energy or time to be duplicitous.

The pharmacy was open for half a day on account of the holiday and fewer prescriptions to fill. When Francine entered, Doc Gallardo was reading. She took a quick look at the title.

"*Rodeos in Calgary*? Damn, you were serious before about being a rodeo man. Is that why you wear a black cowboy hat?"

"It was a long time ago," he said.

"Still in your blood?" she asked.

"I'll always be a rodeo man. There's even a song about a rodeo man that's first-rate by Weldon Henson. 'I've Got to be a Rodeo Man.' Maybe that's really me—'The rodeo's life's got a hold on me and there ain't no way it'll set me free.'"

"I guess that's a calling. Kind of fascinating. Look, Doc, I know it's none of my business but what are you doing today? Got any family?"

"Nope. You're my family." Doc Gallardo gave her a big smile. "Merry Christmas."

Francine and Doc Gallardo were startled out of their pleasantries by the loud clacking of high heels down the corridor.

"Mom!" Rachel shouted from down the hall, followed by the ever-present guard.

"Wouldn't you know," said Francine under her breath as she saw Rachel marching down the hallway, guard at her heels. "Babe, what are you doing here?"

Rachel gave her mother a long, loving hug. The guard was flustered by the abruptness of the affection.

"I've come to take you home with me. For Christmas dinner, remember?"

"I thought I told you I have other plans."

"I checked and you serve Christmas dinner at three. Then you'll come with me."

Doc Gallardo stuck his head back into his book. Francine looked to him for help. A fool's errand.

"How did you get in here?" asked Francine. "You're not allowed."

"I said I was your daughter at the front office. I signed in and the guard knew where you worked."

Rachel became aware of Doc Gallardo and whispered to her mother, "Who's he?"

"Doc Gallardo, get your head out of the book and meet my daughter, Rachel."

"Howdy, ma'am," he said.

"How-do-you-do," said Rachel.

"What are you doing for dinner, Doc Gallardo?" asked Rachel. "Come on over to the house. At least, you'll get a decent meal this Christmas."

Francine was writing out Rachel's address faster than you could say Ulysses Doc Gallardo. She pushed the paper toward him with a stern look as if she had a gun to his head.

"Thanks, y'all," he said.

"Come on, Rachel, let's go see the mess hall."

The guard followed the ladies dutifully as Rachel locked arms with her mother.

～

At five that afternoon, Rachel's warm, cozy, suffering-from-too-much-kitsch home was bustling with activity. A large farmhouse table was covered with an array of traditional Christmas food: two turkeys and two hams, green beans drenched in butter, several trays of veggies with cucumbers, tomatoes, carrots, radishes, and celery stalks. Three dishes of buttery mashed potatoes, mac and cheese, cranberry sauce, and wet stuffing with sausages that smelled like barbeque.

Neighbors and friends were gathered in the kitchen, aprons clinging to their substantial bodies. They were drinking wine, and laughing, and telling jokes.

"Turn up the music," yelled Rachel from the kitchen. "It's from *Oklahoma*."

"Change it to country," yelled a man back at her. "Where's Garth when we need him."

"My, my, it's a full house," said Francine. "I don't suppose you invited Carlos."

"Don't start, Mom. But I probably should have," said Rachel. "Did he have someplace to go?"

"He went to his church. They always have pot luck on holidays. And he does the serving."

"Now I feel terrible," she said. "What a kind thing to do."

"He's kind and thoughtful and would make a good husband if he ever found a girl. I'd love a smoke." Francine walked out of the kitchen mumbling, "Where the hell is Mark?"

Patches of snow spotted the brown grass in the backyard. She saw Mark listening to one of the men who was holding forth on the glories of conservative, right-wing politics.

Mark looked uncomfortable and Francine thought he needed saving. She walked over to him and said, "I'm not interrupting, am I?"

Mark kissed her on the cheek and gave her a hug.

"I got my six-month chip this morning. Mommy dearest is being a good girl."

"What are you up to?" asked Mark. "I miss seeing you. We miss seeing you."

"I'm working in the pharmacy at the correctional facility. No more leading AA meetings. I was promoted."

"Congratulations," said Mark. "Any interesting tidbits at the center?"

"Wouldn't you like to know," she said. "How's Rachel doing?"

"The usual. There's always the stress of her job. She misses you terribly."

"I love her and miss her every day."

"Your eyes are shinning, so you must be happy and proud of all the work you've done this past year."

"I'm doing better than I expected, except I still don't eat right—as you can tell. I still hate everything green."

"I'm proud of you and of Rachel," Mark told her.

"I didn't know how it would go between Rachel and me. We both let go, and I think we are both learning."

Francine wandered into the kitchen. There was good cheer around the center island where the food was displayed. It made her feel warm and fuzzy and want a drink, but the wine bottles cluttering the kitchen counter didn't spark her interest. She thought of Ida and a bottle of Merlot at Chez Moi and suddenly felt grief. *Ida in the ground.* God, she missed her friend.

She heard Doc Gallardo's voice coming from the living room and turned to see where he was. Rachel was all over him, trying to elicit his response to the dangerous effects of opioids on the white population.

They were both talking a mile a minute. It was rare to hear him speak more than one sentence at a time. It was a marathon of a conversation.

"Glad you came over," Francine said as she walked up to him. "You fit right in."

Mark called for Rachel from the kitchen, and she quickly left the conversation.

"Your daughter reminds me of my ex-wife," said Doc Gallardo. "She's got a way about her that's . . ."

"Sexy, beautiful, smart," said Francine. "Any other adjectives you can think of?"

"Yeah, but it's unique to her, like my Adele. She had the same thing going on with that smile and dark eyes."

"Don't get too deep on me, Doc, because I might get jealous and throw you over for my sponsor, Ed."

Francine took him by the arm and led him into the dining area where everyone was gathering. All heads turned his way. One side of his mouth raised and produced his signature smile. That smile was once both enticing and mysterious.

"Garth Brooks," Doc Gallardo said.

"What are you talking about?" asked Francine. "Your name isn't Garth Brooks, whoever the hell that is anyway."

"The music that's playing is Garth Brooks. Famous country western singer."

Francine turned to the gathering. "Hey everyone, this is Ulysses Gallardo, otherwise known as Doc Gallardo who is a pharmacist at the Ebsen Correctional Facility where I volunteer. He's my boss."

A few in the group cheered.

"He's a pharmacist, guys. He's not the second coming."

"Food smells good," Doc Gallardo said as he took off his black cowboy hat.

Mark came over and handed Doc Gallardo a beer. "I'm Rachel's husband, Mark Miller. Nice to meet you."

"Likewise. Thanks for having me. I'm starving, so I'm going to dig in."

"Hurry before it's gone," said Mark. "We're big eaters."

Doc Gallardo stood next to Francine waiting for her to finish piling mashed potatoes on her plate. "How about some protein with those carbs?" he asked.

"You can monitor my smoking patches, you can correct my work in the pharmacy, you can teach me crappy country western songs, but you are not allowed to micro-manage my carb intake." She took a helping of mac and cheese.

Doc Gallardo selected slices of turkey, garnished with cranberry sauce, green beans, and sausage stuffing.

"Does your family ever serve a dish that isn't swimming in butter?" he asked Francine.

"I think you're enjoying yourself," said Francine.

He walked away from the table, grabbed his beer, and settled in a corner of the room. Francine followed and sat next to him.

"I've been thinking of leaving Ebsen next year," said Doc Gallardo.

"I really don't have the energy to pull this out of you, Doc—you being so easy with the words, but try to give me more than a sentence on this subject."

"Eat your carbs; I'll eat my protein," he said, "and then I'll talk to you."

Francine sat in silence fuming. This was a twist. Doc Gallardo leaving. Don leaving. She ate a few bites of mashed potatoes swimming in butter and decided to pretend he didn't say anything. She vowed not to get into a pissing contest with him.

"What I'm trying to say is I want you to come with me. Like a road trip," said Doc Gallardo.

"Are you out of your mind?" she asked. "Hey, Rachel," Francine called out. "I need a little more butter on my mashed potatoes."

Doctor Gallardo sputtered and spit out a bit of stuffing.

Rachel walked over like a matriarch of the house.

"Mom, uncalled for," she said. "Keep it to yourself."

"How can I keep it to myself when even Doc Gallardo noticed the potatoes are floating in butter?"

"Sorry, Ulysses," said Rachel to Doc. "It's Mark that does that. He has never counted a calorie in his life. He works out like a fool and has no calorie issues. How long have you been at Ebsen?"

"Four years," said Doctor Gallardo.

"He's thinking of leaving next year," said Francine.

Doc Gallardo gave Francine a cautious look.

"What's going on, you guys?" asked Rachel. "Are you cooking up something?"

Francine got up and took her plate into the kitchen. She studied the wine labels and twisted and untwisted the caps on several bottles.

"Did I ask the wrong question?" Rachel asked Doc Gallardo.

"No, ma'am, not that I'm aware of," said Doc Gallardo as he watched Francine from across the room as she loomed over the wine bottles on the kitchen counter. "I told her I'm thinking of leaving Ebsen next year."

"She'll be devastated if you leave. Are you aware of that?"

"I'm aware of most things," he replied. "I'm not leaving tomorrow, but when summer is near, it'll be right for me to move, that's all. I've asked her to take a road trip with me."

"It's probably too much for her now to think about a move that big."

"I'm thinking six months from now. June or July."

"You look like a cowboy. Have you always worn that black cowboy hat? Like in the movies, riding on the range, breaking horses in the pen. Maybe you're a rodeo cowboy."

"Something like that," he said.

"Do you like my mother, or do you just put up with her?"

"That's personal."

As Francine lusted over the alcohol, she knew she had a tenuous hold on her emotions. She ripped her smoking patch off her arm, went outside, and bummed a cigarette from one of Mark's friends. She inhaled deeply and watched the smoke swirl into the chilled air as it floated up into the gray sky. She shivered under her pink parka. From behind, someone pulled up the fur-lined hood to her coat and covered her head.

Without turning around, Francine knew it was Doc Gallardo.

"How's it taste?" he asked. "I vaguely remember. The first inhale is like a shot of heroin. Gets you high and the world is right."

"Who knew you were a damn poet."

"Don't get bitter, Francine. It's hard to deal with uncertainty. You've got time to think about coming with me. We all have choices."

"What's that supposed to mean?"

"Uncertainty can be dangerous."

"Did you make that up?"

"Jean Paul Sartre, French philosopher."

"I know who the hell he is. Existentialist. I went to college for a semester."

"All I'm saying right now is I'm giving you a heads up so you can think about going on a road trip with me. I've been looking at you for six months in pain and only you know how long it's been going on."

Francine didn't respond.

"I picked up a sample of your blood when you cut yourself opening a package of vials. I sent it to the lab."

"Liver failure. Too bad you couldn't get to my lungs. I missed my appointment for a chest x-ray. Is that how someone plans to die? X-rays?"

"Everyone plans differently. We'll all take care of you."

"What I want is to take a long trip and make it as much fun as I can. It'll be my last hurrah."

Francine knew it was a trip to nowhere—nowhere was fragile territory. And vulnerable people can't answer direct questions with clarity because they are afraid of being exposed to the possibility of being attacked, or harmed, or abandoned, either physically or emotionally. Maybe in a day or two, she might recover from the sudden change of circumstances. One thing was for sure, she needed another cigarette.

"Before you answer me, put the patch back on," Doc Gallardo said. "One more cigarette is one too many."

After making the rounds at the party and saying goodbye, Doc Gallardo headed for the front door. Rachel was waiting for him. He handed her a card. Their eyes met, silence endured. No one had a playbook for the conversation that needed to take place.

"I want to take your mother on a road trip next year," said Doc Gallardo as he handed Rachel his card. "This is my information in case you need to call me."

"Why would you want to do that?" Rachel asked as she took the Doc's card. "And why do I need your card or your cell?"

"Let me tell you a story about your mother. I liked Francine the moment I met her. It was her humor that first caught my attention. I'm not much on humor as you can tell. I don't know how to use it, and I rarely find anything worthy of a laugh. I was always kidded for my silence and lack of conversational skills. I didn't find it necessary to develop a sense of humor since my looks got me where I needed to go in life."

"Nice story, but what's the point?" asked Rachel.

"When Francine started coming around the pharmacy and I got to know how smart she is, how she makes people laugh, how she nails her observations about people with funny details and spot-on truth, I was hooked. So was everyone else in the facility. The women loved her and got her essence and her humor. It was often instructive. I wondered how anyone could be so sharp and perceptive after living a life in a bottle. There is something deeper in her character, and now that we're friends, I hope to discover what else I need to know about Francine."

"That something deeper was lost on me because I enabled her for decades. I'm jealous that you're going to get to know her better and love her more."

"You know that she's not well, Rachel. She's in pain and time is not on her side."

Francine lit her second cigarette in the backyard. On the third inhale, she put it out.

Strangely, smoking felt like she was headed down the drinking path. No fun smoking without drinking. She turned to see Doc Gallardo leave the house.

Rachel went outside and hugged her mother. She put the patch back on her mother's arm and walked her inside with her.

"So Doc's leaving, but not for a while," Francine said following behind.

"Next year, he said. Let's face it, how long would you stay at a women's prison dispensing pills to felons? He's done his time. It's nothing personal."

"I'm taking it personally," said Francine.

"You're feeling vulnerable, but you'll keep in touch."

"You're assuming I'm not going on the trip with Doc?"

"Mom, I know you are not well. In fact, you're in pain. Doc knows it and I know it. I wish you had gone for testing so we could provide treatment."

"Babe, there's nothing anyone can do. I'm way past medical salvation."

Francine walked into the house ahead of Rachel, picked up her plate of food, sat on a stool at the kitchen counter, and made circles with the mashed potatoes swimming in butter. Mark kept her company and made her smile a few times, but she was somewhere else—in Doc Gallardo's hole-in-the-wall pharmacy behind the green Dutch door keeping track of which pills go to which inmates, memorizing charts and lab results. She was happy there.

A creeping sense of dread and sadness came over Francine. She felt there was nothing more to wish for her in life. She had her share of disappointments and regrets, mixed with selective moments of happiness. That was good enough.

She remembered something Doctor Jerry said, "Happiness comes from the inside, from who you are."

Francine doubted that she could discover the joy of simply being who she was, warts and all. At her age, it would take all the courage and fortitude to resist falling into the same traps and habits that had previously propelled her life.

Rachel put her arms around her mother's frail shoulders.

"Are you cold, Mom?" Rachel asked.

"Cold enough to freeze the balls off a brass monkey," she replied.

Chapter 20

The Lake House

Several months after the Christmas Party, Francine and Doc Gallardo were working silently in the pharmacy. They had not talked much since Rachel's gathering. She was not particularly unhappy or sad; in fact, her emotions were neutral as she went to AA meetings, had lunch with Rachel from time to time, read, and walked Boo Boo. She made many trips to the Elk Lake house, determined to get healthy and get more exercise to help her breathing. But the pain in her abdominal region was persisting. She pushed it out of her mind. What was the point of confronting it?

"Francine," said Doc Gallardo. "It's getting closer to summer, and I'm fixing to leave Ebsen and going on the road trip I told you about. Have you thought any more about coming with me?"

She didn't hear Doc Gallardo at first. Her thoughts were engaged with what to do about her beloved lake house.

"Sorry, Doc. Thinking about something else—about selling my house on Elk Lake. It takes too much to keep it up."

"You didn't answer my question. I'm leaving in a month."

"Where are you going?" she asked.

"To the Calgary Stampede in Alberta, Canada. Going to ride in the rodeo this year."

"I hardly know what to say about that. Sounds interesting, but I've got lots of things on my mind. I'll get back to you."

∽

Francine decided to take a leave of absence and get away from Ebsen, even Rachel and Carlos, and visit the house on Elk Lake to reconnect with a past— a past that had brought her personal joy, fond memories with Jeff Grady, and the summer visits from Carol and Kathy. She had to think about the future. More importantly was her desire to find a way to emotionally commit to Doc Gallardo's road trip. She took Boo Boo to help her make decisions about how the rest of her life was going to turn out. The dog kept her company. They went for long walks during the day and cuddled together at night.

The A-frame house held a deep connection for Francine and her attachment was passionate for this picture-perfect muted green and white cabin with three bedrooms and a studio in the backyard. The land was physically split by the Elk River, and the property was as close to paradise as Francine could imagine. She vowed she would die in that house. Peter bought it for her as a way to contain her energetic need to live surrounded by nature and to have her family and friends gather and commune with her over the summers.

Her memories were vivid of boating and bartending and meeting Sheriff Jeff. However, the lake house also packed decades of negative energy inside the walls. During the early years, Peter wasn't happy that Francine pushed him into buying the lake house. He preferred to sleep in his new RV. But as his health deteriorated, he was forced to spend more time inside. Later, when he was tethered to an oxygen pole, Francine and Peter lost any semblance of being a couple.

As Francine inserted the key into her summer home, the smell of mold permeated the interior. It was a metaphor for its decay. Boo Boo rushed inside and ran around the living room barking and finding a few toys. All that was left of her former life hung from the walls—old pictures of her younger self with her family and Peter, and the musky odors of worn clothes seeping out of the closets after twenty years. It used to bother her when summer residents would come by and ask her if she was interested in selling. They had stars in their eyes thinking of remodeling and or even tearing it down to build a new edifice. Now, she might welcome inquiries about buying—giving her an opportunity to exit the past gracefully and take a leap of faith into the unknown—and go on a road trip with Doc Gallardo. Carol used to say it is more fun to be surprised by life. That's when the light shines and fear recedes.

Carol. The last conversation with Carol at Oak Lane ended badly. It shouldn't have. After the fiftieth reunion, Kathy and Carol promised Francine that they would visit the lake house for a week every summer. In the early years, Francine seemed younger and happier, more her old self, driving the boat to the local club, riding a jet ski back and forth across the lake. They went out to dinner, cooked, and played games. Francine seemed almost normal, although the daily drinking began at mid-day and ended late at night. She slept most of the morning, revived herself, and soldiered on until her girlfriends left for another year.

After four years of meet-ups at the lake, the ritual seemed to take a negative turn. Francine confessed the first fall to her friends, the broken neck, the hospitalization, and her foray into AA, which she recounted as a waste of time. Carol and Kathy were worried about Francine's health. She was thin and not eating much. They talked for hours about counseling, recovery centers, and ran the gamut of reasons to get sober. Francine listened and appeared to understand, then she walked into the kitchen and made another bourbon and 7.

The next summer, Kathy broke her ankle skiing in the spring and had difficulty healing. No one came to the Elk Lake House. Carol visited Kathy in upstate New York. They rarely spoke of Francine. They loved their friend with all their hearts, but it was too painful to yearly dissect the frog named Francine Fisher-Reynolds-Richelli-Freeman.

And there were those damn persistent stomach pains, wherever they came from, that gave her concern. What if she was responsible for holding

Doc hostage to her illness? What if she died and he had to clean up the mess. But he asked her to go on that ride with him anyway. How much grit did she have left? How much time did she have left? How brave was she? Francine didn't have the answers to her questions. She didn't want to wrestle the vagaries of her life at this moment because the truth was clear: she had realized over time that she had already left her summer retreat. It no longer had a hold on her, because she was beginning to see Doc's adventure in her mind. She could already smell the pure air in the mountains of Alberta. She thought of Don as she sat on the sofa and stared at the calm lake water—the buddha. Sit with it. Be with it. Breathe.

To ward off the chill in the house, she wrapped her long, white sweater around her body as if she was a mummy. Francine broke down and cried. She was not alarmed about her feeling of sadness because she understood that she was facing loss—the loss of her addictions, Ida, Don, Rhonda, Ed, Doctor Jerry, the ladies in AA, and even the imminent loss of her life. Once on the road, she hoped loss would turn into clarity about how she wanted her life to end. And she hoped Rachel would forgive her for her making the decision to die on her own terms.

Francine needed to vent. She called Don but there was no answer. She left a message.

"I need someone to talk to, Don. Someone close. I don't know who to call. It's not like I'm going to take a drink in the next ten minutes. It's more like I've come to a moment of decision. Doctor Jerry told us that we should photograph our moments of decision. We would remember them better, or we would remember why we made them. And I'm about to make a momentous decision, dear Donny boy, and exit the premises of my former life.

"Right now, I'm at my house on Elk Lake. I never told you or Doctor Jerry about my green and white A-frame house, but it holds my hidden thoughts, my castrated emotions, and my corroded soul—if I even have one left.

"I've decided to leave my former life within these old, musky walls. Even the furniture is about to collapse, and you can't see out the windows, so dirty with grime and bird crap. The next person who wants to buy the damn place can have it. I'll sell it in a New York minute.

"On another note, I'm thinking about going on a road trip with Doc Gallardo, the pharmacist at Ebsen. He made me an offer I don't think I can refuse. I'm going to a rodeo, not to ride horses—I can hear what you are thinking, know that you are laughing—but to die in the arms of a good-looking rodeo man who wears a black cowboy hat, a black tee-shirt, and creased black jeans every day of his life. Now I call that sexy and consistent.

"My decision to go with him is beginning to feel good and secure. Like I could have been secure with you, except that we're a couple of drunks, and the gods of sobriety told us we couldn't be together. God-damn gods."

There was a click and the voice message ended. Don was listening, stunned, crying, bereft. He wanted to pick up the phone, wanted to talk to her and tell her she has his blessing because that's what she was asking him to do. The stark reality that he was not going to see her again overwhelmed him. There was not a day that went by that he didn't think about her and wonder what she was doing. Night after night he sat on his designated seat at The Sagebrush, his favorite honky-tonk bar in Austin, drank a diet coke, and sang the lyrics to all the country songs he knew. They were all about Francine.

∽

The end of spring pushed against summer. No one came by to ask if she wanted to sell her tear-down cabin during the few weeks she was in self-imposed quarantine. She decided she had to talk to Doc Gallardo. She called him one Friday after work and caught him walking out of the Ebsen.

"Hey, Francine. Good to hear from you. What's going on in your wonderful mind?"

"Doc, I've decided to sell the lake house but before I do I want you to visit me here. Will you do that?"

"Would I? I'd love to. Give me the address and I'll get there tonight with a bag of groceries. Leaving for home now, then the store, and I'll see you at seven for dinner."

Doc Gallardo hung up and Francine didn't know whether to laugh or cry. So she did both.

Francine walked the dog, paced, changed clothes a few times, and put on music—the music of her youth—the rock and roll of the 1950s. She opened and closed the front door and looked out over the lake as a warm breeze blew her way. Finally, Doc Gallardo pulled into the driveway and jumped out with several bags of groceries in his arms. Boo Boo jumped all over his legs. Francine picked up Boo Boo and walked with Doc Gallardo inside.

"No wonder you don't want to leave this place," he said as he put the groceries in the kitchen and opened the slider to the balcony overlooking the blue lake. "This is amazing."

"Want to buy it?" she asked as she joined him on the balcony. "I'll sell it to you cheap."

"You're fooling me," he said as he walked back inside.

"Not kidding. I'm giving you first shot. It's a game changer."

"I don't know what to say. Now you're messing with my head."

"Like you've been doing with me all these months?"

"Point taken. Let's get to fixing dinner. If you go in the white bag, you'll see lemonade and some cheesy dips. I'll tackle the steaks. I assume you've got a barbeque."

"Do I ever. I'll get the charcoal."

They sat out on the balcony eating steaks and corn and joked and laughed about work and family and all the butter sitting in the bottom of the mashed potato plate at Thanksgiving. Francine told him about Sheriff Jeff and how he died one night where Doc Gallardo was sitting. He told her about his four children, two girls and two boys, who were the loves of his life and his devotion to his first wife, Adele.

"The question still stands, Doc. Want to buy the place?"

"I love it. I could love it more. But I've got a journey to take and saying yes to you is a convenient way to stop my plans. Put it up for sale. You'll get a great price."

"The millennial neighbor next door asked me about selling it to him. Of course, that was several years ago and he might not be interested now."

"Makes sense for him to have a bigger lot. It will double his value. Want me to go along with you and act as your agent?"

Francine was pushing back the pain building in her abdomen.

"Let's sleep on it. Tomorrow is another day and I'm tired. Sleep in one of the guest rooms and I'll see you at breakfast."

Doc Gallardo cleaned the kitchen and the grill to the county western station on Spotify and did a little country western shuffle.

The following morning, after coffee, tea, and toast, Francine and Doc Gallardo went next door to the millennial. He opened his door looking disheveled and needing a shave.

"Hi, Josh, so this is my realtor, Ulysses, and we wanted to know if you're still interested in buying my lake house."

Doc Gallardo took off his hat to introduce himself.

"Hi, Josh, glad to meet y'all," said Doc Gallardo in a Texas drawl. "I was wondering how much you wanted Francine's house?"

"I want it a lot," said Josh. "I offered her a price a few years ago."

"Yeah, that's the problem. It was a few years ago. And today is today and the value has gone up—gone up double."

The millennial looked at Francine as if she was crazy.

"It's a tear-down, so suck it up, junior," she said.

"It's still a good buy, Josh. Do a remodel, make your house an Airbnb, maybe Airbnb the big house, and you'll have it paid in two years."

He sucked it up and wrote her a check then and there.

"I'll be back to take what I want," she told him. "You can start moving in anytime."

Francine and Doc Gallardo walked spritely across the boundary between the two houses.

"Ready to go Francine?" he said.

"You bet," she said as she let out her Phyllis Diller laugh. "See you back at the ranch."

Francine carried her suitcase to her ancient, faded yellowish beige SUV with dirty brown cloth seats from the nineties, boosted Boo Boo into the car, rolled down all her windows, turned up the volume on her car radio, and blasted Chuck Berry's "Johnny B. Goode" and all her favorite oldies but goodies from the 50s and 60s on her way back to Zeeland and what was left of the rest of her life. Francine didn't want to second guess herself about whether she had done the right thing selling her lake house out from under the feet of her family. Everyone was busy with work or school or social activities. She would have left the place to her daughter if she had shown any interest in preserving her mother's past, her sanctuary, her heaven on earth. They never knew she worked at a bar on the lake; they never knew she had fallen madly in love with a retired local sheriff named Jeff Grady, and that Jeff, the love of her life, died on the porch of her lake house while he waited for his steak to be cooked.

If living was in the details, Francine had a hell of a lot of details piled up in the cobwebs of her mind. She figured no one gave a rat's ass. No one really cared, so she might as well slip out of Dodge, like in the westerns, when the prostitute got on a stagecoach without being noticed, leaving an empty bed in the bordello. She and Doc would go on an adventure, and she would see rodeos and live like a gypsy on the dusty roads in Oklahoma. Of course, there was no Oklahoma; she was romanticizing the road trip as if it was a movie. If she stood back and watched her life as if it was a movie, no one would believe she had lived it.

The idea of leaving Boo Boo was a heartbreaker. She did not know how she was going to handle her grief. But Carlos was the one left to be the caretaker and he would do a fine job. She should leave the house in Zeeland to him in a level playing field. He deserved it, but what if Rachel would raise holy hell and contest her will in court. It would get nasty. Francine didn't want nasty. *Note to self: call my lawyer.*

When she returned home, Carlos was asleep. She went upstairs and collapsed on the bed. Boo Boo jumped up and cuddled. Her last thought was of Doc Gallardo and his big adventure.

∽

The Charlotte Ebsen Correctional Facility was quiet as Francine drove there a few weeks later. It felt like the prison had been evacuated. Or maybe it was the early morning hour that produced the strange silence. The sun was climbing out of the clouds, and the day was going to be sunny. It occurred to her that she hadn't been awake at seven o'clock in the morning since she worked at the school district. Those were the days of getting up at five, ending her days at three, and pouring her first drink by four.

As she walked down the hallway to the pharmacy, Francine experienced a sense of euphoria, as if she was walking on air. She didn't know where that lightness of being came from. Maybe from disposing of her memories of the lake house, maybe from making a firm decision to go on an adventure, or maybe it was as simple as heading into the last mile of her life. She hoped it was not some kind of existential-bullshit-religious-ayahuasca-hallucination. Steven Shay told her about the experiments with ayahuasca decades ago when they were fucking like cats in heat in a dog-shit generic Motel 6 room off Interstate 95 at Plainfield Avenue NE. They were out of breath and spent when, out of nowhere, Steven asked her if she had tried ayahuasca.

Francine told Steven that he was out of his mind to come up with some obscure reference to the influence of hallucinogens after hours of fucking. He said it's a plant a person drinks that takes the participant to the ends of the earth for hours and hours while having sex. Shamans also used the hallucinogen with people who suffered from PTSD. The drug helped eliminate the poisons in a body that was suffering from shock.

As far as Francine was concerned, they already hit the end of the earth. She couldn't ask for anything more.

Maybe Francine was experiencing an adrenaline rush, a burst of energy and optimism like after she had sex. Or maybe it was the first time she had the ability to repel the negative dynamics that held her in a vise for the last sixty-five years. The anger and bitterness were slipping away. The past traumas were leaving her consciousness, and the stranglehold her parents had over her was becoming a faded memory. Today felt different. She was breathing deeply and thinking clearly, conscious of a different reality. Life was changing.

Doc Gallardo was already at his desk. "You're here early."

"Ye, of little faith," said Francine. "I'm not used to this hour, but I was up and knew you came in at seven."

"What's on your mind?" he asked.

"I'm curious about something," said Francine as she leaned into the pharmacy's green Dutch door. "Did you ever marry again after your first wife?"

Without looking up, Doc Gallardo said, "One more time. But Adele was my great love."

"What happened?" asked Francine.

"She loved the rodeo more than me, I guess."

"Any kids?"

"Two with Adele and two with my second wife, Doreen."

"Damn. Wonders never cease. You're older than I thought."

"I'd say about sixty. Any other questions because I need your definitive answer to our road trip. Are you with me or a'gin me?"

"I'm on board. I thought you knew. We sold the lake house."

"The trip will be good for your spirits, but it won't cure the illness inside you."

They had become friends over the months and had shared details of their lives, inconsequential tidbits, but taken together, the odd couple dug deep into the roots of their respective souls and began to build a Redwood tree that would last until Doc Gallardo was too old to remember.

"When do we leave?" asked Francine.

"In a week. Get your gear packed. Make sure you have your passport with you. Remember Alberta is in Canada."

"Don't be a smart ass," she said. "I went on a cruise to Alaska five years ago. My passport should still be good."

"Write down your address and give it to me. Tell Doctor Stein you're taking time off. Say goodbye to friends in here. Talk to Rachel. You can be in contact with your family with your cell phone. It's not as if you're going off the grid."

Doc Gallardo's crooked smile turned into a straight line. "There's one more thing. We have to fly to where we start the trip. I'll get the tickets. We're going to Spokane first to pick up my new truck, and then we'll cross over into Vancouver. I'll take care of everything."

"Is that all?" she asked.

"That's good for now. Get it together, Francine Freeman. We're going on the road."

The basketball guard standing by the pharmacy followed Francine down the hallway. The smell of cleaning fluids permeated the corridor. One of the inmates was mopping the floor. Francine recognized her as a woman who attended her AA meetings. Ebsen had been good to Francine, and for that, she would always be grateful. She would say a goodbye to Saffron after a cup of the jail's acidic, gut-wrenching coffee.

"Hi, Miss Francine," the woman said. "I'm Saffron. Do you remember me?"

"Of course, Saffron," she said. "How could I forget?"

"We miss you. The lady who took your place is mean and boring. Please come back."

"I'm sorry, Saffron, but I'm leaving Ebsen. I might be back, though. You never know. How about I get a cup of coffee, and we can talk."

Francine watched Saffron walk to the kitchen, head down, wiping tears away. She was reminded about what her sponsor Ed said about change: *Change is good for the soul.*

Francine sat at the end of one of the long tables and sipped her coffee. Her stomach began to burn, and she pushed the coffee away. "Sit down, Saffron, and tell me what you need."

"I don't need anything, but I miss having a good friend. I don't make friends easily. That's why I drank. The bottle was my friend. And now I don't have my bottle. I have a mop."

"Well said, Saffron. Sounds like you've done good work. Honest and true."

"Why doesn't it feel good?" asked Saffron.

"Look, babe, some guru once told me that getting to our truth is easier than hanging with that truth. We have to be clear and conscious at all times and try not to go down the rabbit hole into the darkness and sadness. It doesn't always feel good because it isn't easy."

"Makes sense," said Saffron. "I guess if you want it bad enough, that peace we all talked about, means you have to sit with it."

"And be with it," said Francine. "You have friends, Saffron, but they may not be on the same path as you. You are aware of your emotions, and you seem to want to land on your feet. Don't worry about the others. You are the most important person in your life."

Saffron listened intently. She started to cry again, but stopped, and smiled.

"I can't believe I said that," said Francine. "I must be channeling Doctor Jerry. He was the best. And Don. He was the best, too. I sure miss him."

"Don't you want your coffee?" asked Saffron.

"It doesn't sit well on my stomach. Must be all that acid I have going on inside of me."

It was almost eight o'clock. Doctor Amy Stein usually entered her office on the stroke of eight. Francine heard Doctor Amy's high heels clicking on the concrete before she saw her turn the corner. The woman's steps were quick and efficient as she moved down the corridor. She wore a tight cream-colored skirt and a snug blazer with a soft flowered blouse in light blues and yellows underneath her jacket. A ray of sun streamed through a high window, hit the pin on her lapel, and almost blinded Francine. She thought Doctor Amy had darker hair, but the morning light highlighted her auburn streaks. As she sashayed down the hall, Doctor Amy hummed Lionel Ritchie's "Stuck on You."

"Francine, what are you doing here this early?" asked Doctor Amy as she unlocked her door, stepped inside her office, turned on the light, and walked over to her desk.

"What can I do for you?"

"It's what I'm going to do for you," said Francine as she entered, sat in the hard chair in front of Doctor Amy's desk, then winced.

"You're leaving," said Doctor Amy.

"Does it show?" asked Francine.

"It shows all over your face. Have you put enough thought into your decision?"

"I'm clear about it," replied Francine.

"Are you ill?"

"Why do you ask that?"

"You are thinner than when you came to us. You quit smoking and you should have been gaining weight."

"I can't gain weight, but I'm taking care of myself."

"Francine, that's defensive and a lie. I don't know if you are taking supplements to gain weight, or whether you've seen a doctor, or if you even try to exercise, but if you were my mother, aunt, or sister, I would be all over you because your health is crucial to your recovery."

"I'm eventually going to die no matter what means of resuscitation you'd like to perform on me. And I don't need that disgusting old people's supplement drink to make me healthier. Truth is, I won't be back. Don't save my place. It's not because of you or Ebsen. Actually, my relationship with the women here has been life-saving."

"I'm trying to bring you to some sort of awareness about your physical condition, Francine," said Doctor Amy.

"It's kind of you to want to help, but there's nothing you can do. I know what's going on inside of me. But I'm glad that you guys think I'm smart and could've been a contender, somebody who contributed to this sad planet. But I had no ambition. Never did, and, anyway, it's too late for all that jazz. The good news is that I'm a relatively happy camper. Life is good."

"I trust you know what you are doing and where you are going."

"We can't talk about this anymore, Doctor Amy. I don't want to die at Charlotte Ebsen Correctional Facility, as much as I know I'd get a hell of a send-off. But I'll spare you that and just say thank you. And I think you're a hell of a warrior."

Francine held her head up as she left Doctor Amy's, feeling triumphant despite her self-inflicted wounds. She thought of Rachel, how she raised her to possess good values, to be a successful human being, and how to live and die free.

Of course, she was ill. No one who looked like Francine had long to live. You didn't have to be a genius to see that her body was giving up. But her life was not over yet. She had miles to go before she slept, or at least she was going on a road trip to wherever the hell Doc Gallardo had in mind.

She remembered the poet, Neruda, illuminating the slow-moving signs of dying: "no travel, no reading, no interaction with others, no self-esteem."

Rhonda was coming toward her like she was on roller skates. Her guard couldn't keep up.

"What do you think you're doing, Francine?" asked Rhonda. "Saffron said you're leaving. No, girl, you're not leaving."

"Babe, I have to go now. I'm too attached to this place, and I need distance. I feel good about the job I've done, and I wanted to thank you."

"Girl, I need you. We need you."

Francine hadn't felt so wanted since she left her job at the Walker school district. Her boss had even tried to bribe her to stay because he didn't want to lose her gift of memory.

"I have one last adventure left, and I'm damn well going to take it."

"No, Francine, you have many roads to take."

As Francine's guard caught up to her, Rhonda impulsively threw her arms around her friend, embracing her with all her love. She was crying, then sobbing.

The guards looked around to see if anyone was watching.

"Stay here and get the help you need," said Rhonda.

"It's too late for that. I don't want to spend the rest of my time in a hospital being stuck by needles and attached to an oxygen pole."

"I hope you know what you're doing," said Rhonda.

"Maybe the only right way to know what you're doing is to embrace what sights and sounds of life remain."

"And let others help you," said Rhonda.

"Good or bad, I'm on my own now," Francine said as she took Rhonda's hands.

The guard hovered over Francine.

"I'm saying goodbye if you don't mind," she said to the guard. And with that, Francine hugged Rhonda.

Francine cuddled Boo Boo in her lap as she sat on her bed. Her fingers ran through his white curly hair, cleaned his eyes, and checked his paws. A pervasive sadness engulfed her. She was supposed to be packing her suitcase but had no energy for the task. Boo Boo never took his eyes off her. She started to cry because this was a rite of passage she had to go through to get to the other side. Jolted by abdominal pain, she clutched her stomach.

A long time ago, in her first semester of college at Duquesne, she read a short story about a Japanese family who lived during the early twentieth century near Osaka. Everybody in that family worked blisteringly hard at various jobs: farming, taking in laundry, teaching school, cooking, cleaning. Mundane stuff. The old grandmother lived with them, and nobody paid any attention to the woman. Shrunken, wrinkled, withered, the grandmother moved slowly around the house trying to be helpful, until one day her daughter told her to sit down and rest. She had been helpful all her life, and she didn't have to give back anymore. "Rest and be happy, grandmother."

Several days later, the grandmother packed a few necessities in a rucksack and left the house. She followed a road up a mountain, painstakingly putting one foot in front of the other. A few times she stopped for food, squatting to eat a snack of carrots and cucumbers, and then she continued up the hill to the top of the mountain. She had some strength left in her body, enough to move a few rocks aside to make the outline of a bed. Afternoon clouds were encroaching as she laid down in her makeshift bed. When the clouds turned dark, they began to engulf her frail body. She fell into a deep sleep, and she willingly took her last breath.

It was the way elderly Japanese women took care of their own deaths in the past. Those who were ready to die did so by themselves, of their own volition, because they knew when it was time to leave the earth to others.

The next morning, Francine called her lawyer and made an appointment to change her will. She called Rachel and made an appointment to discuss her plans, finished packing in earnest, fed the dog, and sat down at her kitchen table where she religiously read the morning newspaper, drank tea, and contemplated smoking. The old habit, like her demon lover, was waxing and waning. She hadn't smoked since Christmas, and then it was only one and a half cigarettes. She remembered that the second cigarette tasted like week-old bread with a tinge of mold. She skipped reading the paper. What did she care about the news now? She was leaving. She was leaving her life, her daughter, and everything she held close and maybe going to a far, far, better place.

Carlos walked into the kitchen and made a pot of coffee. He picked up the sports section. Francine set aside three pieces of stationery and began to write.

"Where are you going?" asked Carlos.

"I'm going to a rodeo in Calgary, Canada. It's basically a road trip, Carlos, so don't get your panties in a knot."

"It's the last thing I'd want to do," he said.

Francine kept writing until she finished her letter. She sealed it and added a stamp.

"Make sure this gets in the mail on Friday. That's when I'm leaving."

"All right," said Carlos. "You're very secretive. What's going on?"

"I'm changing my will. You will be allowed to stay in this house for as long as you want, and after a period of time, as Rachel sees fit, the house will be in your name provided you have taken good care inside and outside the house. You'll have Boo Boo to take care of also. This, of course, depends on whether I survive the trip. Do you think you can handle that?"

"Nothing's going to happen to you, so why don't you stop being a drama queen. I'm going to make you some eggs."

"You know I'm not going to eat them."

Francine and Carlos stared at each other like two people who have known each other's secrets for years. He turned away so he wouldn't show his sadness. Francine continued to make notes.

Francine walked up to Rachel's house the next morning. It was crisp and sunny, and the air was full of ions. Before she was about to knock on the door, Rachel opened it and hugged her mother. She brought her inside, sat her down at the kitchen table, and made her a cup of tea.

"What's up with you, Mom," asked Rachel. "You seem to have more time on your hands. Are you feeling all right?"

"I'm taking a break from Ebsen."

"Are you thinking of spending more time at the lake? This doesn't sound like you. What's going on?"

"I want to do something else with my life now," Francine told her. "I've decided to go on the road trip with Doc Gallardo to Alberta, Canada where there is a rodeo in Calgary he wants to attend. There is nothing to worry about. He will take good care of me."

"Mom, you are ill."

"Yes, and that's why I'm going. The last ride. The last look at a sober life. And it feels good. I'll be in nature and there will be mountains and valleys and maybe we'll see some animals."

"What if something happens to you?"

"Doc will call you and you'll come and be with me. But I want no hospitals, no hospice, no assisted living. No long-term insurance, no drugs, no life-saving measures. The reality of life is that you live and then you die. I want to leave Carlos the house, but I can't just give it to him without stipulations. I thought I should have him live there, and you own the house, and that's a comfort. He needs a home and he'll take care of Boo Boo and the cat. I don't know what your situation would be because you would be responsible for repairs or selling it, but you know Carlos will be on top of keeping it in good shape. The other option is to wait a few years, see how he is taking his new responsibility, then give him the deed and title to the house in a few years. They are on my desk. I sold the lake house to the guy next door. The money is in the bank for you and Mark."

Francine got up from the kitchen table and grabbed a stack of papers.

"What are your wishes, Mom?"

Francine sat back down. "In the end, I want him to have the house. But giving him time to adjust to being a quasi-owner makes the most sense. So maybe give him a year or two to adjust."

"That makes sense. I like it and I'll make it work."

"This is the way my life is supposed to be. This is what I want. So much for being clear-eyed and forward march. And remember always that you are the most wonderful daughter a mother could have. I love you to the moon."

Part Five:
Staying Alive

Chapter 21

Into The Future

The summer heat was slowly pushing through the morning clouds. By twelve o'clock, the day would be muggy with a faint breeze. After Francine completed her packing, all she wanted was the peace of silence. Carlos had gone out for groceries and Boo Boo was sleeping. She wanted to go out to the patio and read the paper, but thoughts of Carol and Kathy were first on her mind.

A phone call to both of them was out of the question. It would take too long to tell them each the most recent chapter in her life. A letter was more efficient. She could get clarity by writing out her thoughts to her oldest friends. She went to her old desktop computer, typed a letter, printed out two copies on her dot matrix printer, and read the letter again.

Dear Carol and Kathy,

I feel like I'm in Sister Mary Alberta's typing class when we were juniors, right before Kathy left for upstate New York in the middle of the school year. Kathy, you landed on your feet in your new Catholic high school and became popular the second you walked into the cafeteria and spotted the most popular junior girls. You had the cool ability to make friends easily. Carol and I went along for the ride.

When we were teenagers, nothing could stop us. We were attached at the hip. But, when we went our separate ways, I was never able to fully grow up after that. I reached a level of maturity that didn't serve me well, while you both, as my mother would say, exceeded yourselves. I remained at the level of a high school dipshit adolescent, getting myself pregnant at nineteen, living with an alcoholic, raising my daughter, and finally marrying that truck driver I jokingly said I would marry in eighth grade. What was I thinking? I made stupid decisions. "But you can't go home again," said Thomas Wolfe.

I have a new adventure to go on—probably my last one. I'm going on my journey with the pharmacist at Ebsen Women's Correctional Center. I know that sounds like old Francine, but I've been volunteering in the pharmacy for him for over a year and we clicked. He's about sixty and as handsome as they come. We're going to a rodeo in Calgary in Alberta, Canada, and I'm going on my last ride to see where it leads me.

Don't be alarmed. It isn't the old Francine writing you. It's the new and improved Francine. Although this journey may sound strange—and doesn't sound like me—please believe me. If you love me, you will understand that this is goodbye to the two best friends the world has ever known.

Going to a meeting now, clean and sober. That's the only way to leave this world.

Love always,
Francine

As she put a stamp on the envelope and set it aside with the other mail, the phone rang.

The ring didn't register with Francine right away. Her mind was elsewhere. On the fourth ring, she picked up the receiver.

"Francine, it's Carol. Are you all right? I haven't heard from you in ages. What's going on? The last time we talked we hung up . . ."

"You must be channeling my mind, babe. I just wrote you a letter and I'm about to mail it. It will explain everything."

"Explain what? What's going on? I don't want a letter."

"I'm going to be brief about this because I'll be late for a meeting. I'm going on a road trip. First, I'm flying to Spokane and then my friend, the pharmacist, is picking up a new truck and we're driving to Canada to some kind of rodeo, if you can imagine that."

"I can't imagine how you arrived at this plan," Carol told her. "I'm thinking you are out of your mind. When are you flying? When are you landing? Are you coming in from Grand Rapids?"

"We are flying from Grand Rapids a week from today. We arrive at seven at night on Alaska Air. We're picking up Doc Gallardo's new truck in Spokane, and the next day we're driving to Canada."

"I'll meet you at the airport, and we'll share a room, and I'll stay overnight with you. We can catch up then. Love you."

For the next week, Francine went to two AA meetings a day at the First Baptist Church. She attended out of habit and respect and to talk to her sponsor. Between meetings, she went to the dentist, visited her lawyer again to sign her will, lunched twice with Rachel, and sat with her beloved Boo Boo.

On the last day of life in Grand Rapids, Francine went to what she knew would be her last meeting. It was the place her sobriety began in earnest. She was sure that her demon lover no longer had a death grip on her. All she wanted was to give gratitude and the peace of giving back to those in attendance, to those acquaintances who had given her support, and to the collective unconscious of something called AA. It was time to leave. She walked to the front of the room and whispered to Ed. Then she turned to the group and took a deep breath.

"Ever since sobriety kicked in, I listened to the mantras of gratitude and forgiveness. It was difficult for me to wrap my head around those ideas. How did I manage to live a life full of unconscious decisions that I tried to mask with alcohol? I've had a terrible time trying to forgive my parents and myself. After so many decades of anger, I felt like I could never fully embrace turning the other cheek or letting go of the negative emotions associated with them. It took a lifetime to realize that my parents had opinions about me that had nothing to do with who I am. With sobriety, I can finally separate from who my parents were and what they thought about me from the woman I am today. I speak to those I have gotten to know, and to those I have not met that I can forgive myself for my failings and redeem what's left of my life. Thank you, Ed, and thank you all for your inspiration. I will never forget you."

∽

Francine watched out the window for Doc Gallardo to pull up in a taxi. Tears streamed down her face. Carlos didn't know what to do or how to comfort her.

"Take care of Boo Boo as if you gave birth to him. He needs you. Keep the house neat and in good repair and keep in contact with Rachel. She'll be a solid buddy."

It was a muggy morning, high humidity for the Grand Rapids area, with clouds hovering over the city. Doc Gallardo got out of the taxi, walked to the door like a movie star cowboy, tipped his hat to Carlos, and took Francine's suitcases. Francine gave Boo Boo to Carlos. Her decision was made.

For the first five hours of the trip, Doc Gallardo and Francine flew to Spokane. Francine fell asleep soon after lift-off and slept throughout the flight. By the time she woke up, they were at the Spokane airport gate.

"What happened?" she said. "Are we there already?"

"It was a fast flight. You slept through it."

"Tell me where are we going again?"

"The Calgary Stampede."

∽

Doc Gallardo picked up their carry-on luggage as they went to baggage claim. Carol was waiting. She saw Francine, hugged her, and introduced herself to Doc Gallardo.

"The plan is for us to stay overnight together in the hotel," said Francine to Doc Gallardo.

"I'm okay with that. I've got us rooms at the Holiday Inn. It's near where I'm picking up my truck."

"Perfect," said Carol. "I mean perfect for you and for me because I can take a flight out tomorrow."

They sat at the bar at the Holiday Inn with uneaten hors d'oeuvres in front of them. Carol drank from a glass of wine. Francine had 7UP with grenadine. "I'm happy to see you, Carol, but you're not going to come unglued, are you?

"I know you've been working with this man, and I assume he's a dear, but what about your health? Your family?"

"What's my health got to do with it?" asked Francine.

"Francine Fisher, I know you like a book. This is impulse behavior. You can't go off half-cocked. And where the hell are you going?"

"Calvary Stampede. It's a rodeo. It's perfectly safe. I want to do this trip." Francine winced in pain.

"No, you don't. You're in pain."

"No, I'm dying." Francine sipped her drink and stared at the bottles behind the bar. "I wrote a letter to you and Kathy. It explains everything. All you need to know is that I'm at peace. I'm headed out into nature with a good person who will take me to the end. I won't have Rachel do this, or you and Kathy. I've put Rachel through enough, but she will be with me at the end. Doc Gallardo will see to that. And, for God's sake, don't cry. I'll take you both with me and all our memories. It's all good, Carol. Don't worry."

"What do you mean, don't worry? I can't lose you."

"I'm already lost. Hug me and send me off with good thoughts. We'll always be The Triumvirate."

Carol laughed and they hugged. And they cried.

"Remember the summer of our senior year and we were hanging out at your pool. We were both going off to college in a week and we confessed everything about our lives to each other. I told you I couldn't wait to get out of my house. I told you that the night before at dinner, my father weighed in on my going to Duquesne. He had a few drinks and went after me like a mad dog saying it was a crap school. He was brutal. He told me that I'd never amount to anything. My mother told me not to take him seriously. Then she got out her rosary beads and defended him. It was a sick game they played with each other."

"And I told you that we were going to leave the nest in a few weeks, and we should move on and finally get laid in college," said Carol.

"And what did I say?"

"'You told me that ship had sailed. Robbie—last name ends in a vowel—Sorvino was your first.'"

They held on to each other for dear life and cried and laughed.

"Hardest thing ever," Carol said through her tears. "And I need you to know how much I regret my lack of compassion on the phone about Jeff. I hurt you and I never want to hurt you. I love you, Francine Fisher. I never want to hurt you."

"Oh, stop," said Francine. "It's over now. Your response was probably right. You've been through so many men with me. It was like one more man that I lost. But were you smiling on the phone when I told you because the scene with Jeff on the balcony was so damn funny?"

Carol started to laugh and they both laughed together and it became contagious and everyone in the bar turned to look at these women in their late seventies having a teenage moment.

"I knew it," said Francine, "and I knew it because it was funny the way I told it, even though I was hurting."

"Listen, Francine, when I called you at home, I had something to tell you. I wanted you to know that my mother died recently, and I know you were fond of her."

"Oh, my God, I loved her. She was always there to help without judgment. I'm so sorry. She was one of a kind. You're father, too. They were a pair. I loved them both. Jack was a kick in the pants. So damn funny. He was always there for us."

"Mom was ninety-eight. Almost hit a hundred. I'd love to go the way she did. Peacefully, a bit of dementia, stopped eating, and then, one night, she stopped breathing. That's the way I want to go."

Francine hugged her friend for the last time.

~

The next morning Doc Gallardo and Francine picked up his new shiny, black

Diesel Toyota Tundra and drove through customs at the Vancouver border. Francine examined every square inch of the interior of his truck. It was decked out like a control panel on a jet plane.

"Way cool, Doc. Nothing like I pictured. I thought the rodeos were in Texas, or Oklahoma, or in some God-forsaken southern state where it's hot and dry, and the only vegetation is a tumbleweed."

"If you'd Googled rodeos, you might have discovered that Canada is a country that has some of the best rodeos and roundups in the Western Hemisphere," said Doc Gallardo.

"What's Google?" she asked.

"You're impossible. The Calgary Stampede is famous all over the world."

"Is that something like the running of the bulls in Pamplona?" she asked.

"Either you are pulling my leg, or you have an unsuitable lack of knowledge about horses and bulls. Both are tedious."

"Who put the demon in your coffee this morning?" asked Francine. "I thought we'd have a pleasant romantic road trip like Audrey Hepburn and Albert Finney in *Two for the Road*. But I'm afraid it's going to be more like *Harold and Maud*."

Doc Gallardo looked at her as if she had five heads.

"You're too young to know these films. The comparison is just for me."

"Now that we have that out of the way, I'm going to show you a region of Canada that is one of the most beautiful and sacred parts of the world. This is a trip of a lifetime, Francine. Let's call it epic, not romantic."

"If you say so, but you missed Victoria Island. My dead husband and I honeymooned there. Second happiest moment of my life."

"What was the first happiest moment of your life?"

"When he died."

The drive from Vancouver to Kamloops to central British Columbia in summer was like a dream. Francine wished they had taken the Rocky Mountaineer Motor Coach because she loved trains almost as much as dogs, but such were the conditions of the trip. You can't have it all. She felt gratitude for being inside the cab of his truck, even though Doc was sniffing and snorting his way through the beginnings of a cold.

"It's not a cold, Francine," he said. "It's allergies."

Francine knew that her relationship with Doc Gallardo had changed. At some point, instead of working for him, they became friends—so easy with each other that he asked her to go on a road trip. In the spirit of friendship, Francine decided to call him Ulysses. She wondered if he would notice.

Ulysses was a master tour leader. He knew the landscape along the Trans-Canada Highway like he was born to the life of a Canadian fur trader, or maybe like the explorers, Lewis and Clark, who traipsed the northwest at the beginning of the nineteenth century and discovered the Oregon Trail. When Ulysses passed through the agricultural heartland of British Colombia, he was orgasmic.

"Look, Francine, this is epic. Fraser Valley is a visual feast," Ulysses was on a roll. "The valley is out of this world. Look at the lush green mountainsides. Gaze on the Fraser River off the side of the road. It winds its way through the landscape. And it's full of salmon. We can eat fish every night. Cook it on the fire and fall asleep under the stars."

"I don't do camping," said Francine. "Did I forget to mention that? I hate fish."

"You're impossible," he said.

Francine was fascinated by the canyons carved into the coast and Cascade Mountains. When they came to the thundering waters of Hell's Gate in Southern Fraser Canyon, her heart stopped. Ulysses had told her Hell's Gate was a rocky gorge, the narrowest part of the Fraser River, and it was a sacred place. But she had not anticipated what lay in front of her.

"Let's take the Hell's Gate Airtram to the bottom, Francine," said Ulysses. "It's only five hundred feet down."

The ride was short and sweet and the photo ops at the bottom were other-worldly.

"All this beauty almost makes me believe in God," said Francine. "Note, I said almost. But this beauty is heavenly."

"You have the soul of a poet, Francine. Who knew?"

"It's geological evolution that gets me every time."

Ulysses spontaneously gave his traveling companion a quick hug. He felt every bone in her body. It gave him resolve to make Francine's journey fit for a queen.

There was a suspension bridge and a gift shop, but Francine had no interest in walking on a bridge that challenged her balance, nor did she want to buy overpriced junk.

"I'll cut you a break tonight and we'll stay in Kamloops. I know a great steak house," he told her.

The first day on the road with Ulysses was thrilling. He had everything under control, including finding Montana's, the best steak house in Kamloops. She insisted on picking up the tab on everything along the way to the Calgary Stampede, and they fought over every bill.

"You're exhausting me, Ulysses. Please let me do this. I've got money to burn and nothing but time."

She insisted on two rooms at the Best Western Plus. She wanted to rest and think. Her best hours of thinking were from two to four in the morning. She had no business being anyone's bed partner, with sex or not.

Francine lay on the bed in room 292 of the Best Western Plus, lowered her head onto the pillow, and stared at the cottage cheese ceiling. The mattress was squishy and not to her liking. A sharp pain in her upper right abdomen caused her to double over. This was the third time that day. Although the pain was blinding, she hid it from Ulysses by walking away, or turning around, or distracting him from taking notice. Fluid was building up in her otherwise flat stomach and feelings of nausea induced the need to vomit, but she willed otherwise. Her breath smelled like the bottom of a sewer.

Thoughts of drinking had long since passed—she couldn't remember the last time she wanted a drink, and the drinking dreams were gone. The alcoholism that drove her life for decades was in a coma, never to awaken again. When she got her bearings after the overpowering pain, what concerned her most was Rachel, and how she would cope with her journey. Would she check in with Carlos from time to time? Hopefully she won't smother him too much—simply be a needed support. Carlos was trustworthy and consistent in his care of Boo Boo and the house. He'll be a good manager. They'll make a good team eventually.

That first morning at the Best Western Plus, Francine ate the biggest breakfast she had eaten since she was sixteen. Ulysses watched her wolf down the pancakes, eggs, bacon, and toast with astonishment.

"Slow down, cowgirl," he said. "You're not mounting that horse just yet."

"The altitude is making me hungry. And fresh air. Clean water. Besides, what makes you think my bony ass is going to sit in a saddle?"

"There is a remote possibility," he said. "Ever hear of padding?"

"Look at me, babe. What do you see? I'm a physical disaster. I can barely pee, or bend over, or get out of a chair. You know what's going on as well as I do. And you damn well can see the yellow in my eyes."

"I'm not taking pity on you, my friend," said Ulysses. "I'm taking care of you."

"Let's not get maudlin, babe. We can now see the forest through the trees."

Chapter 22

Harold and Maude

Francine watched the Rocky Mountaineer train depart Kamloops for Jasper in the cold, misty morning. The magnificence of the silver train showed brightly under the thin clouds covering the sun.

They planned on driving through Jasper National Park, and Francine prepared herself for the five-hour journey by studying a map she purchased at a convenience store. She asked Ulysses if he would stop by the train station so she could watch the Mountaineer's departure.

Before long, they were traveling along the shore of the North Thompson River, through charming rural communities, up into the Rocky Mountain trench. Francine was surprised to find herself interested in the geological changes evident in the two higher and imposing ranges: the Monashee and Cariboo Mountains. Ulysses told her about the peak known as Mount Terry Fox, named after the legendary fundraiser, Terry Fox, who attempted to run across Canada with his prosthetic leg before losing his life to cancer.

They passed Moose Lake and Pyramid Falls before coming to a campground in Jasper National Park. Francine freaked out.

"No camping, Ulysses. I don't do camping."

"I don't care what you want, Francine, you are going to camp under the stars tonight. I've got sleeping bags and blow-up mattresses in the back and all the necessities for cooking dinner. I even brought a tent if you're too scared to endure the nature of the night."

"You're damn right I want a tent," she said. "I don't like bears or critters. I'm not happy about this."

"First, we're going to the sky tram lift. You can get a better view of all the beauties in Maligne Canyon, including the magnificent waterfalls. The view will solidify your belief in a higher power."

Francine had the time of her life on the sky tram. The scene was stunning, breathtaking, awesome, and every other superlative that came into her mind. The adventure was worth everything she had been through in life. Disappointments disappeared, sadness and loss vanished, and she felt born again in body, mind, and spirit.

When they got off the tram, Francine took a deep breath and felt the peace of being surrounded by exquisite beauty.

"You're free, Francine," said Ulysses, "as free and as strong as these mountains."

Ulysses reached out and squeezed her hands.

Francine and Ulysses ate and slept under the stars, unafraid and open to another universe, far away from what she knew as her old reality. The taste of charbroiled steak cooked over the fire, the juicy corn, and old-fashioned beans reminded her of all the westerns she watched as a young girl growing up, from *Red River*, to *Stagecoach*, to *My Darling Clementine*. Her mouth watered when the cook brought out food from the chuckwagon and threw it on the flames of a nearby fire, charring the meat. She realized that she should have developed a taste for travel decades ago. Not that RV monstrosity Peter trotted out as the climax of his life. If she lived another year or two, she would become a wandering gypsy, a nomad without roots, without ever feeling pain.

Francine hardly slept that night. The sky was a cluster of bright stars, electric ions, and streaming comets. She breathed deeply and smelled the ozone. From time to time, she recognized she had to go to the bathroom, but she hoped she could wait until the sun rose.

As they drove southeast down Icefields Parkway, the glaciated peaks towering over the roadside reminded her of pictures she saw of the Matterhorn in the Swiss Alps. They stopped to view the Athabasca Falls, then on to the Athabasca Glacier, where they boarded the Ice Explorer and traveled right onto the ice. Their guide explained the geology of the region, but Francine did not hear a word he said.

"I'm blown away, babe," she said in a whisper.

Ulysses did not hear her. He, too, was in his own world, taken far away from any connection to his life as a father of four, twice married, a pharmacist by trade, and a rodeo man by nature.

When they returned to the truck, Francine was nauseated. Ulysses found a café and helped her inside to a red leather booth that had seen better days.

"Smells like bacon in here," said Francine. "I love bacon. It reminds me of home cooking, which reminds me of a joke. I once loved a man named Jeff Grady. He was a sheriff up at the lake and hung out at the bar where I was a bartender."

"You've got to be kidding me, lady," said Ulysses.

"Hang in, will ya? Jeff was a storyteller, a raconteur if you will, and one night he was talking about the FBI, an agency he loathed with a passion. He asked everyone at the bar what were the three most overrated things in the world. Before anyone could respond and ruin his joke, he said, 'home cooking, home fucking, and the FBI.'"

Ulysses laughed so loud all conversations in the café stopped. Then Francine brought Phyllis Diller to life and the room erupted in applause.

The waitress came up to take their order. "The lady will have ginger ale, and I'll have a cup of coffee."

"There is so much beauty in life. I've had tons of time to think since I became sober. When you're drunk, you don't think. You go unconscious. Life stands still, frozen in time. My soul is worn out, which reminds me of a line of poetry Walt Whitman wrote in 'Song of Myself.'

I celebrate myself, and sing myself,
And what I assume you shall assume,
For every atom belonging to me as good belongs to you.
I loafe and invite my soul,
I lean and loafe at my ease observing a spear of summer grass.

"My friend, Don from rehab, quoted the same poem to me one day when I was crazy with wanting to drink. He told me to celebrate me, sing, and the world belongs to me. Instead of self-sabotaging. I embrace, therefore I am."

Ulysses couldn't take his eyes off his traveling partner. What nature wrought, Francine perceived as salvation.

A peaceful silence enveloped them on their drive to Lake Louise and Banff. Once they arrived at one of the most beautiful lakes and landscapes ever to evolve in nature, they decided to spend the afternoon touring Banff National Park's highlights, which included Moraine Lake and Yoho National Park.

"I'm toured out, Ulysses. Let's do this day in less than two hours, then take me to a campground, stuff me inside a sleeping bag, and leave me there."

"I overexposed you, but I didn't want to stop the stream of natural beauty," he said. "I'm starved. There are hundreds of hotels in Banff."

"No hotels. Nothing to remind me of modern society. Let's find a cheap dive. Burger and shakes."

It didn't take long before they came upon The Eddie Burger + Bar. It was not much on décor, but the smell of hamburgers being fried in grease was mouth-watering. They ordered burgers and milkshakes.

They ate like cowhands on a summer cattle drive across the plains. Laughing and eating became a bond, a connection between two disparate people, fifteen years apart in age, without any connection to each other's lives except a stint at Charlotte Ebsen Women's Correctional Facility.

Francine pushed her plate away. She couldn't finish her burger. Her appetite was spent. All that was left was sipping the milkshake in fits and starts.

"Our trip is straight out of *Harold and Maude*. It's a movie and you're too straight-laced to know about it, but the story is about an eighty-year-old woman and a twenty-year-old kid. They go on a road trip, like us, but it's a train ride. They fall in love and explore life from a different perspective."

"I'd sure like to see that. Sounds kinky."

"No kink. Just friendship and all the stuff that goes along with caring for someone.

Speaking of which, I'm curious. You were married twice, have four kids, mostly all grown up, and you're plying your trade at a jailhouse pharmacy. How did you end up with that resume?"

"I don't have a resume," he said. "I have stuff I did, but not a coherent, professional path that would allow me to make six figures a year. I was sloppy about my life."

"How did you get off track?" asked Francine.

"Made bad decisions."

"We all made bad decisions, and what a coincidence that you and I ended up together in prison together. I'm thinking you have trouble with women."

"Two wrong marriages and two good women. Fifteen years and nothing in common except for the kids. The first wife was too young for me. But I loved Adele more than life and still do. She was a rodeo queen. That's where we met and that's where we left each other. She didn't mean to run back to the rodeo after five years of marriage, but it happened in a flash. I'm not sure if Adele loved the rodeo more than she loved me and the kids. That's open for debate. Then I married again to a kind woman, but not for love. She helped me with the kids. And then we had two more. She was the wrong woman at the right time, and we crashed."

"Where did you end up?" Francine asked.

"In a psyche ward. Two months observation. After they drugged me that first night, I knew I wouldn't make the two months. I told the shrink I wouldn't take the drugs, and by the fifth session, we had it out. The shrink told me to leave."

"Did you learn anything about yourself?" she asked.

"I learned I have a charm over women that's addictive. It gets me going sexually. I can't blame the women since I initiate it. But I needed to change my behavior patterns, where I was going, and what I was going to do to get there."

"What about your children?" asked Francine. "How did they cope with all that drama?"

"They're doing fine—all went to college, all found good jobs. I don't talk much about the past with them. They've moved on and live their own lives now."

Ulysses picked at the burger on Francine's plate and twirled the fries in ketchup. "Time to talk about the elephant in the room, Mrs. Freeman. You want to know why I asked you to come with me on this trip?"

"Maybe I know and maybe I don't know. Does it matter?"

"It matters to me," he said. "This is my healing journey as much as it is yours. I wanted to share my passions with you because you're special to me. And I wanted to show you a world of beauty. I thought you might want to know that. Now, let's go find a place to gaze at the stars."

After stopping off at a local grocery store for dinner and breakfast food, Ulysses and Francine drove into the Tunnel Mountain Village Campground.

"We're going to get a spot with a tent and fire pit," he said. "All the comforts of home."

Once they made it to the campground and got set up, Ulysses cooked steaks and beans. Francine didn't eat much, which didn't surprise Ulysses.

She was getting thinner, her eyes were yellowish, as was her skin, and her cheeks were devoid of color. He wrapped another blanket around her body and moved closer to her so he could keep her warm. Francine laid her head on his shoulder and fell fast asleep. He sipped coffee and gazed at the stars dotting the midnight blue sky. In time, his lids got heavy, and he slept for a few hours until his arm felt numb. He laid Francine down on the blow-up mattress, put her sleeping bag over her, slid into his own bag, and he slept like a baby in a bassinet.

The following morning, Francine walked out of the restroom refreshed from her shower.

She felt relaxed and of sound mind. The state of her body was another issue.

"I've got an idea," she said between bites of scrambled eggs. "Let's go straight to Calgary. We'll drive through the mountains of Rundle and Tunnel Mountain Drive, ride to Sulphur Mountain, and take in the panorama of the Bow Valley. We don't have to take a gondola, just push on forward to the Stampede."

Ulysses was not surprised by the request. Francine needed to get somewhere and rest in comfort and watch the world circle around her. And Ulysses needed to call Rachel. She had called him four times, and he could imagine her concern.

"Wait until you see this eighty-six-year-old woman race in the barrel event. She reminds me of you. Feisty and funny as a crutch."

"So, this isn't your first rodeo at Calgary?" asked Francine. "You strike me as a Southwest kind of rodeo man."

"You got me wrong, ma'am. I love the Northwest. It feels cleaner, purer in spirit and heart. The places I lived in in Texas were dry and hot and made my skin itch. When I got out of the psych ward, I packed a duffle bag and headed north to Grand Rapids because it's a medium-sized city surrounded by gorgeous lakes and bass fishing, and it's reasonably close to the Canadian border, and the Canadian Rockies is where God resides."

The drive from Banff to Calgary was approximately one and a half hours via the Trans-Canada Highway, and they had plenty of time to pack leisurely. Ulysses loaded the truck meticulously while Francine studied the map.

"We'll get to Calgary before the opening night festivities," said Ulysses.

Francine had purchased a travel book on Alberta, Canada, in the last gift shop she visited. There was a phrase she repeated to herself as they drove straight through to Calgary: *Canadian ranches meet the Rockies in Alberta.* The landscape was magical and possessed a beauty that had to be experienced with all five senses while you inhaled the rarefied air.

"What's with you and this Stampede?" asked Francine.

"I've participated in the Calgary Stampede three times. Each time, it gave me a sense of accomplishment, along with a sore back, and a crippled body. Once, I broke my arm riding a bronco."

"I bought a book on the Stampede, but what's your take on it?"

"It's a brutal ten days if your body holds up. And there are tons of things to do and see. Tourists go there from all over the world. It attracts over a million people. That's epic for a rodeo. It's the greatest show on earth for rodeo cowboys with big parades and miles of exhibition tents. Crowds are everywhere on the grounds."

"It says in my book that this guy Weadick—the guy who started the Stampede—was like the PT Barnum of the rodeo world."

"Yep. He started off as a trained trick rider and ended up as a one-man rodeo producer. Back in the day, everyone was hungry for entertainment, not just in America but in Canada as well. And there was a long history of political infighting and financial kickbacks with these kinds of events. Make no mistake, Weadick made money the first time out."

"But he only had one stampede in 1912," said Francine. "What happened after that?"

"He attracted big money the first time out, but big cattle people were only willing to invest in the one-time event. Cowboys from all over Western Canada, the U.S., and even Mexico came, and it was so successful that Weadick put on another Stampede in 1913, but it was in Winnipeg, and it failed. In 1923, when the stampede returned to Calgary, it combined two events—the rodeo and the Calgary Industrial Exhibition. History was made again."

"When you're old and gray, you can lead tours for the Stampede," said Francine. "The history is in your bones."

Ulysses drove steadily into the cosmopolitan city of Calgary, with its multiple glass and steel skyscrapers plunging through the clear blue summer skies.

"Last time I was here five years ago, this was still a mid-size city. Damn. Looks like the tourists bought and paid for the expansion."

Ulysses pulled into the entrance of Suite Digs Arriva, a four-star hotel near the arena. "This place has class, no doubt about it. Sure you want to stay here?"

"See if you can get me into a room as fast as you can," said Francine. "I'm feeling like I need a nap."

"No lunch?" asked Ulysses.

"You get something to eat and get the lay of the land," she said as she opened the truck door, looking pale and frail.

∽

Ulysses walked to the arena and called Rachel. "I'm sorry about not calling you back promptly. We were always together on the road. Now we've hit Calgary and she's resting in her room at Suite Digs Arriva. It's a first-class hotel."

"How is she? You know I'm worried as hell."

"Hanging in with fits and starts."

"That's it? Fits and starts? Can you be more specific?

"Look, Rachel, it's minute by minute. There is pain, then it goes away; eating, then the appetite goes away. Nothing is normal. If she was in a hospital, she'd be hooked up to machines that collect data every second. Your mom doesn't care about that now. She's living without tubes and she's happy and that's what counts."

"Yes. Yes. You're right. I'll try to relax. Call me if anything changes."

"Of course. Take care, Rachel.

Doc Gallardo walked through the arena gate and picked up the smells of hay and horses, along with the cattle and feed. He was home at last—standing in one of the most impressive rodeo arenas in the Northern hemisphere. Although the size dwarfed him, he felt invigorated by the prospect of getting on a bucking bronco again. He had been avoiding it for ten years, trying to change his ways and not pursue Adele. Until he stood by the entrance to the main gate, Ulysses had no idea how much he missed the rodeo circuit and how much he loved Adele. Somewhere along his journey, he stopped listening to his heart. That was his one regret in life.

On previous visits, Ulysses established a rodeo ritual. He walked through the horse stalls where he scuffed up his boots and kicked the hay. As he nuzzled the horses, he would talk riding techniques with some of the handlers, and then he'd search out some of the better bronco riders to discuss the best horses to ride.

He played out that ritual again and felt at home. He tried to find some old cowhands in the business, but most of the rodeo helpers were new and young. It made him feel old.

When Ulysses returned to the hotel to check on Francine, she was sound asleep. He thought it prudent to have another key made for her room so he could keep a close eye on her. It was late afternoon, and the evening's festivities were going to begin in another hour. He figured Francine was not going to be staying up late, so he returned to the stadium. It was already packed with partiers, some already drunk and disruptive. He looked over the schedule for the next day and thought Francine would like the women's barrel races.

He went back to the corrals and spotted one of the horse trainers. Tom Costello was close to seventy, skin withered from the daily pulverizing of the sun, and in need of a new pair of cowboy boots. He also needed a cowhand's shirt that wasn't fraying at the cuffs and collar.

"Hey, Tom, it's me, Ulysses. How are you doing? You look good after all these years."

"Great to see you, cowboy," said Tom. "It's been some time. I'm hanging in there. We started out in this life together, remember?"

"How can I forget? You taught me everything I know. Got a question. Can you check out a few horses I might like to ride in a few events and tell me what you think?"

"I'll give you the stats on a few, but a young beauty name of Natchez is one of the best."

"Thanks, I'll take a look, but first I need the registration office," Ulysses said. "Where'd they locate it this year?"

"Southside of the arena," said the trainer. "What's your specialty? It's been so long, I forgot."

"Barrel racing," Ulysses said. "Maybe I'll get thrown off by a bucking bronco just to see if I survive. I can also rope a cow with a little practice."

"What about driving a wagon?" asked the trainer. "If you've got the agility with the reins, you might do well. All it takes is guts and strength."

"Thanks. I'll think about it. One more thing, Tom. Have you seen the eighty-six-year-old woman barrel rider?"

"Word has it that she died last year," said Tom. "She'll be missed."

After registering, Ulysses went in search of Natchez's owner. He wanted to put time in on roping in order to increase his speed and physical flexibility. There was plenty of time to think about driving a wagon because it was the last event of the rodeo.

Ulysses spotted Natchez in the back corral. She was a beauty and sure-footed to the ground. The lady had talent and so did the rider exercising the horse.

The owner of Natchez was a woman in her late fifties, fit, and full of confidence about the pedigree of her horse. She was dressed in full western wear with a black felt hat firmly placed on her head and a red scarf around her neck.

"I'm Ulysses Gallardo, ma'am," he said. "I'm wondering if you might allow me to ride her in a few of my events. She's a beauty for sure."

"I haven't seen you around the circuit, cowboy," she said. "By the way, I'm Mrs. O'Connell. If you're thinking of riding her for the barrel racing, go ahead and try her out."

"And roping," he said. "I'd be pleased to take her for a ride if you don't mind."

Mrs. O'Connell nodded her head. "I'm sure you can handle Natchez, Mr. Gallardo."

Ulysses mounted the horse and smiled to himself. This was one perfect horse. He practiced roping because he was rusty, and Mrs. O'Donnell was generous in her compliments along with giving him some pointers.

"How are you on the barrels?" she asked.

"It used to be my event back in the day," he said.

They went to the barrel practice area, and Ulysses showed his expertise cutting around the barrels with precision.

"You haven't lost your touch, Ulysses," she said.

It was turning dark, and the fireworks were beginning. He remembered a cowboy bar a couple of blocks away from the arena where the entrants drank and cavorted. Ulysses knew of no better way to learn a few rodeo secrets than hanging with the colorful locals. He wanted Francine to enjoy the Stampede, and hoped she would be up for looking at the exhibition tents in the following days.

The cowboy bar was less honky-tonk and more dive bar. There was no stage, no place for country bands to play—just an old jukebox from the sixties, a long bar with no light to see your drink, and sawdust floors that hadn't been swept since the early eighties. The men who frequented the bar were not rodeo riders. They were more like drifters and grifters from another century. Ulysses was not going to learn any trade secrets in. Hanging around derelicts was a sucker's game.

Down the street, there was a line of people standing outside what was probably the real deal honky-tonk bar, complete with live music. He thought he'd take Francine there one night and teach her the country western two-step.

He could feel the phone ringing in his pocket on his walk back to the hotel. It could be no one but Rachel. Ulysses could feel her anxiety and worry. He pulled the phone out of his pocket and answered. Just as he did, he heard the click that ended the call.

Chapter 28

Coming Home

A burning sensation in her stomach woke up Francine in the early morning hours. She turned on the light and glanced at the bedside clock—5:00 a.m. If she read her book, she might go back to sleep. She didn't care for the book. It was a story about a girl growing up in the Louisiana bayou who exceeds her circumstances beyond her own expectations. Francine had read hundreds of these memoirs, and they all had the same happy endings. She threw the book on the bed—the end. Ashes to ashes, dust to dust.

Rachel must be worried by now. Her phone was on the nightstand, but she forgot to charge it. She was always forgetting to charge it. She hoped there was enough battery left.

"Hi, it's your mother. I'm calling so you won't worry. The trip, the beauty of nature brings me a special feeling of peace and gobs of happiness. I'm not going to worry about what happens at the end. I'm sure Doc will call you if I will be walking down the slippery hill, but let's not count those chickens before they hatch. Everything is taken care of. Be patient and know that I will be going in peace. You are loved, my heart, always."

Francine fell back to sleep and dreamed of eagles flying high in the clear blue sky above the Canadian Rockies. One of the eagles picked her up, from where she did not know, and they flew next to each other. Her eyes connected with the eyes of a bird, and they blended into one eagle, exploring the vast expanse of the universe. She flew high, so high she couldn't see the earth any longer. The updrafts and downdrafts were carrying her into a space she never knew existed. Her wings never moved because she was one with the wind—her friend, the wind.

A knock at the door awoke her.

"Just a minute. I gotta get out of bed. It'll take an eternity."

With extreme effort, Francine hobbled to the door, opened it, and turned back to bed. "Don't bother with me, babe, I'm doing great."

He gently put his arm around her and helped her sit down on the bed.

"Darlin', I'll help you get dressed, and we'll go to the expensive coffee shop for eggs and toast. You always have an appetite for that."

In the stillness of the morning light, Ulysses slipped her nightgown above her head and saw the ravages of her illness on her skeletal body. Long ago and far away was Francine. Putting weight on her body was not a possibility.

"I need a shower," she said.

"I'll draw you a bath," he said as he wrapped a thin robe around her pale white body; her skin folded neatly like ripples in a stream.

He slid her into the bathtub, which was filled with bubbles and soothing aromas. She laid her head on the back of the tub and closed her eyes.

"Feels good," she murmured.

Ulysses was a healer by nature, and he knew what to do. He dipped a washcloth in the bubble bath, and with the care of a surgeon, stroked her shoulders and washed her. It was a labor of love for a man with a calling.

"Breathe, Francine," he said. "You'll feel better."

"It hurts."

"Please, breathe."

After the bath, he managed to get her dressed, into the elevator, and with effort, walked her into the coffee shop. He ordered her tea and toast, plus a plate of scrambled eggs.

"I'm doing it, babe," she said. "This is a momentary setback this morning. I'm still doing the Stampede."

"Glad to hear it."

∽

Francine ate everything on her plate and asked for another order of toast.

"What's on today?" she asked.

"The women's barrel race is still on. Finish up, and we'll walk over."

"I need the exercise," said Francine. "Will we see the eighty-six-year-old ride?"

"I'm afraid she is no longer with us."

"That's sad," said Francine. "Or maybe not. She lived her life the way she wanted to."

Francine put her toast down and sipped her tea. "You're a natural, Ulysses."

"A natural what?" he asked.

"Healer. You know how to care. That's a rarity."

"It's what I feel," he said.

"Are you getting all romantic on me?" asked Francine.

"Just getting all *Harold and Maude* with you."

"But we aren't having sex," said Francine. "Did I ever tell you how I learned about sex?"

"No," he said, "but I'm sure you'll tell me."

"Funniest damn story. You see I went to a co-educational Catholic high school, but we never had classes together except for sex education in our senior year. It was a watered-down version of sex ed. What else would it be with boys in the room? We were taught how to get pregnant as outlined by the rules of the Catholic Church, so we didn't take it seriously.

"A priest, a psychologist, and a medical doctor met with us every Friday afternoon. That sounds like the beginning of a joke from a Jewish comic in the Catskills and, unfortunately, it was a joke. The boys and girls ogled graphics of the vagina, fallopian tubes, and uterus. The girls never saw a drawing of the penis. I thought it was unfair to the girls, even though I had seen my boyfriend's penis a month before the last semester of my senior year."

"Did you go to confession and tell the priest?" he asked.

"Are you crazy? Why would I do that? Anyway, we were told to practice abstinence because birth control was forbidden. It was 1960 and birth control pills hadn't been invented. Girls couldn't figure out what a diaphragm looked like or how to use it, but since it was a form of birth control, it didn't matter. According to the church, the only way to regulate having babies was the rhythm method, which rarely worked. No student spoke out or asked a question until one day, close to the end of school, Carol raised her hand. She was steaming. Carol said she didn't understand if two married adults don't want children right away, why should they? What's the big deal?

"The priest almost came unglued and the doctor intervened with the suggestion that the male wear a condom. It was a free-for-all from there. Father Ryan exploded—it's against the rules of the Catholic Church—and the psychologist was out of his league. Carol wanted a definition of family planning according to the rules of the Catholic Church."

"That's pretty bold for a high school girl to say," said Ulysses. "Where did she pick up that idea so young?"

"Her mother. She was channeling her non-Catholic, progressive mother. Ester was actually Jewish, but no one knew that except my anti-Semitic father suspected it. Every student in the class was cringing after Carol questioned the gurus in the classroom. But nothing happened to Carol, except that she became the most admired girl in her senior class. That moment was worthy of a homecoming queen crown. Ester died recently. That's why Carol came to see me in Spokane. Her mother helped me through the most difficult time of my life. I'll never forget her."

∾

Ulysses took Francine into the arena and walked her down the stairs to seats that were in the shade of the cool morning. He brought a pillow with him for her to sit on, and she was grateful. The noise from the packed arena was enticing and filled her with newfound energy.

"I've got to go look at a horse for the men's barrel event tomorrow, so hold the fort."

"I want to see your horse."

"Later. Then I'll put you up in the saddle so you can feel what I feel when I ride, only it will be more gentle. Watch and tell me who's in the lead. The finals are this afternoon."

Ulysses made his way to the stalls behind the arena. He tried to push the fear down that his body was not going to hold up. Years of healing and longing plagued him. But it was time to take a risk and challenge his afflictions. Inexplicably, Francine inspired him to go after his dream.

Mrs. O'Connell was standing by Natchez, holding the reins.

"She's saddled and ready to give you a good ride, cowboy."

He put a foot in the stirrup and threw his other leg over the saddle. It had been a long while since he was a rodeo cowboy, but he was finally back home.

"Jeez, Ulysses, it looks like this is your horse," said Mrs. O'Connell. "Perfect fit for your tiny ass."

Tom came by to admire Ulysses sitting on Natchez.

"Looks like old times," said Tom as he picked his teeth with a chewed-up toothpick.

A skinny rodeo dog began sniffing around Natchez's legs.

"Don't mind him," said Tom. "He's looking for scraps."

"Aren't we all?"

"Take a practice ride around the ring and make it feel like home," said Tom.

Sometimes home is a saddle; sometimes home is eight seconds on the back of a bull; sometimes home is a pharmacy dispensary in a women's correctional facility; sometimes home is in front of you, but you haven't had time to open the door.

"What's going on, cowboy?" asked Mrs. O'Connell. "You got stage fright? Ride that horse like you mean it. You're going to win this race hands down on Natchez."

"Maybe too much time has passed since my rodeo days. I started out riding at sixteen in Odessa, Texas, and never looked back until life's obligations took over."

"You talking about Adele Simpson?" asked Mrs. O'Connell.

"How do you know about her?" he asked. "Well, hell, I guess everybody knows about Adele Simpson. I fell head over heels for her when I first met her at twenty, but that redhead didn't give me the time of day."

"She was known as a cracker-jack barrel rider around the circuit," she said. "Only her reputation as a prized prick teaser preceded her riding abilities."

"Yep, took me a couple of years to catch on to her, but one day I volunteered to shoe one of her horses, and to everyone's surprise, Adele took to me shortly thereafter."

Ulysses got off Natchez and checked his saddle cinches and the horse's bit.

"It was plenty more years for her to say yes to my marriage proposal. By that time, I was twenty-seven and fighting physical pain as a constant companion. After Adele got pregnant, we retired from the rodeo circuit."

"It's hard to live with the punishment of the rodeo," said Tom. "It takes everything out of you. I still got pain from a broken hip."

"I was pretty tired after two broken arms, a fractured hip, and a cracked knee," Ulysses responded.

"What'd you do after you left?" asked Tom.

"I tried a few jobs, construction and I worked on cars, but they were jobs and not a career. While Adele and I were raising two children, I went to night school, got a degree in pharmacology, and the rest is history, except that Adele split after five years and went back to the rodeo."

"Figures," said Mrs. O'Connell. "It's an old story, but usually the husband leaves."

Ulysses mounted Natchez and took her for another ride to the back of the stables and ran her through the paces of the barrels again. She moved quickly on the turns and switchbacks. He was pleased with their performance. They fit together like a hand and glove.

When Ulysses returned to the stands, he handed Francine a hotdog, fries, and a large iced tea. Her eyes lit up, and she ate like she had not seen food in a week.

"Listen, I've been reading about the horses and riders in the men's barrel race, and besides you, I've got my favorites. I'm seriously considering placing a bet tomorrow."

"You can't place a bet, Francine. It's not like we're at the racetrack."

"Sure, it is. They're riding horses."

In a moment's flash, Ulysses stopped hearing anything Francine was saying. His face turned chalky white as he looked at the gate across the arena with his green eyes boring directly at someone or something.

"Hey, Ulysses, are you listening?" she asked. "What's up? What are you staring at? You look like you've seen a ghost."

"What the hell?" he remarked to himself.

"Come on, Ulysses, what's up?" she asked.

"A full head of red hair," he said.

"Is that something important?" she said.

"It's Adele," he said as he got out of his seat and trotted like a horse toward the gate. "Stay put. I'll be back. Enjoy the women's barrel race."

"My, my, it'll be old home week with you two."

The women's barrel race began, and Francine was laser-focused on the event. The race was fun to watch at first, but it was never-ending, and she started to get bored. Some of the riders looked as if they were construction workers or sumo wrestlers. She'd had enough.

She took her pillow seat and walked unsteadily up the stairs, resting several times before she made her way through the exit.

Outside the arena, there were dizzying rows of exhibits filled with tchotchkes, none of which interested her. She threw her food carton into a trash bin and took an old San Francisco Giants baseball hat out of her purse. It was not sticky hot, but it was warm enough to cause her to take off her sweater and tie it around her thin waist. It was the heat of the day, and the sun hung over her head like a fist.

Francine ducked inside a tent that sold Calgary Stampede T-shirts, hats, and sweatshirts.

The pretty young girl almost took a fright when she saw Francine. Maybe she was all of twenty, and she wanted the world to be beautiful.

"Sorry if I frightened you," said Francine. "It was too hot for me to stand in the sun, and this booth has the most shade."

"Are you okay, ma'am?" asked the young woman. "I'm Janine."

"Do you have a chair to sit on, Janine?" asked Francine. "Just for a sec."

Janine took a chair from behind the cashier's desk and helped Francine sit down.

"Thank you, and nice to meet you. I'm Francine."

Janine poured Francine a glass of water from her thermos and then said, "You don't look well, ma'am. Go ahead and drink some water and breathe deeply."

Francine sipped some water. "This helps. Thanks again."

"Please stay here for as long as you want."

Janine looked at Francine and had an idea. She picked up a Calgary Stampede t-shirt from a stack on one of the tables, brought it over to Francine, and urged her to put it on.

"While you are here with me, you might as well help us do some advertising."

"Nice touch," said Francine. "Will do."

Francine put on the T-shirt over her blouse. It looked like a nightgown on her small frame, and it surely made a statement about the biggest and best rodeo in the Western hemisphere.

Chapter 24

Rodeo Girl

Adele was a woman who loved red lipstick any time of day or night. She wore tight, faded jeans, ripped in the right places—on her thighs and knees—complete with a dark brown belt with a sterling silver buckle that Ulysses remembered giving her.

He watched her for a few minutes and tried to gauge her mood and energy. Adele had plenty of both. Ever since the day Ulysses met her as a young rodeo rider, he had been obsessed by her vibrancy—until she wore him out. He couldn't satisfy her drive, neither could their young children. She was not interested in full-time parenting, even though she wept when she left her young daughter and son. In private, she told her husband that she couldn't cope, and besides, she missed the rodeo. "I'm just a rodeo girl," she told him. Ulysses was devastated.

Adele's horse was let out of the chute and into the arena with a seasoned rider in the saddle. She was so excited, she almost followed the horse into the arena. The applause and cheers were deafening as the female rider took the barrels. Adele's rodeo cowgirl was riding at peak performance, satisfying not just Adele, but hordes of fans. It was a winning moment, and Ulysses didn't want to bring her down by intruding on her joy. When Adele turned around to celebrate with another rider, she saw him.

It was all there in that moment—that damn chemistry, that crooked smile. She felt the sex settle in the right places in her body as she surveyed him in his black cowboy hat, black t-shirt, and black jeans. He would never change.

Adele walked toward her ex-husband like a stripper getting ready to offer a lap dance. Her sexy smile was meant for an old lover, not a husband. Ulysses met his muse halfway and took her in his arms. They held onto each other with old longing, as if they were going to die without each other.

"What are you doing here, baby?" Adele whispered.

"I'd like to say it was to find you, but I didn't know you were still on the rodeo circuit."

"A friend needed my help."

"Same with me. I'm riding the barrels and a bronco, then roping a calf, and maybe doing the wagon drive for old time sake."

"Good choices, except for the bronco and the wagon," Adele said. "You can't do that. Eight seconds of hell and then who knows after that. And driving the wagon is plain dumb. At your age, you don't need more broken bones."

"Maybe I have one last ride left on the bull."

"No, baby, you don't. Do the barrels and the calf roping event. You were always good with a rope." Adele smiled at her sexual innuendo.

"I'll take it under advisement," he said with a kiss. "I want to ask you a hundred questions: What have you been doing? Do you see the kids often? What city do you live in? Who's in your bed lately?"

"The last question is none of your business, cowboy," she said, "but you probably know the answers to the other questions since you talk to the kids regularly."

He couldn't believe his luck. Seeing Adele like this was more exciting than getting on a horse again. He had no idea what he was going to do with all the emotion surging through him.

"El Paso," said Adele.

"You live in El Paso? Jeez, Adele, you can't get out of Texas for the life of you."

"I like the border city. The kids hate it. They'd rather meet me in Austin, but you know that."

"I guess I know more than I let on. And you? How much do you know about me?"

"Darlin', we have kids together. You think they don't talk to me about you? Silly man."

He kissed her flat out on her beautiful red ruby lips. She tasted like cherries and root beer.

"Listen, baby, I'm with someone, and I'd love you to come with me and meet her. I'll tell you the story on the way, but I can't leave her alone too long. Poor health."

Adele's assistant was at her side with a flick of her finger. After a few words of instruction to the handler, Adele took her ex-husband's arm and fast-walked out of the chute. Along the way, he explained Francine in broad strokes.

"You'll see when you meet her."

As they entered the spectators' area in the rodeo arena, Ulysses scanned the seats. Francine was nowhere to be found. A sense of panic stopped him in his tracks. He turned around to the upper stands, hooding his eyes to cover the glaring sun.

Adele was standing by the side of the entrance. She grabbed his hand as he passed, and asked, "Ulysses, what's wrong? Why are you hyperventilating?"

He took Adele's hand and led her to the exhibition tents. Ulysses was not daunted by the dozens of long rows of tents on a large field because he knew Francine wouldn't get far. He saw her in the front corner of the first tent. Her body was slumped over on a chair, her beat-up baseball hat covered her eyes, and her T-shirt was soaked with sweat.

Adele ran after him and witnessed something unfathomable in the life of the silent cowboy. He was cradling an aging woman and crying.

"Francine? Do you hear me? Please answer me. Damn you, wake up!"

Francine stirred, opened her eyes, and instinctively fought off Ulysses. He released his arms.

"It's me, Francine. Doc. I'm Doc. Ulysses."

Adele got a water bottle from Janine and gave it to Ulysses. He held it to her mouth as she greedily drank half.

"Oh my God, what happened?" Francine asked. "Where am I?"

"You're at the Stampede. You must have wandered off."

"She came into my booth and fell asleep," said Janine. "I'm sorry I didn't check on her more often."

"It's fine," said Ulysses as he and Adele helped Francine to her feet. "Let's get some food. This is Adele, in case you're wondering."

"I've got the picture," said Francine. "Pleasure to meet you, Adele. You've got a fine man here."

"It's a big day tomorrow," said Ulysses. "I'm riding in the men's barrel race, and you've got a front-row seat."

"Can't wait. I'll be ready, cowboy."

They left the exhibition tent and made their way to the front gate. From there, they took a taxi to the hotel and ate at the coffee shop. Francine gobbled a plate of macaroni and cheese with two pieces of garlic bread and downed a full glass of iced tea.

"I feel great," said Francine. "Except I need a bath. I feel like I've been rotting in a chicken coop for a week."

"Come on, Francine, I'll draw you the best bath you ever had," Adele told her.

"Keep the bubbles to a minimum," she called back as she walked ahead.

Although Francine was unsteady on her feet, she was a trooper as she made her way to the elevator with Adele who was laughing by the time the elevator closed.

Adele drew a warm bubble bath. Francine walked into the bathroom wrapped in a towel.

"Close your eyes, honey. I don't want you to faint."

"Don't worry about me," said Adele. "I'll help you into the bath, so you won't slip."

"I'm as strong as an ox," Francine said as her towel dropped to the floor. "I warned you, babe."

Francine bathed for the good part of an hour, dozing frequently. Adele woke her up and tried to get her to come out of the tub. On the third try, she was able to lift Francine and carry her to bed. She found her nightgown under the pillow, slipped it over her head, and tucked her in.

Adele heard a soft knock at the door. Ulysses entered with a bottle of wine and two wine glasses.

"Have you been hanging out in the hotel bar? You smell like a brewery."

"I'm mourning her loss."

"Not yet, my love," Adele said. "What's her condition?"

"Last stages of cirrhosis of the liver."

He poured the wine and studied the liquid as it filled the glasses. He held up his glass.

"I'm not doing this. I'm not toasting anything. Francine is still kicking, and for the moment, she lives. Let me help you get her to the arena tomorrow so she can watch her rodeo man win the barrel race."

He drank his wine slowly, thoughtfully.

"Is your room next door?" asked Adele.

"Don't screw around with me, Adele. I'm in no mood."

"I'll be gentle."

∽

Two sets of eyes stared at the ceiling. Neither the cowboy nor the cowgirl moved a muscle as they held hands. Adele took a deep breath in an effort to speak, but she could not utter a word. She was overcome by memories of their marriage, two adult children, and a roaming energy that brought her back to her cowboy. All that time, all that living, all that distance, and it brought her back to loving Ulysses more than anyone on earth. If truth be told, she prayed he would be at the Stampede every year. This is what it must be like to witness a miracle.

"How many were there?" he asked her.

"Why is that always the first thing out of a man's mouth? Don't be so predictable."

"In seventeen years, there must have been plenty," he said.

"I don't know," she said. "I didn't count them."

"You're right. I don't need to know. I married Doreen and had a few other relationships that amounted to nothing."

"Let's cut this conversation short," said Adele. "I've always loved you, and still do. Some things don't change."

"What do we do now?" he asked.

"First, we have to tend to Francine," she said. "Let's get her up and see how we can get some food down her. And get her into the arena."

Ulysses wanted her, wanted to feel her warmth, but that would be for another night.

Adele slipped out of bed, washed up, dressed, and left the room. She entered Francine's room and was relieved that she was still breathing, even snoring. They would have another day all together.

Breakfast was a lively meal. Francine was in a joking mood, self-deprecating as usual.

"You two made a major mistake way back when," said Francine. "You shouldn't have left each other. Don't mind me. I'm great with being a Monday morning quarterback."

"I made the mistake, not him," said Adele. "I got restless, like a gypsy, except I was a rodeo rider, hooked on the circuit. I knew I was going to leave the children with a good man and that they would forgive me in time. They did and came to live with me when my body couldn't ride another horse. My bony ass was screaming to stop the madness."

"When did that happen?" Ulysses asked. "It works fine as I can see."

"Adele, you left that one wide open," said Francine. "Now what time is the event?"

"Soon. Let's get going," he said. "Adele, darling, please do me a favor and hold my horse before the gate opens."

"Anything else you want me to hold?" she asked.

"You stole my line, babe," said Francine.

Francine sat on the shady side of the arena surrounded by a sea of early morning rodeo fans. It was nine o'clock on the dot, and Francine watched the rodeo gate eagerly while she held a box of popcorn. Her stomach was fluttering, and she felt some nausea. She wanted her rodeo man to do well. It meant so much to him. He was still the cowboy pharmacist with the black hat and twinkling eyes who was kind to his core.

The barrel races started, and the crowd roared. The first four riders bounded out of the gate, but their times were mediocre. Ulysses was the fifth rider, and he came out of the gate like a cat pouncing on a rat. He sat his horse to perfection, whirling around the barrels, cutting corners, swaying his body from side to side while keeping his arms tucked in close to his center. He was making a clean sweep with precision. He even had time to crunch his black hat on his head between barrels. She wondered if he took his hat off to sleep.

As he rounded his mount to the other side of the barrel circle, Francine held her breath. He was doing so well that Francine thought if she moved, the spell would be broken. Ulysses pulled up his reins as he finished rounding the last barrel. He had a big smile on his face.

"Oh baby, oh baby, oh baby," she whispered. "You did it, you precious thing."

The stands erupted with applause and cheers. He was their favorite. He was their hero—the unknown sixty-year-old cowboy with more tenacity than brains. As Francine wept, she was certain that Adele was weeping, too. There were seven more riders to go, but Francine didn't care. Blurry with happiness, it didn't matter to her who won. She knew that her rodeo man was the winner.

And what she knew turned out to be true as the announcement was made that Ulysses had won his event. His was the best time, beating out the nearest competitor by three seconds.

They celebrated at a steakhouse next to the hotel. Francine wanted a drink so badly she could taste it. And a cigarette. But both desires faded fast with a stabbing pain in her stomach.

Adele went around the table to sit next to Francine and held her.

"I'm okay now. The pain reminds me that when I get the craving to drink and smoke, the forces of darkness try to conspire to take me back to my old ways. It's not going to happen."

Sit with it, be with it. Did she need this meditation crap? She closed her eyes and drew her attention to herself, and it worked. The darkness receded like a cloud passing in front of her. Her napkin was in shreds; her back was soaked with sweat, but she was going to make it without giving in to her demons.

"What did you like the best about the barrel event, Francine?" asked Ulysses.

"You were the best part of the barrel event. Rode like a Trojan and you won, babe."

"You are my lucky charm, Francine. I couldn't have won the barrels without you and my darling Adele."

Adele grabbed his hand and stared down at her plate.

"I'm going to my room to nap," Francine said. "I want to be fresh for the bucking bronco event. And don't get on my back for not eating all of my steak. I'll eat it for dinner."

The waiter handed Francine a Styrofoam box for her leftovers. Francine was not going to eat the remains. She was nauseated and about to vomit.

"Will you pick up a stopwatch for me?" asked Francine. "I want to feel like I'm sitting on the bull, you know? Eight seconds and all that jazz, and don't forget to wake me up in a few hours so we can walk over to the arena together."

Francine left the Styrofoam box on the table.

Adele and Ulysses held hands. It felt warm and familiar.

"I know what you're doing, baby, riding the bull," said Adele. "But why punish your body like that now?"

"It's the last opportunity to challenge myself. Hey, baby, everyone deserves eight seconds of torture. Even so, if I make it to three seconds, I will have won."

"You always were like this. I thought you aging and all might make you rethink your competitiveness."

Ulysses unclasped his hands from Adele.

"You should talk, Adele. You were the one who couldn't let go of competing. That's why you left me and the kids, right."

"That's unfair," said Adele. "I told you I was restless."

"And I told you to get your fill of the rodeo and come home when you're done. And you never came home, damn you."

"I wanted to come home, but every time I started out to catch the last train or a bus out of a rodeo town, I couldn't get on it."

"I don't know what that means," said Ulysses.

"It means I was homesick and didn't know how to get back. You married again, and then years went by, and I was lost."

"That's not knowing your own mind."

"Leaving you was a wrong-headed decision and I regret it. The rodeo game was addictive. You might not believe this, but I didn't mean to come back to Calgary. When my friend asked for help, a familiar emotion resurfaced."

"You want my forgiveness?" he asked. "You have it. You have it because I've never stopped loving you."

"And I love you, and I'm proud for so many reasons, especially for what you are doing for Francine."

"I'm riding it out with her. The woman has heart and deserves a peaceful end."

"You think there's hope for us?" asked Adele.

"You never did anything wrong, darling. The way I'm looking at it is that you had an itch and left for a time. Now, I want you back if you'll come home."

"I'll put my things in order, and I'll come back to you."

"I live in Grand Rapids now," he said.

"I've always known where you live, baby," Adele said. "Now I'm going upstairs to help Francine, and you get her that stopwatch she wants so much. See you soon."

Chapter 25

Leaves of Grass

Marble floors glistened and the chandeliers glowed above the gray and white lobby as Ulysses entered the souvenir store to buy Francine a stopwatch. The surrounding glass gave the shop a futuristic quality as opposed to a traditional western theme. Nevertheless, the cowboy spirit still reigned in Calgary.

He stepped into the souvenir store and his phone rang. He picked it up and walked out of the store and paced, then sat on a purple felt sofa at the far end of the lobby. He took off his hat and continued to listen.

"I feel like I have to come to Calgary now," said Rachel.

"Pack your things and be ready. You can even get a ticket, then change it at the last minute. Let her have a little more time if she needs it. We're not in emergency territory yet."

"I want to talk to her."

"Francine is having a blast. She is currently at the hotel resting."

He heard Rachel crying.

"It will be soon," he said. "I'm sorry you're in pain. For now she has full capacity. Even though her energy is dissipating and she can't much feel hunger, she manages to gobble up every third meal. we, Adelle and I, my ex-wife, are taking good care of her, and we are diligently watching over her. She loves the rodeo, and I'm buying a stopwatch for her so she can follow the times of the bucking bronco event."

He heard Rachel laugh. Then a whimper. Then a laugh.

"Has she seen a doctor?" asked Rachel.

"I'm going to call a doctor when I see the end coming. Once she stops eating altogether, then it's time."

"Mom called me and left a message saying she was happy. It frightened me that she sounded so normal and at peace."

"It's time for you to be happy. Try not to think of an outcome. Take this journey moment by moment. I'm a pharmacist, so when the pain gets too much, I have what is needed for her. I fully intend to do right by her wishes. She's one of a kind, a big-hearted, complicated woman who walks her own walk. Rest easy, now."

He lowered his head, put his black cowboy hat on, and shoved the phone into his jeans. The cowboy sauntered back to the souvenir store and aimlessly ran his eyes across a table of Calvary medallions. Keepsakes for the rodeo. Ulysses had his own keepsake, and he would remember celebrating the rodeo with Francine for decades to come. He bought her a stopwatch.

Adele and Francine snuck up behind Ulysses in the souvenir store and both took an arm as they started to leave.

"Wait," said Francine. "I want to buy a new hat. What I have left of my hair looks like it was on the spin cycle of a washing machine."

Francine had fun trying on hats, laughing with the sales lady. By the time she decided on a natural straw cowboy hat, she was pleased with her new look.

"Damn, I look like I should have had a part in a Wyatt Earp TV show, or at least *Gunsmoke*. Yep, that's it. I should have played Kitty to what's his name, oh yeah, James Arness, and I would have had a go-around with Dennis Weaver. Old Chester and I could have had a threesome with Sheriff Matt Dillon. Brilliant concept, don't you think?"

Customers were gathering around for the Francine Show as Adele and Ulysses escorted her out of the shop with her cowboy hat jauntily tipped to the right on her head.

"This is my homecoming crown, don't you know," she said. "I look better today than I did back in 1960 with Danny Trevino on my arm. What a night. To think I was once a homecoming queen."

Before they left the hotel, Ulysses gave her the stopwatch and showed her how to use it. He also bought a hamburger to go in case she got hungry. They headed out to the arena, laughing and carrying on like teenagers going to a Friday night football game.

∽

It was three o'clock in the afternoon and the stands were filling up. The three musketeers edged their way over to the shady side, and Ulysses placed a pillow down on a seat. Several people obliged to accommodate the strange trio. Francine sat next to a weathered, skinny old man wearing a beat-up, dirty beige cowboy hat. He was studying the roster of riders for the bucking bronco event.

"Wish me luck," Ulysses said. "I'm still wearing number twelve."

"You've got this event covered, Doc, and I'm in your corner all the way."

Francine inched closer to the old cowboy next to her. "What's so interesting on that page?" she asked.

In a raspy voice, he answered, "Studying the riders."

"Wanna make a bet my rider wins the bucking bronco event?"

"I wouldn't mind," he said. "Name is Tex."

"I'm Francine. How far from home are you, Tex?"

"Not far enough. How much you wanna bet?"

"My rider is number twelve, and the bull is named Harry, and we are going to win this event. How about a hundred?"

"Can't take your money," said Tex. "He won't win. There's a sure winner named Kevin Bartolo. He's won this event every time out in the last three years."

"Let's make a bet anyway," she said. "I'm feeling lucky, and my stopwatch is at the ready, Tex. Let the games begin."

"Okay, Francine, you're on," said Tex.

"Looks like you have company, so I'm going to check on Ulysses," said Adele.

"Don't distract him, babe," said Francine.

"I shouldn't. You're right."

"What's up with you love birds?" asked Francine. "And don't give me any breeze off because something's up."

"Honest to God, Francine, the old feelings we both had for each other are still there. He asked me to come back and stay with him, but I don't know where home is or what's in his mind."

"Who knows what's in a man's mind," said Francine. "Hell, I don't even know what's in my mind."

Francine tried to laugh, but instead, she winced and doubled over with stomach pain.

"What's happening, Francine?" asked Adele.

"Pain. It's passing. I did some reading when I found out that my liver was corroded, and it suggested marijuana, like eating the stuff in food. What do you know about it?"

"I've been around the rodeo circuit long enough to know that rodeo jocks get hurt all the time and they smoke a joint or two to ease the pain."

"I think I'm ready to smoke a joint," said Francine.

"Ulysses has meds for you when it gets too intense," Adele said.

"I'm not ready to take the morphine, so I'm going to ask Ulysses to score me some dope."

Adele couldn't keep a straight face. Although many states in the U.S. had decriminalized medical marijuana and it was legal in Canada, hearing this granny talk like she was in a scene from *The Mod Squad* made Adele let out a hoot.

Francine started to laugh as she realized how she sounded.

"I'll see what I can do to get you some, or maybe Ulysses can get edibles at the dispensary."

"Hey, Francine," said Tex. "Your man is at the gate."

"Shoot, my stopwatch," she said as she pulled it out of her purse.

She looked at the starting gate across the arena and saw that Harry the bull was bucking his way into the stall. He was mean-looking and irritable. It took Ulysses a little time to hitch up on the wooden slats on the sides of the gate and drop onto the bull.

"He's out of breath and low on energy," said Adele. "He's not at his best. Riding a bucking bronco was not a great idea."

"Too late now," said Francine. "But I've got hope."

Ulysses was out of practice. His legs felt like jelly as he gripped the girth of the bull. His arms didn't have the strength of past rides. The goal of the rider was to stay on the bull for eight seconds, and Ulysses lasted four seconds before the bull bucked him off. He scrambled away from the bull and lost sight of him. Although he landed hard on the ground without injury, his body was in a state of mild shock. Ulysses didn't want to be trampled, so he struggled to get up and look normal. He took his hat off and tried to cover up a limp on his way to the exit. He looked up into the stands to find Adele and Francine, but his vision was slightly blurry. He recognized painful discomfort in his hip, but he didn't care because he rode the bull and that was all that mattered.

"He did it," shouted Francine. "Four seconds of bliss."

"The rider has to sit that bull for eight seconds to win," said Tex.

"It doesn't matter," said Francine as she gave Tex the hundred dollars. "My guy won for me."

Kevin Bartolo won the event, but Ulysses came in dead middle. He might not have won, but he gave Francine a thrill. It was all for her anyway.

Adele and Francine were anxious for Ulysses to return to the stands. Adele asked Tex for his program and noticed that the calf roping contest was next up.

"Damn that man," Adele said. "I know what he's going to do. Better get out your stopwatch because I fear that big lug of a man is entering the calf roping contest. He's a natural roper, you know. He's got more first places in that event. That and barrel racing. Ulysses wants a win today, and he's damn good as a roper. He could rope a bird sitting on a horse. So, what he's doing right now is entering an event that he might win. Righting the wrong. That's my guy."

An hour later, Ulysses came out of the gate on Natchez twirling a rope and chasing after a black calf. He twirled his rope three times and caught the calf around his neck. He dropped off the horse and tied up the calf.

"That was five seconds, Adele," screamed Francine. "And five more riders to go."

It was a nail-biting ten more minutes until the announcer came on and informed the audience that number twelve won by a second. Adele grabbed Francine's arm, hugged her, and screamed.

That night, the trio celebrated at a country western bar appropriately named The Roping Bull. Francine had never heard live country music, nor was she interested, but she wanted to experience the entire rodeo world.

It was semi-dark inside, with low lights, washed-out red walls, and a small stage in front of a well-worn concrete dance floor that was dimly lit. Francine could still see the rivets and holes made years ago by the boots of thousands of country western dancers. Red fabric with silver tassels hung from the back of the stage.

Instruments were casually scattered on the floor at the ready when the musicians entered the stage. Two bass guitars, an acoustic guitar, a drum set, and a steel guitar rounded out the instrumental collection. The leader of the group came on stage alone with a fiddle. He looked barely old enough to drink. Francine was fascinated by the way he plucked the strings, flipped the fiddle, and how lovingly he caressed his instrument—like it was a beautiful woman.

Wooden tables were randomly spread around the room, fully occupied by rodeo riders both male and female. A long bar was off to the left side of the dance floor. It was crowded with men in dusty cowboy boots and sweat-stained hats. It reminded Francine of a scene out of an old John Ford western.

"Where is the mechanical bull?" asked Francine.

"That's so eighties Urban Cowboy, Francine," said Adele.

"Excuse me," said Francine. "I'm out of touch with the comings and goings of the shit-kicker-cowboy world."

They found a table with two older men already seated, and Ulysses asked to join them. He brought over another chair, and they crowded together. The barmaid, definitely under twenty-one, came over and took their order. Francine ordered iced tea.

"We don't have iced tea," the barmaid said. "This is a bar. We've got Coke, Diet Coke, Sprite, and ginger ale."

Ulysses could feel Francine's rising anger. "She'll have Sprite," he said.

"And add a few cherries with the juice, please," she said. "We're celebrating."

"You were crazy as all get out," said Adele. "Roping that bull to prove a point."

"But I did prove a point, didn't I?"

"You're incorrigible," replied Adele as she kissed him on the cheek.

The rest of the band walked on stage, picked up their instruments, and talked and laughed while they took their time tuning. One of the men in the room lost his temper at the delay and shouted at the band to "get your act together and play." Other patrons booed and clapped and cheered.

Francine got a kick out of the spirited response as she listened for the first country western song. Ulysses was as excited as a kid.

"That singer and the band knocked the hell out of the song," said Ulysses. "It was a Garth Brooks tune called 'Ain't Going Down,' in case you were wondering."

The five-piece band followed it up with Dwight Yoakum's "Honkey Tonk Man."

"Where are the women in this male pit?" asked Francine.

"There's a female country singer coming on in a few minutes," said Adele. "She sounds like Patsy Cline."

"I know her," said Francine. "She had hit songs in my time, way back in the late fifties. My favorite was 'Crazy.'"

Francine started to sing "Crazy" and the men at the table cheered her on. She knew all the lyrics—*Crazy for feeling so lonely, I'm crazy for feeling so blue. I knew you would love me as long as you wanted and then some day, you'd leave me for somebody new.*"

Ulysses and Adele danced two-step to a few honky-tonk songs. He twirled her and held her close, and they looked like they had danced together forever. Francine figured that their attraction worked on many levels, and she was feeling quite proud of her role in bringing them together, even though it was accidental, or serendipitous, or fate.

While she was still lost in thought, Ulysses was at her side and lifting her out of the chair. Francine looked at him with fake shock.

"We're going dancing, Francine," he said. "Hang on to your cowboy hat."

Francine walked onto the dance floor like she owned it, like it was second nature to her. Ulysses took her into his arms and began a slow two-step.

"You're pretty good," he said.

"I watched everyone dancing, babe, because I knew you'd get me out here."

"Ready for a swing step. That's what we do in Austin. A two-step swing."

"Go for it. I'm in the mood to dance the night away."

One of the men at the table asked Adele to dance. She accepted and winked at Ulysses.

The next hour was full of changing dance partners, plenty of laughs, and flirting with men like she did at the high school sock hop.

∾

For the next three days, Francine attended seven of the rodeo events listed on the roster. Her favorite was the bareback ride and saddle bronc. She lived through her pain, fortified by marijuana gummy bears. The afternoon before Ulysses entered the calf roping event, he brought Francine to the horse stables. She held his hand as they walked past each stall. Francine gave every horse her attention, fed them carrots, and greeted the handlers who were hanging out.

She stopped in front of a stall with Natchez on the nameplate. "This is your Natchez, Ulysses," said Francine.

"Want to ride her?" he asked.

"I'll never get up there."

Ulysses opened the gate to the stall and led Natchez outside. He saddled her and padded the seat with a few extra blankets. He brought a portable step to the left side of the horse.

"Mount your steed, my lady," said Ulysses. "I'll help you up if you'll give me your hand."

Francine mounted the horse with effort. She had trouble getting her leg around Natchez's girth. Adele was there on the other side to help.

"Sit up as tall as you can, Francine," said Adele, "and hold onto the reins."

"I'm on top of the world," said Francine, laughing, tepidly at first, then, as she gained confidence, she let out a *whoop*.

Ulysses walked Francine and the horse around a ring next to the stables until he noticed that Francine was losing energy. He tied Natchez to a post and lifted Francine off the horse. He carried her to a nearby chair as Adele attended to Natchez.

"How did you like your ride?" asked Ulysses. "Pretty cool, huh?"

"Best feeling ever. I finally got to ride a horse. It's the beginning of my new career."

Each day, Francine's body grew a little weaker, but she was still able to remain focused on the task at hand. Even though she was rarely hungry, and she slept most of the morning, she rallied in the afternoon. Ulysses and Adele took turns with her needs.

On the fifth day of the Stampede, Francine woke up to ankles swollen to the size of oranges. She panicked and called Ulysses. He was not picking up the phone in his room. She called his cell phone. Adele had insisted she have his cell number for emergencies. She called Adele—no answer. She thought they must be at lunch.

She was thirsty. The water pitcher on her night table was empty. Francine willed herself to sit up, then slid down the bed. The steer wrestling started at two. She had to be there to support him. Of all the days to get this swelling. She had no strength to pull herself back up onto the bed, so she crawled to the bathroom to get her diuretic pills. With no strength left, she sat on the bathroom floor and waited.

Help came in a few minutes. Ulysses lifted her off the floor and onto the bed.

"What do you need?" asked Adele.

"Diuretic pills," Francine whispered. "Water. So thirsty."

Adele gave her a large glass of water and Francine swallowed her pills. She closed her eyes, leaned back on the propped-up pillow, and took deep breaths.

"I have to get to the steer wrestling event," she said. "And you did great on the calf roping. Did I tell you that?"

"We'll get there," said Ulysses. "Adele, would you be so kind as to bring Francine food? Something soft."

"A burger and fries and a Doctor Pepper, please, Adele, and use my credit card," said Francine. "It's in my purse."

"Right," said Adele as she left the room without Francine's card.

Ulysses piled extra pillows at the end of the bed and raised Francine's legs onto them.

"The swelling is common with your condition. I'm going to order a wheelchair from the lobby, and we'll get over there sometime before two."

"That's a great idea. It'll take time for the diuretic to kick in. I don't suppose you could get me a Depend, otherwise, I'll need an out-house. Don't worry, Doc. I don't have much pride left right about now."

"I'll take care of it."

Ulysses opened up a paper bag and unfolded a napkin. There were two brownies inside.

"Take one of these," said Ulysses.

"Are these better than the gummy bears?" She chewed the brownie with pleasant sounds. "Can I have the other?"

"Let's wait to see how you feel."

Adele returned with the food and was pleased that Francine had an appetite. While she was eating, Ulysses went down to the lobby to arrange for a wheelchair. At one o'clock, he pushed the chair into Francine's room.

"Those brownies were bitchin'. I'm feeling like I could ride a bucking bronco."

"Don't get ahead of yourself; we've got a long day."

Negotiating the logistics of getting the wheelchair into the rodeo arena was a challenge. Ulysses found a row of four handicapped seats in the shade. She saw Tex walking up the stairs with a program in hand.

The bareback riders were already lining up for their competition, and Francine was anxious to make a bet with Tex for the steer wrestling event.

"I'm going to run an errand before my event," said Ulysses. "Adele will be here in a few minutes. Enjoy."

"No worries. I've got Tex to keep me company."

"Hi, Francine," said Tex as he walked over to her. "How's my betting partner?"

"Good. Don't mind this wheelchair. I got swollen ankles."

Tex handed her his program and sat down on the stair next to her.

"Damn boney ass," said Tex to himself. "You got a favorite for the steer wrestling?"

"Betting on my man, Ulysses," she said. "Another hundred?"

"You're on a lucky streak, little lady," Tex said, "And I am hesitant to bet with you. But you look so adorable today, I think I'll make it another hundred."

Adele was out of breath as she ran to the bleachers, relieved to find Francine in good shape.

Ulysses returned to the horse stalls in less than an hour and got to the gate in time to saddle Natchez, test the reigns, and ride into the arena in the midst of rousing cheers, his black hat firmly on his head, and gaining speed on the steers.

Adele screamed out when she saw Ulysses jump off the horse and wrapped his arms around the steer, wrestled him to the ground, grabbed his legs, tied them together, and raised his hands to indicate he was finished. It was pure magic. The arena erupted with cheers.

After the steer wrestling, a rodeo clown came out to entertain the crowd. He rode bareback, fell off his horse numerous times, and saluted Francine in the stands.

"Hey Francine, your rodeo cowboy says hi," said the clown as he blew her a kiss.

The crowd around Francine stood and applauded.

After the exhilarating day, they had a quiet dinner. Everyone was in a mellow mood. Ulysses took Francine upstairs and gave her a brownie for dessert. Her swollen feel had gone down in the last couple of hours, but her general breathing had shortened.

"Hey, babe. How do your chances look to win the chuckwagon race?"

"Why? You got a bet with the old man who sits next to you in the stands?"

"You mean the handicapped guy?" she asked. "He's kind of sweet on me."

"Everybody's sweet on you, Francine."

"I've won about five hundred off him."

"I'll make another hundred for you," he said.

"Good. I need the money," she joked. "Don't worry, Doc. I'm in a good place."

He stayed with her for another hour, afraid she was not going to make it through the night, desperately hoping he would be with her at the end.

When she was sound asleep, he went into the bathroom to called Rachel.

"Time to get ready and come to Calgary, Rachel. I have one more event tomorrow, but she's been in and out of increasing pain."

"I'm packed and have an open ticket. See you tomorrow."

Ulysses laid down on the sofa next to Francine's bed. Before he fell asleep, he worried about transporting Francine's body back to Grand Rapids and how it was all going to work. Exhausted, he fell asleep and dreamed of flying like Superman in the old television series. He could see from above everything happening on Earth, and he could save people from danger and tragedy. He felt free and happy.

Early the next morning, Adele entered the room, wearing pajamas and a sweatshirt. She watched Ulysses sleep on the sofa. She loved the man with all her heart and hoped she'd never be so foolish as to leave him again. Without regret for the life she had lived, Adele was grateful for a second chance with him.

When Adele laid down next to Ulysses on the sofa, he stirred, responding to her distinctive, lingering smell: jasmine mixed with gardenia. He spooned her body as they fell asleep.

Several hours later, Francine woke in pain.

"Babe," she said, "I need a morphine shot. Pot isn't going to cut it."

Adele climbed onto the bed with Francine as Ulysses went to his room to get the medicine. Rodeo life was hard, but dealing with Francine was harder on his heart and spirit than living daily with his worn-out body.

Damn, Francine, stay with us for another day so we can celebrate your life.

∽

It took some skill to lift Francine out of her wheelchair and into the stands and settle her next to Tex. Adele was afraid Francine would slip out of her arms.

"I need something to drink, and you need popcorn," said Adele. "Hold the fort down with Tex."

"Put your money up, Tex, because I got this one today," she said. "My man is going to win the wagon train race."

"Hope the animals don't get injured," said Tex. "You know what they do to the horses that get injured."

"What are you talking about, you old fool?" Francine asked.

"Since 1986, seventy horses have died in the chuckwagon event," said the old man. "The event is an accident waiting to happen. They've got new regulations and things like that, vets all around, but it still happens. Two died this year."

Adele brought popcorn and drinks to Francine—she refused the food.

"What's wrong, Francine?" asked Adele. "You look upset."

"I was excited about this race, but Tex said horses were being killed."

"I'm afraid there have been injuries to horses through the years, but now they have new regulations."

"Please tell Ulysses that I don't want him to do it. I can't bear animal cruelty."

"I think it's too late."

"Please, Adele. Try."

Adele ran up the steps as Francine turned to the old man next to her.

"All bets are off Tex. I didn't come this far in my life to see animals slaughtered because they are injured and unfit for work. That's no way to treat a human being. That's no way to treat any living creature. We're supposed to leave this earth with dignity, no matter who you are, no matter what you've done. We make mistakes, but we are sorry for those mistakes. So a horse gets injured, and it isn't their fault. Why in hell would somebody put down an animal for that?"

"Because it's the way they do it and ain't nothing we can do about it," said Tex.

"It's cruel, and if there is one thing I hate most in life it's cruelty," responded Francine. "And you can take that to the bank."

Ulysses looked over the holding lineup for the chuckwagon event. Racehorses were attached to flatbeds. These wagons were not as heavy as those used in the old west. They had been modified for safety, so the Thoroughbreds were not pulling a wagon that was too heavy for their weight. And they could run faster.

Thoroughbreds were high-spirited creatures and easily excitable. They were relegated to chuckwagon racing because they had suffered an injury that made them ineligible for the racing circuit. Ulysses knew the statistics on the deaths of horses in the event over the decades. The stats did not give him a good feeling and neither did the volatile energy of the corral. The horses were jumpy, and the drivers were aggressive.

One of the handlers gave him a wagon assignment. Ulysses hesitated as he took the ticket.

"You're Gallardo, right?" asked the handler.

"Yep," he said, "but I'm not sure I can or want to drive the wagon."

"Fine, we got plenty of drivers who want your spot. Next time, do your homework."

Adele's voice interrupted his response to the handler. From the sound of her tone, there was trouble.

"Ulysses, you can't do this," she interrupted as she ran up to him.

"I'm not doing anything. It's over." Ulysses squeezed her until she thought she would break. "I couldn't be in a race like this. It's suicide."

"Francine was beside herself. The old man in the next seat gave her the stats on horse injuries and how many are put down because of being of no use anymore."

"Yes, my Adele. No more events. We're done here, darling."

When they got back to Francine, she was nearly unconscious. The old man next to her was taking a nap.

The chuckwagon race started, and it was apparent that Ulysses had made a good decision. The horses raced at top speed as the wagons behind them flailed from left to right, often colliding because the drivers were blinded by the dust. He was grateful Francine didn't have to witness the accident waiting to happen.

While everyone's attention was on the arena, Ulysses and Adele carried Francine to her wheelchair and got her back to the hotel, where Rachel was waiting for them in the lobby. She rushed to her mother and took her hands.

"Mom, Mom, I'm here. It's Rachel."

Francine opened her eyes and smiled. "That's my girl. Always here for me."

They took her upstairs, lifted her out of the wheelchair, and laid her on the bed.

"First things first. Let's watch her in shifts," said Ulysses. "Adele, you get something to eat, and Rachel and I will wait here."

The hours dragged on. Adele switched shifts with Ulysses. Rachel refused to leave. If her mother woke up, she wanted to be there. At six o'clock, she finally spoke with a raspy voice. "Babe," she said. "Rachel."

Her daughter had fallen asleep next to her in the last five minutes, so Rachel barely heard her. Ulysses went to her other side and held her hand.

"What can I do for you, Francine?" he asked.

"It's coming to the end. A shot won't help."

"How much pain are you in?"

"I can't feel much. Hard to swallow."

"Maybe it's time I get you a doctor. He'll know better."

"No doctor. I'm doing this my way."

"Tell me about the pain?" he asked again.

"What I'm feeling—this pain I have—is no more or less than the pain I've had all year. You lean to forget. I don't have enough inside of me to fight it."

Francine closed her eyes and fell in and out of consciousness. Rachel never let go of her hand.

Ulysses left the room and asked the front desk to recommend a physician. The doctor on call was unavailable. It was a sign that the next hour or two he would be providing her care. It was the reason he took her on his journey—to bring her to the end.

When Ulysses came back to Francine's room, Adele and Rachel were sitting on the edge of the bed holding her hand.

"How are you feeling, Maude?" asked Ulysses.

"I'm just peachy, Harold, in case you're confused by my looks."

Ulysses stifled a laugh. He knew where she was coming from. The original Francine was still inside her. He took out a few instruments to check Francine's vitals.

"Francine, I'm going to take your temperature and listen to your breath—give you an assessment," said Ulysses as he did his work quickly.

Francine closed her eyes. Her face was turning alabaster as she began to take the journey to the other side. When Francine finally spoke, her voice was as quiet as a whisper. Her language was faltering, but her memory was as clear as always. She licked her lips a few times in order to begin her soliloquy with determination and heart.

"I've got a few more things to say before I go to sleep, y'all," Francine said. Her voice was low with hints of strength. "I'm speaking Texas now, babe, just for you. And I've got to say goodbye to a few people in my life. First, you, Ulysses Doc Gallardo, for this beautiful journey to another land in another life I was happy and grateful to live. Thank you, my wonderful Rachel for not standing in my way when I told you I was going to a rodeo. You didn't put a restraining order on me, and you allowed me to have my last and final journey. How lucky am I. And Adele, for your love and care.

Be good to this guy because he's one of a kind. I'm getting sentimental, but I mean it. You know my memory, Doc, and I remember my life as if it were yesterday—my Carol and Kathy—we had a bitchin' life together as the best of friends. Smoking Kent cigarettes and going to Drake's after school, mooching rides in Dick's Model T and Tim's Studebaker, sneaking out for dates through my bedroom window so Colleen-the-bitch wouldn't catch me; but she did, and I was always on restriction. Except for the night I was once crowned the homecoming queen."

Rachel took her hand while Ulysses prepared the syringe.

"Lay back and rest, Francine. Please close your eyes and breathe deeply."

"No morphine, Doc. I see you doing it. I'm going out in style. My way, if you please."

Ulysses put the morphine away and glanced at Adele. He could hear his heart pounding.

"Oh, my Rachel, so strong and smart. And Mark is a gift of a husband and father—and my Ari and Douglas—tell them they will have success and happiness. Be kind to Carlos because he was loyal and loving to me and the dogs. Boo Boo, my heart, Sasha, and my forever Ida. And an old cat who came in one day and never left."

Adele held her hand, trying to control an avalanche of tears. Ulysses took her other hand and watched her trying to whisper out her last words.

"Get the stopwatch out, Doc, and time my death. I'm trying to set a record. I've got the power now. I own my power."

"You got it," whispered Ulysses into her ear. "Take your time leaving your strength and wisdom to the ages. Ride high. And know that you are loved by all—you're a force to be reckoned with in life and death."

"That's the best that can be said for a life," whispered Francine.

"I love you forever and to the moon, Mom."

Rachel and Ulysses laid down on either side of Francine and made a cocoon to give her a sense of security. They spooned her with love and protected her with their bodies and souls. Adele held Ulysses on his other side.

The final journey of Francine Fisher was beginning. As her spirit retreated from her body, she saw an apparition of her image shining in the spotlight and wearing her homecoming crown.

We were together. I forgot the rest.
Walt Whitman

Thank you so much for reading *Once a Homecoming Queen*. If you've enjoyed the book, we would be grateful if you would post a review on the bookseller's website. Just a few words is all it takes!

Acknowledgements

Gratitude to the generosity and support of those who contributed to *Once A Homecoming Queen*:

Pat Jackson
Cheryl Miller
Mark Malatesta
Michael Groff
Paige Ripperger
The Witches Coven: Elif, Heather, Leslie, Nazan, Kathrine, Pauline, and Debbie whose support carried me through my writing journey.
Nancy Cushing-Jones
Jerry Schmidt
Eric Kaufman
Edd O'Donnell
The tribe at The Broken Spoke, Austin, Texas, with shared inspiration from Country Western singer, Weldon Henson.

Made in the USA
Middletown, DE
09 April 2024